"So if the Great Birds did not send me, then who?"

His index finger  her chin until Samantha met his mesmerizing eyes. her face and she dr He moved no close desire was so strong the buzz of danger. felt it and shook off the dreamy lethargy.

Samantha pressed both hands against his chest to hold him back. Alon paused and gave her a quizzical look.

"How do you know what I am?" she asked.

"I can sense you, little shifter, feel you with every pore and every tiny hair on my skin. I can feel the emotions pouring through you like floodwater and I can feel the worth of your soul, because that is what I do."

What the hell was he?

Books by Jenna Kernan

Harlequin Nocturne

*Dream Stalker #78
*Ghost Stalker #111
*Soul Whisperer #126
*Beauty's Beast #158

*The Trackers

Other titles by Jenna Kernan available in ebook format.

JENNA KERNAN

writes fast-paced romantic adventures set in out-of-the-way places and populated by larger-than-life characters.

Happily married to her college sweetheart, Jenna shares a love of the outdoors with her husband. The couple enjoys treasure hunting all over the country, searching for natural gold nuggets and precious and semiprecious stones.

Jenna has been nominated for two RITA® Awards for her Western romances and received a Book Buyers Best Award for paranormal romance in 2010. Visit Jenna at her internet home, www.jennakernan.com, or at http://twitter.com/jennakernan for up-to-the-minute news.

BEAUTY'S BEAST

JENNA KERNAN

Recycling programs
for this product may
not exist in your area.

ISBN-13: 978-0-373-88568-8

BEAUTY'S BEAST

Copyright © 2013 by Jeannette H. Monaco

All rights reserved. Except for use in any review, the reproduction or utilization of this work in whole or in part in any form by any electronic, mechanical or other means, now known or hereafter invented, including xerography, photocopying and recording, or in any information storage or retrieval system, is forbidden without the written permission of the publisher, Harlequin Enterprises Limited, 225 Duncan Mill Road, Don Mills, Ontario M3B 3K9, Canada.

This is a work of fiction. Names, characters, places and incidents are either the product of the author's imagination or are used fictitiously, and any resemblance to actual persons, living or dead, business establishments, events or locales is entirely coincidental.

This edition published by arrangement with Harlequin Books S.A.

For questions and comments about the quality of this book, please contact us at CustomerService@Harlequin.com.

® and TM are trademarks of Harlequin Enterprises Limited or its corporate affiliates. Trademarks indicated with ® are registered in the United States Patent and Trademark Office, the Canadian Trade Marks Office and in other countries.

Printed in U.S.A.

Dear Reader,

I'm so pleased to introduce my final story in The Trackers series, featuring a world that is loosely based on Lakota myth.

My first three romances introduced two feuding Halfling races who now unite to face the Ruler of Ghosts. This time Nagi has built a deadly army of the newest Halfling race, his offspring—the Ghost Children.

Only one Halfling recognizes that her people will fail without the help of the loyal Ghost Children. Samantha Proud is a remarkable Seer. Like her father, she has the ability to shift. Unlike her father, she is willing to leave her people and risk banishment to get help.

Alon Garza is the son of Nagi. Like his father, he has the power to destroy living souls. Unlike his father, he loves the living world enough to protect it from his father's dark ambitions.

Many call Alon a monster, but Samantha sees what others cannot—a brave man who is unafraid of dying if it will protect the world from the dark ambitions of his sire. Together they will bring the Ghost Children to the battle for the Living World.

I hope you will visit me at www.jennakernan.com, follow me on Twitter at Twitter.com/jennakernan and come see what I'm up to on Facebook.

Jenna Kernan

This story is dedicated with much gratitude to my editor, Ann Leslie Tuttle, whose insight and advice has been a gift beyond measure.

Chapter 1

The fear made changing into her animal form easy. Transformed into a grizzly bear, Samantha Proud charged across the frozen lake as if the devil himself was on her tail—for soon he would be. The March wind blew at her back as she hurdled across the Great Slave Lake in Canada's Northwest Territories.

What have I done? What have I done? The thoughts echoed with the rhythmic strike of the pads of her feet on the frozen ground. Her stomach twisted with fear as she galloped along, her claws tearing the ice. Should she warn her family or protect them by running in the opposite direction?

Home, she thought. It was the only home she had ever known. Miles blurred together and she reached familiar territory, out of breath and dizzy from her exertions. It was Blake who saw her first. Her twin brother was older by only seven minutes, but that was enough to establish him as her elder and she as his little sister, if you could call a nine-hundred-pound bear little.

They had spent a lifetime running and had run too far and too long for him not to understand the meaning of her panicked flight. On sighting her, he bellowed at the top of his lungs and bolted with her to their parents.

Their father, Sebastian, a great healer, bellowed in return and charged out to meet them, arriving in the yard to their cabin just as Blake and Samantha rounded the woodpile. Her mother, a Seer of Souls, was not a Skinwalker and so could not take an animal form. She was last to arrive, appearing from the cabin as she drew on her black down coat over a lavender turtleneck, her long dark hair falling in disarray about her pretty face.

With one look at her children, she broke into a sprint. "What's happened?"

All three of them, her father, brother and herself, shifted to human form with a flash of light and the now-familiar surge of energy that pulsed from her core. An instant later and their great bearskin coats transformed, at their direction, into their preferred attire. Jeans and a red fleece jacket for Blake and jeans and a brown-and-green plaid flannel for her father.

Blake now stood seven feet tall and possessed a heavy musculature, just the same as their father. His straight, shaggy brown hair was lighter than Samantha's and far shorter. They both had golden-brown skin and the high cheekbones of the First Nation, though her eyes were more cinnamon and his deep brown. Blake's square jaw was clamped tight, and his eyes narrowed on her in disapproval. Here was another difference. Blake's face resembled their father's, especially when he scowled like that, while Samantha's heart-shaped face, generous mouth and pointed chin resembled their mother's.

"What did you do?" Blake whispered. He knew where she went and why. His disapproval did not prevent him from guarding her secrets, as always.

"In the Dogrib fishing camp," she puffed, out of breath. "An evil ghost had possession of a child."

Her parents went still and stared at each other in deadly silence. Samantha snatched another breath as her courage fled entirely. Dread settled on her, pressing her down. She needed to tell them the rest. Needed to warn them. Looking at their worried faces, she felt the groundswell of regret. Why couldn't she have done as she was told for once?

"You were in Yellowknife?" Her father's words were more accusation than question. She knew the danger of going where people lived, because where people lived, ghosts could be found.

"I *told* you not to go," Blake said.

"What good are my gifts if I am not permitted to use them?"

"What good are they if you're dead?" he countered.

She glanced at her parents, shifting uneasily under their silent condemnation.

"I only go there once a year, at the spring equinox. Just to do some healing." As if when she visited made any difference.

"Showing off," said Blake.

"I'm not!"

Her mother was not so subtle. "Please tell me you did not expel a ghost. That you did not send it for judgment."

How could she leave a child in torment, when she knew how to free him?

Samantha wanted to tell her parents that she was tired of hiding, tired of living on the run. That up until today she had never, ever even seen a possession. But instead, she bowed her head.

Her mother's voice rose an octave. "Did you?"

Samantha nodded.

Her mother's sharp exhale sounded like a hiss, and her father's jaw tightened. They shared a look. Her parents had done nothing but try to protect their children, though lately their protection felt more like a great, frozen cage. All Samantha wanted was to be useful.

"I'm sorry, Mama," she whispered.

Michaela Proud had once been the last Seer of Souls, but with the birth of her twins, she had become the mother of the only other Seers left in the world. The three of them formed the last of the Ghost Clan.

Michaela's knees gave way but Sebastian caught her. Samantha would never forget the shattered, desolate look upon her mother's pale face. It only added to Samantha's terror.

"No," her mother whispered.

"Nagi will know," said her father, voicing what they all knew.

Her heart thudded as she watched her strong, capable mother cling to her father like a child. "What should we do?"

He did not hesitate. "Run."

Michaela shook her head. "But he can track us. Send his ghosts after us."

"Not together. But as we planned. We separate. He can't follow us all."

Samantha stood motionless as she watched the chaos she had wrought. She had destroyed all her parents' efforts to protect them because she could not turn her back on one human child.

"I'm sorry, Mama," she whispered.

Her mother cried as she drew Samantha into her arms. "Oh, my precious girl."

Her father, the great bear and master healer, encircled them both. But Samantha knew even he was not strong enough to defeat Nagi. It was why they never used their gifts and why they had spent her entire lifetime in hiding.

Blake moved closer and her mother snatched him up as well, gripping him in an embrace that was a useless defense against their enemies. At twenty-two, Samantha was well past cowering in her parents' arms, wasn't she?

Her father stepped back.

"We have to divide to the four directions. Quickly. Before he comes."

"No!" cried her mother. Her opposition frightened Samantha almost more than Nagi.

"Mother, he's coming. We have to go," said her father, his voice now low, coaxing. "One to Nicholas, one to Bess. We agreed."

"But Bess? They won't be safe there."

Bess Suncatcher was the raven who flew to the Spirit World. Her power was dark and dangerous. Samantha's heart crashed into her ribs in wild, painful drumming.

"She knew this would happen. She warned us."

"You know what she does! You know who she calls family." Her mother's voice held both fear and anguish.

Samantha held a hand to her throat, trying to draw a breath past the terror.

Her father's voice radiated a calm certainty that did not reassure. "My friends will keep them safe if anyone can."

"Which one?" she asked.

Their father stared at them both and then fixed his gaze on his son. "Blake to Nicholas. He's the oldest and a leader. Blake will bring the Niyanoka to our cause if anyone can."

Her brother nodded, accepting the responsibility as easily as if he had been preparing for it all of his life. Samantha did a double take. Had he? Did everyone know of this escape plan but her?

Realization hit, dropping hard and cold into her stomach. Her parents had discussed this plan, laid out this last desperate measure to protect their children. Blake knew, too. It was clear by his grave expression and complete lack of surprise. They'd told their dependable child and kept it from their reckless one.

Michaela clung to Samantha. "She can go with him."

Where were they sending her that made her mother so frightened? Fear lifted the hairs on Samantha's neck. To Bess Suncatcher. Samantha searched her mind for details of her father's friends whom she'd never met.

"No," said Sebastian. "Two would leave a brighter trail. He'll find them. She goes to Bess. Bess and Cesar will protect her and prepare her. She knows our enemy better than any of us."

"What if you're wrong?"

He smoothed Michaela's hair and gave her a brave smile. "I may be. But the Thunderbirds do not make mistakes. They know the fates of us all. If it is not safe, then they will bring her somewhere else. Remember they brought Nicholas to Jessie?"

"And she nearly killed him!" she cried, then buried her face in her hands and wept.

"It's the last way I know to protect them," he said, his eyes full of sorrow. He reached for his wife, and she threw herself against him. "We have to hurry, Mother, and pray the Thunderbirds leave no trail."

Sebastian took hold of his twins, gripping the outer

shoulder of each. "No more hiding. Your mother goes to her people in the east. I go north to rally the Skinwalkers to fight. Blake goes to my friend Nicholas Chien, a wolf and great tracker. His wife, Jessie, is a Spirit Child." He stared at Blake. "They knew this day would come. His wife will help you bring the Niyanoka to join us. Blake, do you remember all I have told you?"

Samantha's suspicions were confirmed at the nod of her brother's head. She felt hollow inside. She wasn't trustworthy. She'd sneaked away to work her healing arts and endangered them all. Blake had a purpose. They all did. All but her.

Her father continued his instructions. "Convince your mother's people to join us by any means."

Blake stood, his body straight and tall, but his dark eyes filled with uncertainty. "I'll try my best, sir."

Their father squeezed Blake's shoulder and then released him. "Succeed. You must." Her father turned to her. "You go to my friend Bess Suncatcher, a raven. Her mate is a Spirit Child, a Soul Whisperer."

Her mother's words echoed in her mind. *You know who she calls family.*

A Soul Whisperer? Her eyes rounded and a buzzing began in her ears. Her mother had taught her that this was the most cursed of all Niyanoka, unclean for speaking to the dead. Her blood slowed like water turning to ice, but she did not object. How could she when she had brought this Armageddon to them?

"Bess has some dangerous ideas, but none know the Toe Taggers better than she. Find her. Learn what you can. Tell her it has begun and ask her to join me. But be watchful for Toe Taggers. If you see one, run. If you cannot run, kill it before it kills you."

Her eyes rounded and her stomach dropped.

"Do you understand, Sammy?"

She shook her head. What did he ask her to do?

But he was already looking to his wife. Samantha's lip trembled as she held back tears. Her parents had never left them and never felt they could not protect them, until now. Blake and her mother would rally the Niyanoka and her father would bring the Skinwalkers. To what? For what? Samantha began to shake.

Her mother grabbed hold of her husband in a last embrace. Tears choked Samantha so she could not speak. Their auras flared, suddenly visible even in the fading daylight. She knew her parents were true soul mates, with the bond of shared emotions and thoughts. She longed for such a connection.

"What if we're wrong?" Michaela whispered.

Sebastian stroked her glossy hair. "It only works if we split into four. He can't follow four, not all at once. Some of us might…"

His words faded. Samantha's breath caught as she realized what he meant to say. *Some of us might escape.* Whom would Nagi follow? Which one of them would die? She hoped it was her. She could not bear being responsible for their deaths. Was that her purpose, to lead Nagi from those she loved? Calm crept into her heart like cold crystals of ice, but she was no longer afraid. She would be last to leave. She'd see to that.

Her mother cradled Samantha and kissed her hair. It felt like a final farewell. Samantha lifted her gaze to stare down at her mother, who was average height but not tall enough to meet the eyes of her daughter, now six feet three inches tall. The two embraced and then drew apart.

With her eyes still pinned on Samantha, her mother

spoke to her husband. "Call the Whirlwinds and pray they can carry us to safety."

Sebastian lifted his arms to the heavens, chanting a prayer Samantha knew by heart. Dark, menacing clouds swept in from the north. A storm blew, lifting the rocks and sand to pelt them. All four turned their backs to the wind.

The Thunderbirds had long ago taken the Skinwalkers into their hearts. These Thunderbeings had the power to harness electrical energy on earth and stir the winds into storms. For reasons none could recall, the Supernaturals would carry the Skinwalkers in their claws if they deemed the matter grave. Apparently, at some point, the Spirit Children had decided the Supernaturals were a private jet service and were now on the no-fly list. But no Skinwalker *ever* called a Thunderbeing unless his or her life depended upon it, for all recognized that such an arrangement was not to be abused.

"Look," cried Blake, pointing to the sky.

Samantha craned her neck and thought she saw the great beating wings of a huge eagle sweeping down upon them.

Her mother screamed and pointed. Samantha turned to see the gray billowing smoke of evil, disembodied ghosts surging toward them from the south. Samantha and Blake transformed instantly into their bear forms, standing before their mother as she gasped with one hand over her heart.

"We are found," she cried, her words all but lost in the raging winds.

Samantha stared in horror at the approaching horde: Nagi, his evil ghosts and something hideous. She knew what these must be, felt certainty swallowing her up. They were, for she had heard of them, the living offspring he had sired. Toe Taggers! Nagi's children were pale and brutish, living monsters, all teeth, claws and quills. She covered her face and turned away.

Sebastian howled, releasing the beast within. He could not fight ghosts unless they took corporeal form and, not being a Seer, he could not even spot them. But he could make out the Toe Taggers and Nagi drawing nearer. He stood between his family and attack as he called to the heavens. The dark clouds rolled in, blotting out the stars. The shriek of the wind screamed in Samantha's ears, but she could make him out, there in the south, advancing like death.

Samantha moved to stand beside her father, but he pushed her back with one giant paw, sending her tumbling along the ground. From this vantage she clearly saw him—Nagi.

The Ruler of Ghosts rose up before them, billowing as black as the smoke from a burning oil rig. He was dark and deadly with yellow cat's eyes, just as her mother had described. He reached for them, claws extending from his undulating body. Samantha forgot how to fight. She forgot every single thing her father had taught her about how to survive. This was her fault. All of it, because she had wanted to try her powers instead of doing as she was told.

Something snatched her up, tearing her from her mother's arms, dragging her from her twin brother, sweeping Samantha into the sky.

She howled her dismay, wanting to be left behind to give her family a chance to escape.

Below her, she saw the Toe Taggers attack her father, falling upon him like a pack of wild dogs.

She screamed as the ice pelted her, as the great claws gripped her, as the mighty wings beat the skies into a whirlwind.

Chapter 2

Nagi reached the Skinwalker as his Ghost Children carried the grizzly backward to the ground.

He felt certain his offspring could best the Spirit Children born of Niyan, and they grew ten times more quickly. The Skinwalkers, born of Tob Tob, would be more challenging. Here was their first test.

The old male had stayed behind to defend, and Nagi's own children were too stupid and too vicious to resist the temptation to fight. So instead of pursuing the Seer, as ordered, they were distracted by the only one of the four he did not want to kill, which was likely the old bear's intention.

Nagi had no ability to track the Seer unless she revealed herself. His Ghostlings were squandering this golden opportunity.

"The Seer!" he hissed, motioning to the sky.

His children continued their useless attack.

Why had the Seer, who had not sent one evil ghost to his Circle in all these years, suddenly done something so reckless?

Then an unexpected answer struck him. Could it have been one of her children?

Was it possible that she had offspring old enough to use their powers?

That meant they would be old enough to reproduce. Three Seers was bad, but he did not relish the prospect of contending with another generation. Not when he had so methodically exterminated the Ghost Clan. Well, all but one, and that one had been female, curse the luck.

He glanced at his snarling, snapping children and repressed a shudder. If not for the Seer, he would have no need of a living army.

For now he would settle with the grizzly. Past time to take his immortal soul.

Nagi hovered over the great bear, who writhed and strained against the deadly grip of Nagi's children. It took all six of them to hold him. He was strong, this one, but not immortal. Nagi could feel his soul, firmly attached to this body and to this world. Well, not for long.

"Where have you sent them?" he hissed.

The bear bellowed and the clouds above them turned black. The wind rose and Nagi watched in horror as his children were swept aside with the blowing rain. The Thunderbirds reached their talons down and snatched the bear from their midst as easily as Nagi might pluck a soul from a living body.

"No!" he shrieked, rising to follow the retreating storm, only to be tossed back to the ground by the thumping hooves of the Thunderhorses. He had never suffered such an indignity. The audacity of a Supernatural touching a true Spirit enraged him. But still he lay impotent in the mud as above him the bear disappeared into the same vortex that had taken the Seer and her offspring.

"Follow him!" he shrieked, but his words were lost to the roaring wind, and his children rolled past him like tumbleweeds.

Two of his children managed to change into their essence, billowing upward into the storm like a volcano erupting below the sea. But they were blasted apart and fell in pieces all about him, dead or dying.

"Useless, brainless fools!" he roared at his fallen children.

The last mighty Thunderhorse galloped after his brothers, the great eagles who carried the old bear. Nagi watched them go, unwilling to chance pursuit.

The massive storm above him broke apart, sweeping away in the four directions. Nagi turned in a slow circle.

Which storms carried the Seers?

Samantha spun in space. She had long ago stopped fighting the winds that tore at her, tossed her, tumbled her like clothing in a dryer. Instead, she gave herself over to the whirlwind and found she could breathe and that the needles of ice did not chill her or cut her skin. She was as dizzy as a child barrel-rolling down a hill. And when she spilled onto the ground, she fell hard, tearing the clothing from her knees and scraping the skin from the palms of her hands. The pain came a moment later. Samantha glanced at her stinging hands in time to see the blood welling from multiple tiny abrasions.

She groaned and rolled to her back, closing her eyes against the spinning sensation that continued even though she was now still. Gradually the wooziness receded and she opened her eyes. Above her, tall trees towered, elephantine trunks with deeply grooved reddish-brown bark. She recognized them instantly even though she had never seen them in person. These were the mighty sequoias. She breathed deeply, scenting pine, moss, the sweet fragrance of rich soil and the ground squirrel that had recently passed this way.

In what seemed moments, she had flown from above the Arctic Circle to California. She braced, waiting for Nagi to appear, but the minutes ticked by, birds flitted through the forest and she sensed no threat.

She glanced at her palms, now sticky with blood. A sweep of her hand brought an electric zip of energy as her clothing transformed. Her boots, snow pants, parka and gloves reconstituted to create a fairly respectable copy of the uniforms she had seen the foresters wearing, with serviceable work boots, olive-green slacks and a tan jacket with the familiar white patch on the left sleeve.

The soreness of her muscles and the annoyance of the blood on her palms brought her to her feet to search for sixteen stones. She placed them in a healing circle and managed to repair the minor damage to her body even without the tobacco and sage needed to sanctify the circle or the feather she used to focus her energy. Her stomach knotted as the gravity of what she had done settled on her like mist.

Were they safe?

Had the Supernaturals done as her father requested and taken her to the raven, or carried her elsewhere? Her father said the Thunderbirds knew the fates of us all. Where had the Supernatural beings taken her?

The crack of a branch brought her about. Nagi?

Someone or something was here. She inhaled, finding the new scent of another creature, but she could not identify it. It was sweet, like the rich soil and the autumn leaves. This was not the scent of any animal she knew. But it certainly was alive. She could hear it breathing.

Samantha weighed her options—attack or run.

She crouched, preparing to change and charge. There were few creatures who would face a charging grizzly, especially one who was frightened and without her family for the first time since birth.

What was hiding behind that massive trunk? A Toe Tagger? Her father's warning bounced up in her mind. *If you see a Toe Tagger, run.*

Something stepped into tall ferns. She hesitated as she realized it was a man, a hauntingly beautiful man with fine silvery blond hair that swept the shoulders of his charcoal-gray wool sports jacket. His slacks and fitted cashmere sweater were also gray, but more the color of a mourning dove. An odd choice of attire for a hike in the woods. He dressed like a walking shadow.

Samantha sagged with relief at finding a man, rather than one of her dreaded enemies. Was he human? The light played tricks because his aura seemed only a gray shadow, which wasn't right. No living thing had a gray aura. It was too bright to clearly see in any case. The late-afternoon sun sent golden light down to the forest floor in bright, wide beams.

She needed to find Bess before she ran into one of Nagi's hated spawn.

The man stepped closer. His features were similar enough to her own to make her believe he was of the First Nation. But his pale skin tone and that hair, it did not fit. The texture, the color was all wrong. She stepped closer, drawn by his ethereal beauty and her own curiosity. He glanced back, as if considering retreat.

"Hello," she called.

He frowned, his dark brow lowering over his blue

eyes. She'd never seen eyes that color. They reminded her of glacial ice, and when he fixed them on her she felt a little charge of excitement buzz inside her. He moved with a grace and power that brought a trickle of fear to her belly. Her instinct told her he wasn't human. His scent told her he wasn't a Skinwalker. Niyanoka? She tried again to see his aura, looking for the distinctive golden cap that marked her mother's people, and failed once more.

She stepped back and he closed the space between them, the flat heels of his boots sinking into the soft earth. She inhaled his scent, searching for what he really was, and the sweetness of him made her want to move closer. She held herself back.

"Where did you come from?" he asked, his voice a rich, velvety bass that rumbled through her belly, making her insides quiver.

He stood with a relaxed confidence she found unnerving. His eyes swept her body, making her skin tingle and her muscles tense. Was he friend or foe? She could not tell. She only knew he was not Nagi.

"I'm doing some work in the forest." She tapped the patch on her left sleeve.

The man's eyes narrowed. "Rangers in California have yellow patches and they carry sidearms. So, I'll ask you again, where do you come from, little Skinwalker?"

Her arms dropped to her sides and a shiver of panic went through her. He had her at a disadvantage, for he knew what she was.

What was he that he could so easily spot her? Niyanoka, she decided. Must be. Those born of the race of Children of Spirit could see auras and easily recognized Skinwalkers from their brown aura visible in all but the brightest of light.

Her parents said she must find Bess Suncatcher. Did her father really have friends so old and so true that they would welcome such trouble on their doorstep? Samantha did not think so.

"What are you doing in my woods, little one?" he asked, stepping closer.

She shook now. The fear, the journey and the unknown were all swirling inside her to form a perfect storm.

He moved forward. She stepped back, uncertain what to do. Changing shape before a human broke one of the two rules by which the Skinwalkers lived. First, protect the Balance, the finely spun web of the natural world, from all threats. Second, do not let the humans know what you are except to save your life.

He wasn't exactly threatening her. But somehow he was. His stare unnerved her. Why did her breathing accelerate at his approach until she grew dizzy again?

"That's a Canadian uniform. Why would you think you were in Canada?" His questions were casual, as if he did not expect an answer but preferred to puzzle out his own. His eyes narrowed and dark lashes descended over pale eyes. "Unless." He glanced at the skies, putting it together. "The storm." His gaze shot back to her. "So it's true, then. The Thunderbirds *do* carry you. But why here?" He stared up at the sky. "They couldn't have meant for *me* to find you. There's been a mistake."

She retreated another step, thinking that she had to agree with him, but instead she repeated what her father had said.

"The Thunderbirds don't make mistakes." *They know the fates of us all. If it is not safe, then they will bring her somewhere else.*

She stared up at this stranger. They had brought her to him.

He flicked his gaze back to her, and she felt her throat go dry.

"Ah, it speaks. Well, then. Now we are getting somewhere."

Was it his presence or his looks that made her so anxious? He wasn't human or he wouldn't know of the Thunderbirds, unless he was a shaman. He didn't look like a holy man. More like a hunter.

"I'm Alon," he said, pressing an open hand over his heart and inclining his head. His feathery hair brushed his cheeks.

She stared at his long pale fingers, cushioned now in the gray fabric of his sweater and thick muscles of his chest. Her ears tingled at the rush of blood pouring through her.

"Samantha," she managed.

His smile revealed dazzling white teeth but failed to have the desired effect. The baring of his teeth only made him look more dangerous. White teeth and that strong, square jaw. She briefly considered the possibility that he might be a Toe Tagger, but she had seen Nagi's children as they attacked her father. They were terrible to behold. While Alon looked more like a statue carved by a master's hand, almost too perfect to be real.

His eyes twinkled now, the menace vanishing as he seemed to transform again into someone she could trust. He moved closer and she held her ground. Something about the way he looked at her now seemed so reassuring, but she held on to her distrust.

He reached, offering his open hand. She stared, wanting to take it. She had to struggle not to. What power was this? She tucked her hands behind her, pressing them to the rough bark, preparing to push off and run if need be.

"Go on," he urged, tempting her with the rich timbre of his deep voice.

She did. Her hand slid over his, palms pressing one to the other. His skin was cool. An instant later a flash of energy surged from the point of contact, lifted the tiny hairs on her forearm and caused her skin to tingle. His eyes locked on hers, and she saw the first glimmer of uncertainty there. Was he as surprised as she?

Her mouth dropped open in a little O as a buzzing started in her ears as the unfamiliar energy lifted the hairs on her neck before it cascaded down her spine. She shivered.

He frowned and tightened the grip on her hand. "Cold?"

She shook her head. *Afraid, delighted, anxious as a polar bear stranded on an ice drift.*

He tugged, exerting a slow, insistent pressure that she was strong enough to resist, but somehow did not wish to. He lifted his opposite hand and crooked one finger, using his knuckle to stroke her cheek. Her body hummed in response, her skin flushing in a way she had not experienced but instantly recognized as sexual.

His index finger then settled beneath her jaw, lifting her chin until she gazed up into those mesmerizing eyes. Her heartbeat drummed in her ears.

"So if the Great Birds did not send you to me, then who?"

His sweet breath fanned her face, and she drew in the fragrance of him.

He moved no closer. The beating of sexual desire was so strong that it almost drowned out the buzz of danger. But not quite. She heard it, felt it and shook off the dreamy lethargy.

Samantha pressed both hands against his chest to hold him back. He paused and gave her a quizzical look.

"How do you know what I am?" she asked.

His half smile showed a lazy quality. Her mouth dropped open to stare as her heart continued to slam into her ribs like a handball batted against a cement wall.

"Do you know how animals can sense earthquakes?"

She had that same ability herself. She nodded.

"And how sharks can sense the vibrations of an injured fish from miles away?"

She nodded again.

"And how a spider knows the instant a fly lands in his web?"

She did not like the way this conversation was going at all, and fear now gripped her middle in a fist so tight she could scarcely breathe.

"I can sense you, little shifter, feel you with every pore and every tiny hair on my skin. I can feel the emotions pouring through you like floodwater and I can feel the worth of your soul, because that is what I do."

What the hell was he?

Samantha struggled for clarity against the honeyed breath and entrancing gaze. The stranger's hold was light at first, but then turned possessive. When he tried to draw her body to his, the desire fled and survival instinct engaged. What was she doing?

He pulled and she pushed with all her might. It was a thrust that would have sent a human airborne. Yet he only stumbled a few steps before recovering his balance. He stared, his head cocked to the side, assessing her. Instead of anger or menace, she saw only confusion followed immediately by the quirking of an eyebrow as if she intrigued him.

"Strong, very strong for one so small."

There was that word again. *Small.*

"Why are you here, pretty one?"

Ironic for him to call her pretty, for his appearance was so striking as to make even the most attractive man she had ever laid eyes on pale in comparison.

"I'm looking for Bess Suncatcher."

Both brows shot up. "How do you know my mother?"

His mother?

A child of the raven would be an ally, wouldn't he? She wasn't sure.

"Mother?"

He nodded.

She inhaled again, but his scent held no trace of any animal shifter she had ever encountered. She sensed so much danger here it hindered her thinking. The Skinwalker inside her urged her to run, taking charge as her thinking brain struggled to maintain control.

Was he a Skinwalker raven then? But he wasn't. She could tell from his scent, and he lacked the brown aura. So how then could he be born of a Skinwalker?

She won't be safe there. If you see a Toe Tagger, kill it before it kills you.

She glanced about for any sign of the horrible monsters that her father said lived in this place.

"She did not mention you."

And then it came to her. Bess was married to a Niyanoka. Was this Cesar's son? A chill rippled through her. Soul Whisperers spoke to the dead. They were dangerous and avoided even by their own kind. Samantha took another step back.

"My father sent me."

"His name?"

She hesitated, not wanting to give a potential enemy any information that could help him. But if he was whom he said, he would learn this soon enough. Should she trust him? She didn't trust easily and rarely outside the family. She had trusted Nôdi, the chief of the Dogrib fishing camp, and look what had happened as a result.

Her upbringing had made her paranoid, but it had not given her the skills necessary to tell truth from lies. She wished she were a Truth Seeker. Those Niyanoka could always tell if someone was lying. Her entire life had been about lies and running and hiding. She was sick of it.

Alon waited for her answer with a stillness that unnerved her. Samantha drew a deep breath, as if preparing to bungee jump from a bridge.

"Sebastian. That's his name." Now she waited. First Alon's eyebrows lifted to still greater heights and then his mouth tipped down as he nodded.

"I can bring you to our home. But unfortunately my parents are not here." He motioned to his right.

"What? Wait. My father asked them to bring me to Bess."

"And she is not here. Only *I* am here."

"But…why…" Her words fell off.

"As you said, the Thunderbirds don't make mistakes. So it must be that you are meant to be here with me. Ill-conceived choice, I fear."

"Can you contact her?"

"Not at present."

She didn't know what to do now. She couldn't go back.

"I can offer you the hospitality of our home, but we best get there before dark."

That snapped her from her musing. Why before dark?

Alon started off, and Samantha had to stretch her legs to keep pace while trying to keep from staring at him as he moved with such perfection. "So you are the firstborn of the first two Halfling races, a Seer of Souls and a great bear. Is that correct?"

It was a detail Samantha never spoke of, a secret that could bring death to her family. Just the mention of the word *Seer* caused her to stumble. He caught her before she fell, swinging her ahead of him as he captured both her upper arms.

Again that awareness tingled from the point of contact.

This man knew her most dangerous secret, yet she knew nothing of him but his name.

"I am the second born. My brother is first by several minutes," she whispered. "They told you?"

"My parents trust me. Where is your twin?"

Again she equivocated. "He was sent to a friend of my father's."

"Nicholas Chien or Tuff Jackson?"

Samantha blinked in astonishment. She did not know what to say. Alon knew the name of her father's three closest friends. Was the son of a friend also a friend?

Chapter 3

Samantha didn't know what to do. She had never been on her own before and wouldn't be now if not for her own willfulness. Because she had saved one human, her family were all running scattered to the four directions and at the mercy of strangers.

She had to find Bess Suncatcher, and she was not certain that Alon was really the Skinwalker raven's son.

"If you are a bear like your father then can you also heal wounds?" asked Alon.

Samantha hesitated and then inclined her chin. One corner of his mouth turned upward as if this pleased him.

"I am also a twin."

"Identical?" she asked.

He shook his head. "I have a sister."

"Older or younger?"

His mouth went grim and he did not answer, but instead turned away. "Follow me."

She didn't, so he stopped and turned back, his face now somber and his eyes troubled.

"Samantha, don't be so frightened."

She straightened. "I'm not."

His eyes rolled skyward at the lie. "I can hear your heartbeat."

She glared but did not deny her disquiet again.

"I will see you safely to our home. You have my word."

She believed him. But why did she believe him?

"You are a Halfling?"

He glanced back and then blew out a long breath. "Yes."

"What are your gifts?" she asked.

His eyes shifted to the undergrowth and then flicked to the branches.

"I do not consider them gifts."

She waited but he said no more. He cocked his head. She listened, scented the air and found no threat.

"Best be off." He set them in motion again.

Samantha thought back to her mother's teaching. Niyanoka could be born with any gift, not just the ones of their parents, and there were so many. Some were born with more than one. She strode beside him as she tried to recall them all. Clairvoyants, Truth Seekers, Dream Walkers, Memory Walkers, Peacemakers... And then she recalled something else. He had said she was born of the *first* two Halfling races. She stared at this man, heeded the warning that prickled over her skin and dropped back a few more steps.

"Why did the Thunderbirds carry you?" he asked. "What threatened your life?"

"Ghosts," she said. "Ghosts and the enemy of my mother, the Spirit Nagi, Ruler of all Ghosts."

This time it was Alon who lost his footing. He drew up short and turned to scrutinize her.

"Nagi?" he asked as if for confirmation.

She nodded, studying his drawn face. He was right to look so concerned. The ruler of the Circle of Ghosts was a dangerous foe. Merely helping her placed him and his entire family at risk.

"I understand if you do not want me near you, Alon."

"You are worried about *my* safety?" His voice rang with incredulity. He closed his eyes for a moment and braced his hand across his forehead as if suddenly struck with a terrible headache. "He is not near. That much I know." He remained where he was, motionless, his head bowed as if in deep thought. "And there are no ghosts about."

She gaped. "How…how? Do you see them, too?"

Only Seers and Skinwalker owls could see ghosts. And only Seers could send disembodied spirits to the Ghost Road, though her father said that an owl could sometimes trick a ghost into leaving a human host. Terrible possibilities emerged in her mind.

"I can see them." His hand dropped to his side. "And I can feel them on my skin."

Tingling fingers of terror danced like ice water down her spine. He could feel the presence of ghosts?

"What are you?" she asked, unable to keep the panic from creeping into her voice.

He did not answer, only jerked his head to scan the open meadow beyond the line of trees, catching the movement an instant before she did.

Something flashed before them, diving into the open space. Samantha stifled a scream until she recognized the brown and white feathers of a swooping harrier hawk. This was no threat, at least, not to her.

She crouched, still looking for ghosts. They appeared to her as wisps of smoke of various colors, usually at the periphery of her vision. The sunlight that streamed down on the grassy field made spotting them much more difficult than in the darkness and clear cold air of the north. It was another reason her father kept them so far north—so they could see the ghosts before the ghosts saw them.

Before them, the sun streamed down on an open field. At the center of the meadow the snow had receded completely, and lush green shoots sprang up amid the bowed yellow grass. The lush landscape reminded Samantha again of how far the Thunderbirds had carried her.

It took only an instant for the raptor to snatch up a hare. The rabbit screamed pitifully as it was whisked without warning into the sky. But the hawk had managed to sink only one set of talons into the rabbit's back, and so it kicked and writhed. The hawk flapped and flew in a crazy pattern as the struggle continued. Samantha and Alon watched in fascination.

The hawk released the hare. The rodent fell against the trunk of a downed tree and then rolled beneath. The hawk shrieked and flapped, but it could not fly beneath the thick cover of broken branches to reach the wounded hare.

"No dinner for him tonight," said Alon, revealing that he had been rooting for the hawk, while Samantha favored the hare.

She stepped out from cover, crossing quickly to the downed tree. The hawk knew her on sight, recognizing the superior predator, and quickly turned tail.

Samantha reached between the cage of dead limbs and retrieved the dying rabbit.

"Broke his back," said Alon, considering the creature.

Samantha carried the hare by the hind legs. Bleeding, torn and broken, it still waved its front paws in a pitiful effort to escape.

"Do you like rabbit?" he asked, as if she planned to make a stew. But she had no appetite for this little creature.

"It's in pain. Help me find some stones," she said.

He cocked his head, obviously confused. "Stones?"

She nodded, laying down the rabbit to search.

"How big?"

Despite their speed, by the time she had the healing circle ready, the rabbit was no longer breathing. Samantha chanted, hopeful to find the creature's heart still beating, but when she had healed the rabbit's wounds and repaired its spine, it was very definitely lifeless.

"Damn it!" she cursed.

"It looks good as new."

"It's dead," she said, pointing out the obvious.

"And you don't like rabbit stew?"

She made a sound of disgust.

"Its soul is gone," he said.

"Yes, I can see that. Thanks."

She met his aggravated stare with one of her own.

"It's just a rabbit," he said.

"And you're just a man."

His mouth quirked at that. He rose. "Wait here. It didn't go far."

What didn't? she wondered.

She watched him stride a few steps away and scoop down to snatch something that she could not see. When he turned, she saw why. There was nothing in his clenched fist.

He returned to her and sank to his knees before the little corpse. Then he shoved his fist right inside the rabbit without making a mark. His hand now seemed as insubstantial as smoke. Samantha gave a little shriek of surprise and tumbled to her hindquarters. He opened his hand and withdrew it.

"What in the name of…"

But before she could finish, the rabbit sprang to its feet and darted to cover. She gaped at the place where it had vanished before turning her attention back to him.

She pointed. "It was dead."

He nodded.

"You brought it back to life."

"No, you did that. All I did was return its soul to its body. If you hadn't fixed it, the soul would have just leaked out again." He placed his hands on his muscular thighs. She stared at those hands, which now seemed as substantial as her own, but bigger, broader and more threatening. "I can remove souls the same way."

She swallowed back her rising panic. She knew of only one creature who could harvest souls. She rolled to the balls of her feet, now in a low crouch.

"Just what the hell are you, Alon?"

"Exactly what you're thinking. I'm a Halfling but not like our parents. I am born of Nagi. A Naginoka, Samantha."

Samantha shot to her feet as if fired from a gun. A Toe Tagger! How could Alon be a Toe Tagger? Toe Taggers were ugly, hideous. She'd seen them attacking her father, seen their quills, gray skin, bulbous yellow eyes and their long, vicious fangs.

Why would the Thunderbirds bring her to him?

She stared at Alon. He was so attractive that his gaze brought her pulse racing even now.

Samantha rose and backed awkwardly away, her fear making her joints stiff.

He followed her slowly, hands open, extended—hands that could retrieve a soul or remove hers.

"Samantha, stop."

She didn't. Instead she did what her father had told her to do, what she had been doing her entire life. Samantha turned and ran.

She plunged through the forest, dodging about the huge trunks of the sequoias, thrashing through the underbrush, tearing up the ferns in her wild flight.

Nagi. He was the son of Nagi. The child of her enemy, the Spirit who had hunted her family throughout her entire life. A Toe Tagger, like the nightmare creatures she saw bearing down on them.

Why would the Thunderbirds drop her like a live rabbit into the nest of a hungry hatchling eagle?

She stifled a sob as she raced on.

Her heart beat in her temples as she tried to pull the air past the fingers of dread closing her throat. She gulped, gasped, wept as she ran. She understood now why her mother had not wanted to send her to Bess Suncatcher. Why she had asked which one would go to the raven. She had known.

Why had Alon said he was the son of Bess Suncatcher? He wasn't, couldn't be.

The brush slashed across her legs as she fled. Still in human form, she ran with the speed of a bear, thirty miles an hour, charging through the woods, snapping branches the thickness of her wrist as if they were swizzle sticks.

Was he still behind her?

She chanced a glance over her shoulder and saw nothing.

How far had she come? Far enough for the adrenaline to ebb, deserting her now, turning her knees to water.

The drum of her heart yielded to the buzz she recognized as dangerous. She'd run too far, too hard. Her body demanded rest. She could hear nothing but the unnatural hum in her ears brought on by a lack of oxygen to her brain. Samantha glanced about, slowing, gripping the tree trunk before her for support.

Where was he now?

Sweat soaked her clothing, trickled down her back and beaded upon her face. She used her sleeve to wipe her forehead, and she realized her fingers were tingling.

But she'd escaped him.

"Samantha?"

She jumped, spun and faced him. He stood some four feet before her, in a grove of ferns that brushed his bare hips. From what she could see he was naked. His mouth now dipped down in an expression of disapproval. Why wasn't he sweating? Where were his clothes? She must have sprinted six miles, and yet his breathing was normal. He had not a hair out of place, as if he'd just dropped from the sky. She glanced up.

Had he?

"Leave me alone." She managed the words between gasps for breath.

He stepped closer, leaving the ferns and giving her an eyeful. His skin was flawless, he was extremely well-endowed and his abs were as taut and defined as a male cover model's.

Samantha crouched. If she couldn't escape, she'd attack. She swung at him with one arm, a blow that would have sent any ordinary man flying, but he absorbed it without even rocking on his feet. Instead, it was she who ricocheted backward, something that had never happened to her before.

She turned and fled again, back the way she had

come, the surge of adrenaline buoying her up, giving her energy. How had he caught her? Why hadn't she heard him coming?

This time she ran until she dropped, falling to her knees behind the cover of a downed tree. She waited, listening, but could hear nothing but the roar of her blood and that warning buzz in her ears. She wondered if she might faint.

She crouched, trembling like the rabbit she had become. Gradually the sounds of the forest returned—bird song, the whine of insects, the wind in the treetops.

She placed her hands on the rough, damp bark and lifted her head like a prairie dog searching for her pursuer.

He appeared a moment later, his hair looking mussed as he drew on a gray T-shirt and slipped into his long-sleeved dove-gray shirt. When he'd fastened the second-to-last button and tucked the shirt's hem into his gray jeans, she noticed his feet were bare.

He stared directly at her as if he knew where she hid. She was on her feet and running again before he spoke, but she heard him calling for her to stop. She'd die running first.

The sudden weight of something striking her lower back hurdled her forward. His arms wrapped about her and they toppled together onto the loam of needles. He took the brunt of the fall but then rolled her so fast the world blurred for an instant.

Samantha found herself lying on her back, staring up at Alon, who now straddled her hips. He'd hooked his lower legs across her shins, pinning them to the earth. He had already gained possession of her left wrist. She took a swing at him with her right, but he blocked the blow with disquieting ease, securing her other hand. He trapped her wrists above her head. His wide torso was now poised above hers, his breathing slow and steady, as she gasped for the air she lacked.

She bucked and he shook his head in disapproval. Did he expect her to surrender just because she was beaten? She writhed in a vain effort to dislodge him. He tilted his head to study her, his expression confused.

It took only another moment to recognize that she had found a man who was stronger than she. Her brother, Blake, could pin her on a good day, as could her father. But she had never met an outsider with the strength of a bear who was not a bear. Her body went cold and her stomach cramped at the realization. She was dead.

She strained her arms, twisting, but his easy grip did not yield.

"Stop. You're hurting yourself."

Why didn't he move to finish her?

The dread ebbed against a groundswell of anger. This was not some game, at least not to her. Finally, she laid her head back, gritting her teeth against the fury of her defeat. Samantha went still, but her muscles remained taut, ready for any opportunity.

He was a Halfling, but like none she'd ever known. Born of Nagi. Born of a living ghost.

He gave her a pleased smile. To her absolute shock, she felt a flash of heat in response. Gradually she became aware of the fit of his strong legs on her hips and that weird hum of sensation where he touched her wrists.

Was this why he pursued her? Was he after her body, or was it that the idea of killing excited him? She shivered, wondering exactly what kind of a monster this might be.

He dropped to his elbows, pressing his chest to hers. She waited for the heaving revulsion she expected. But to her dismay the sensation of his warm chest pressing her to the earth set off a tingle of excitement that rippled over her skin, making her breasts sensitive.

No, no, she could not be aroused by this spawn of her enemy. She squeezed her eyes closed against the horror. When she opened them it was to find his clear blue eyes staring down into hers.

Why was he so perfectly made? This was some cruel trick of nature.

His smile made her stomach twitch. He nestled his hips against hers as if they were lovers, instead of enemies, and her body responded, becoming wet and tight in preparation. She prayed he did not have the acute sense of smell that she did, for then her humiliation would be complete.

"Kill me or let me up," she ordered.

"Neither. I'm not trying to kill you, little shifter. I am trying to keep you from killing yourself. So we'll just wait until your heart rate returns to normal."

Her brow furrowed. That would never happen. Not with his big male body blanketing her while his intoxicating scent played havoc with her senses. This was more shameful than her capture. Nothing had ever outrun her before.

She let her head drop to the earth and accepted defeat. Spots danced before her eyes and her chest ached from her exertions.

"That's better. Rest. You were running yourself to death. I stopped you."

She didn't try to hide her annoyance. "If you were so concerned, why didn't you just let me go?"

He shook his head, his expression somber as if he was sorry.

"No, it's not safe in these woods."

"I was born in the woods. I can defend myself."

"These woods are not like the ones you have known." He glanced about, scanning their surroundings. "Not at all."

She shivered at the edge in his voice and the terror his words evoked. What was here that could be more dangerous than he was?

Now Samantha did not know if she should try to escape him, or ask for his protection.

Nothing could ever catch her when she ran. Nothing and no one, until today. She had finally met her match, and he could do anything he liked to her. The realization filled her belly with terror and her heart with a thrill of anticipation.

She bucked again. His attention fixed back to her.

"Let me up," she demanded.

He shook his head, sending his white-blond hair cascading over his forehead. How could a man this appealing have been spawned by something as repulsive as Nagi?

"Not until you are rested."

"Let me up!"

He shook his head. "If I do, you'll run again. Won't you, rabbit? You're a good runner. I wonder what would happen if you ever turned to fight?"

He was right again. Her entire life had been one long game of hide-and-seek against Nagi and his ghosts.

Alon's attention strayed from her eyes, wandered lazily down her face and then fixed on her mouth.

Her lips parted as she recognized the blatant desire written on his face. His mouth quirked and his gaze slid to her throat and then her breasts before returning to fix on her eyes. The intent stare made her tingle all over.

She writhed against him, side to side, feeling his erection growing as she did so. He winced as if in pain.

"You should stop that," he said, his voice now no more than a growl.

Samantha ceased fighting.

"That's better." His voice mesmerized, his eyes hypnotized.

"What are you doing to me?"

"The same thing you're doing to me, I think."

The desire beat inside her like a living thing, demanding she yield.

"You're putting these thoughts in my head."

It had to be his thoughts. This feeling could not be coming from inside her. She could not be physically attracted to her enemy. He must be sending them to her, invading her mind as she had heard some Niyanoka could do.

He shook his head. "This does not come from me. It comes from us. It is unwelcome."

"You said it, buster."

"I meant that *I* find it unwelcome."

That shocked her into silence.

His fine hair shimmered in the sunlight, his eyes narrowed and he stared a long moment. She felt he was deciding something and found herself holding her breath.

"You were sent to my mother. That makes you my responsibility. So I place you under my protection."

"She's not your mother."

His eyes went cold then and his mouth turned hard. "What do you know about anything?"

He rolled away but held control of her wrist. She tried and failed to break his grip as he dragged her to her feet. She made an attempt to run, and he yanked her arm so that she collided with his torso. A moment later he had her in his arms.

"Stop acting like a child. I didn't invite you here," he said. "And I don't want you here. I just want to be left alone." He gave her a squeeze, pressing the breath from her. "Can you understand that? But neither of us gets what we want. I'm stuck with you. And you're stuck with me. Got it?"

"I don't need your help," she said and tried to prove it by jerking her arm free of his grasp. She failed again.

"You wouldn't last ten minutes. Now stop making a nuisance of yourself and start acting like what you are, an uninvited guest who is a pain in my ass."

She was about to laugh in his face. Did he really think she was that helpless? She was a grizzly bear, for heaven's sake, fully capable of defeating…

Some of her bravado ebbed away and she stilled. She couldn't defeat Alon. Were there others here like him?

Chapter 4

Alon held tight to the little Skinwalker, who had finally come to accept that he was stronger than she. How he'd love to just let her go. But his mother would skin him alive. Alon knew Sebastian by reputation. His mother would want him to protect her friend's child.

"If I release your wrist will you promise not to run?"

"Why? I thought you could catch me so easily." She tried for a fierce look that only put a wrinkle in her pretty brow. This game wearied him.

"Perhaps I will tie you to that tree," he said.

That arched an eyebrow as she turned to consider the tree in question. He didn't have any rope, but she didn't seem to realize that.

She held on to her anger, gnawing her full lower lip, but she conceded. "I will not run."

He released her instantly, happy to be away from the

softness of her skin and the scent that drew him like nectar.

Now he could not feel her yielding curves. But he could see them. Samantha Proud was tall for a woman, reaching nearly to his chin, and he found that he liked the way her body fit to his as much as he admired the grace of her movements.

She had an extremely pleasing feminine form, full and shapely at the breast and hip, and narrow in the waist. Her thick dark brown hair had come loose in her wild run, and she no longer wore the ridiculous ranger hat. Where had it gone? The thick strands now cascaded in a tangle over her shoulder, spilling over her full breasts and curling at her waist. Her mane framed her heart-shaped face. Her large eyes, high flushed cheeks and pointed chin combined to be more than their parts. His stomach twitched as he studied her, resisting the urge to advance. Her full lips could not be pressed into a flat, grim line, though she tried. She narrowed her cinnamon eyes at him. The unspoken threat and obvious displeasure amused him, and he felt an unfamiliar smile tease at his mouth.

"Now what?" she asked.

It was an excellent question and one to which he had no answer. He wished Aldara was here. His twin sister was the more vicious, but she was female and might know what to do with Samantha.

Alon could think of only one thing. But he knew his mother would not approve. He cast aside his baser instincts for the moment, though he had captured her fair and square. With her, he forgot his moral objections to taking a woman and began to consider how it might best be done.

"Alon?"

He had to shake his head to drive off the lustful images. Why did she have to smell so intoxicating? Why was her hair all rich brown and falling about her shoulders in a curtain. Her long lashes made her eyes even more entrancing.

"Now, I take you back to the house and…"

She raised her sculptured brows, hanging on his words. When he stopped her expression turned to disapproving.

"And?"

"Contact your folks? I'm not sure. I've never found a Skinwalker in the woods before. Why did the ghosts attack you?"

"No offense, but I don't know you. I want to speak to Bess."

He shrugged and then motioned in the direction of home. The woman was a pain, but she was also pretty, tall and strong. Any male would find her attractive. Any who was looking for companionship.

He was not. He had to remind himself again. He never would be.

"So your mom is gone. What about your twin sister and Bess's husband, Cesar Garza?"

"My sister and I are gathering the remaining yearlings." He lifted his nose, searching for Aldara's scent, but did not find it. She'd promised to stay close. "My parents took my pack north to relocate because ghosts have been seen close to this place. Neither will come back here."

"Nagi's ghosts?"

"We've known for some time that a war was coming. My parents warned yours. They warned everyone. Few would listen. Nagi is recruiting us to join his army. Your father knows this. Your family may have been the first to be attacked, but they won't be the last. An army of Ghostlings will be hard to defeat."

"Ghostlings?"

Had she not heard the term?

"Naginoka, children of Nagi. Bess calls us Ghostlings or Ghost Children. What do you call us?"

Samantha glanced away. Had she heard the other words, the ones that marked them as what they were? Walking Dead. Toe Taggers. Alon ground his teeth to keep them from lengthening. Strong emotions brought the change.

It was why he needed to be rid of her. He did not wish to admit it, but she affected him, aroused him and brought him one step closer to his most savage self.

But when he touched her, the sensation was like nothing he ever experienced, hot and cold, desire mixed with panic. She was dangerous, this one, because she threatened his control.

"What does that mean, that he's recruiting Ghostlings?" she asked.

"He's hunting us."

Samantha stopped walking, and he was forced to stop again. He didn't like talking, and he especially did not like talking about this. But he did find pleasure in her voice. The resonance and timbre hit him in the chest.

"Hunting? What happens when he catches one?"

"He gives him a choice. Join his army or die."

Her face went pale. "How many have joined?"

"Ah," he said. "For a moment I thought you sympathized with our plight." He turned away.

She trotted to catch up.

"I might be more sympathetic if they hadn't attacked my family. My father stayed behind to fight. They were slashing at him with those razor claws when the Thunderbirds took me. I don't know if he's alive or dead."

He paused so she could draw even with him. "How many Ghostlings?"

"Maybe a half dozen."

"He's dead."

Samantha staggered. He reached out to steady her. The instant his fingers brushed her hand the electric surge returned, stronger than before. His heart sped, blood roared and his arousal stirred. He broke away.

Dangerous. She was all that, and in ways he had never imagined. She looked stunned, as well. She drew her hand to her chest, cradling it as if his touch had burned her skin.

"But my father has never been defeated," whispered Samantha.

"Then he has never faced a Ghostling." This time he saw his words strike her like arrows. Her mouth dropped open and her eyes went glassy. He recalled his mother saying he was too blunt and that the truth, especially a hard truth, needed to be delivered with care.

"My father stayed to protect us, to give us time to flee."

"Then he did his duty as a father, defending his young."

"I want to go back for him."

Alon's expression was serious. "But did he not fight so you could live? To go back would be to throw away his sacrifice."

Her eyes welled with glistening silver tears, and she dashed them away as they fell.

"He asked you to find my mother. That is what you should do."

Her nostrils flared as she narrowed her dark eyes on

him, but she nodded her consent. Perhaps she did not like him reminding her of her duty to her parents.

He brushed the hair from her face, the backs of his fingers grazing the high angle of her cheekbone. The rage caught him like a blow. Was that his anger or hers?

His claws emerged from his fingers and his skin tingled with energy. The change was coming. He released Samantha and took several steps back. He needed to calm himself or she'd see him change.

"The Thunderbirds might have saved him," he offered, squeezing his hands to fists and willing himself to take slow, steady breaths. Each one brought the floral scent of her to him. The sharp claws retracted and he let his shoulders sag.

She blinked at him with those impossibly long lashes, and he was hit with another emotion—lust, deep and red. He was not touching her, so he knew that this reaction was all his. He tried to move away, but she reached out her hand. The only way to control his response was not to touch her, yet he found his arm lifting, his fingers lacing with hers. How could the simple pressing of palm to palm raise every hair on his body?

"Do you think so?"

The hope flickering in her russet-brown eyes did something to his insides. It felt as if she squeezed his heart instead of his hand. What was happening to him?

"They protect Skinwalkers. He is a Skinwalker. Therefore they protect him." The logic that so annoyed his mother seemed to help Samantha, for a smile broke like the dawn across her lovely face.

She lunged at him, and he had time only to brace himself before her arms wrapped about his neck as she hugged him. He stiffened as she pressed to him. His body sprang to attention with a rush of blood and surging need.

What madness was this? Why would she hug him now that she knew what he was?

She seemed to come to her senses in slow degrees. Did she notice that he did not hug her back? That his hands stayed in fists at his sides and he held his body rigid as a corpse? She slid off him, her toes returning to the earth as she pushed away.

He found his breath again, but each time he inhaled, the air was full of her arousing, alluring scent. He growled.

"I'm sorry, Alon. I didn't mean to upset you." She stared up at him. "What's wrong with your eyes?"

They were likely changing color, turning from icy blue to the sickly yellow of his first form. He spun, giving her his back, and stalked away.

This time *she* pursued him.

"Do you really think that he's alive?"

He would do nothing to crush the hope he now heard in her musical voice. But neither did he want her joyful again. It was too dangerous for them both.

"It's possible."

She trotted behind him in silence for a shockingly short time. Then the questions began again.

"You don't look like the ones that attacked my family. Why are you so different?"

He cast a glance back at her.

"Nothing personal, but I'm not inclined to answer your questions, either. Two-way street."

Her brow wrinkled and she stopped again, pressing both hands to her hips in a posture that reminded him of his mother when she was on a tear.

"Fine. What do you want to know?"

What she looked like naked. He paused, weighing his options, knowing he should leave her, knowing he would not.

"Well?"

"Nothing. I don't want to know anything about you except how to get rid of you."

Her hands slid from her hips and dropped to her sides. Her chin trembled for a moment before she bit down on her lower lip with straight white upper teeth. Did she use the pain to keep her from tears? He stepped closer, fascinated. His sister never cried.

"I didn't ask to come here."

"Neither did I invite you."

She folded her arms over her chest. Her breasts squeezed upward from the constriction, and he forced himself to look away an instant too late. Damn, he wanted to see what she had under that stupid uniform. He wanted to pin her to the earth and...

"How much farther?"

He didn't know if he should shake her or kiss her. He wanted to do both. He stared at the trees and prayed to the Great Spirit to send him control.

"Four hundred and fifty meters," he said.

"Do you have internet? I want to write my family and tell them I am all right."

That might be premature, he thought. If Nagi was after her, he might be following her. If he found her, Nagi would find him and Aldara and all the young ones hidden in these woods. He and Aldara were the eldest. It was their duty to keep them safe.

"To get to the computer, we have to move that way." He thumbed over his shoulder. "And you keep stopping."

Samantha continued beside him without pausing or asking her endless questions. Alon listened for the yearlings while scenting the air for their trail. For some reason they were not in their usual territory. Perhaps Aldara had succeeded in communicating with them. If anyone could, it would be his sister.

The packs roaming the property concerned him deeply. Samantha had been very lucky that he found her first.

Or was it luck? He thought of the Thunderbirds dropping her practically at his feet.

He didn't take it as some grand sign. The Supernaturals had correctly determined that he was the creature least likely to kill her on sight and placed her accordingly.

But then, why hadn't they taken her to Bess as her father had wished? They could have. They could find anyone anywhere. So why hadn't they? The reason for their action eluded and troubled him.

They broke from the trees a few moments later and entered a wide alpine meadow.

"There it is." Alon pointed.

At the crest of the rise sat the impressive log structure that looked large and grand enough to be some sort of lodge. In fact, it had been so before Bess repurposed the building into a living space for her adopted horde. When they outgrew it, Cesar built the dorms and later the school behind the main house. Alon glanced toward the clapboard construction where he now lived and then flicked his gaze at her. She'd be safer in the house. None of the yearlings ever ventured there.

"You'll stay in there," he said.

She lifted a brow as if to argue. He narrowed his eyes.

"It will be more difficult to keep you alive if you leave this place."

"The only threat that I've seen so far is you."

He didn't argue the point. He was a threat but not the only one here, regardless of what she had seen. Something about this little Skinwalker interested him, and that was dangerous for her. Alon knew what he was capable of, even if his parents did not. They had a blind spot for all their children, denying their true natures and giving them high ideals. Alon feared his parents would soon be disappointed. The prospect of Bess and Cesar seeing their "children" for what they truly were troubled him, as well.

"And how do I know that Suncatcher lives in that house?"

Alon paused. He'd never been called a liar before and found it irritated him.

"Where is she exactly?"

"Moving north with the eldest of my siblings. All that would go have gone. Aldara and I stayed behind to try to convince the others. The Beta, Gamma and Delta packs."

"Packs?"

"We run in packs with those of our approximate age. I'm Alpha. The Betas are near their final change, approaching fifteen. The Gammas are less than ten, and the Deltas only babies, two and under. The Betas have roamed too far for us to easily find them. The Gammas refuse to leave this place because they cannot conceive a threat. It is not in our nature. The Deltas are not old enough to understand what we ask. At so young an age their needs are…basic. Aldara believes we can convince all of them to follow."

"But you do not?"

"My kind is not open to persuasion. They are influenced only by superior force. To the young ones all creatures are either predator or food."

Samantha frowned at this answer.

He motioned toward the house. "Inside there is a phone, computer, food, facilities for washing. Take what you like and stay inside until I return for you."

"When will that be?"

"After nightfall."

He turned to leave her.

"When will Bess be back?"

"She has abandoned this place. When I have finished with the packs, I will bring you to her."

That did not seem to please Samantha, judging from the pinched expression and the line that now formed between her elegant brows.

"Why don't you just tell me how to find her?"

He shook his head. It was a miracle one of the packs hadn't discovered Samantha already. He wasn't about to cross his fingers and point her north.

"No."

"My father told me to find Bess."

"You can wait or you can die. Your choice." He stalked away.

Chapter 5

When Alon reached the cover of the trees he turned back. Samantha stared at the place where he had vanished into the forest. Finally she turned toward the house and marched up the front steps.

Alon lingered, watching her, fearing she would leave the house. There was some pull between them. Even from this distance he felt drawn to her. He wanted to go back, and it mattered not at all that she didn't want to speak to him or that he had business elsewhere.

What was wrong with him?

He placed the back of his hand on his brow as his mother always did when he was acting strangely. No fever. But his blood felt fevered, and his skin tingled with a soft buzz of energy that warmed him like a fire. And each time he touched her soft skin his stomach grew tight.

The door closed behind her. Only when she was out of sight was Alon able to move in the opposite direction.

He removed his clothes, folded them and set them in the crook of a tree. Then he transformed into his flying form and rocketed through the forest. In this form he was least substantial. The billowing smoke made it easy to fly in tight places but impossible to fight. But for fighting he had his first form. That was what his mom dubbed it—first form or fighting form.

Alon just called it his monster form.

Samantha stepped into the vaulted foyer of the Garzas' empty home and paused as the unexpected surrounded her.

She had thought to see an abundance of wood and rustic furnishings. Instead, she was greeted with a contemporary stairway that seemed to float upward as it was anchored only to one wall. Clean plaster and elegant molding had been painted white. Before her hung a long Japanese scroll that stretched from the second story and nearly touched the floor. The brightly colored silk edging framed an ink painting of many blackbirds rising through the air.

She peeked into the living room, taking in the sleek white leather sofa set before a glass coffee table facing a hearth with a mantel of white marble, black granite and obsidian. The elegant room had no clutter, but several unique objects of art. A splash of color came from a painting of pink cherry blossoms above the hearth and wilted red roses on the mantel.

She continued through the foyer, finding the kitchen and informal dining room filling the back half of the enormous house.

Reaching the center of the stainless-steel and black

granite kitchen, Samantha realized how thirsty she was. She cupped her hand and drank from the faucet. Only when her thirst was satisfied did she explore the offerings in the kitchen.

She felt like Goldilocks raiding the pantry of the three bears, but then remembered she was also one of the bears. Alon had invited her in. Dropped her at the door like a bad date, actually.

Bess Suncatcher kept a full larder, and Samantha had no trouble making a meal. When she had satisfied her hunger, she turned to the computer set up on a counter between two flanking pantry shelves in the walk-in larder. She'd seen such an arrangement in decor magazines, described as a place for the owner to look up a recipe or read emails.

The internet connection was surprisingly strong. None of her family had mobile phones, because changing from bear to human forms made it impossible to carry such things. But they did all have email accounts.

Samantha checked hers for news and was disappointed to find nothing from any of them. She told them of her safe arrival and where she landed. She paused before telling them about Alon, not knowing what to say. She told them she had seen their father attacked before being torn away from them by the whirlwinds and that she feared for his safety. Finally she said she had not yet found Bess but was in her home. Samantha pressed Send and glanced around, noting that the bare windows had gone dark. Nightfall, she realized.

When would he be back?

She headed upstairs to one of the bathrooms and took a moment to wash then transformed her bearskin into fitted jeans and a gauzy peasant blouse. She wore no underwear, socks or shoes. She had preferred it that way since she was a child. The less restraining her garments, the better.

"Now, let's just see who lives here."

When she was finished exploring the house, she reached the conclusion that Cesar Garza and Bess Suncatcher did live here until quite recently. So Alon had not lied about that. The Thunderbirds could find people, especially people who were not where you expected them to be. Yet they had plunked her here in this empty house.

It made no sense.

Samantha stared out the picture windows into the night. Should she stay or go? Alon could be bluffing, but thus far everything she could verify had been true.

The yearlings were out there. How dangerous could they be? She was a grizzly bear for goodness' sakes. Nothing could defeat her.

Alon had.

Samantha sighed and decided to check her email again. Perhaps there was some word. The inbox popped up with one new message.

Samantha saw Blake's address and suddenly she could breathe again. Her brother was alive.

A moment later she scanned his message. He had arrived uninjured at the home of the wolf and the Dream Walker. Nicholas had left Blake in charge of his family as he went to search for their father. Samantha sagged in her chair. The wolf was going to help her father. He'd find him. She knew a wolf's gifts. Nicholas could track down anyone he had ever met. But would he be too late?

The worry gnawed at her like termites in dry wood as she read on. Tomorrow Blake would meet the chief of the Northwestern Council. In less than an afternoon he had found whom he sought, been trusted with Nicholas's family and begun the process of becoming a member of their mother's people, while she had spent the afternoon running through the woods like a headless chicken and creepy-crawling a stranger's house.

Samantha wilted a little in her chair.

Oh, and let's not forget that she had met a Toe Tagger who could steal a creature's living soul. She shivered.

"What's wrong?"

Samantha exploded out of the chair at the same instant she recognized Alon's voice. She clutched her chest with both hands as her gaze snapped to his. He stood in the door to the pantry, arms folded over his chest, his silvery blond hair now pulled back into a neat ponytail.

Samantha gasped. "You might have given me a heart attack."

"Your heart is strong," he said.

Was he referring to the self-imposed stress test she'd given herself in the forest?

Why hadn't she heard him or smelled him? Her senses were excellent, far better than a human's. Nobody sneaked up on her, yet he had gotten all the way to the doorway of the pantry before she'd noticed him.

And now he blocked the only exit.

The hairs on her neck lifted.

His broad shoulders did not leave her enough territory to squeeze by him. She did not like the way he stared unblinking at her. It made her feel…hunted.

"Step back, Alon," she growled, lowering her chin as she prepared for a fight she would likely lose.

His smile widened as if anxious to answer the challenge in her voice.

He arched a brow. "Or what?"

Samantha lowered her chin a notch. "Or I'll make you step back."

He didn't move for a long, silent moment. Then he

stood sideways and swept a hand toward the opening, like a courtier moving aside to let a lady pass.

He gave a half grin that made her stomach flutter and churn all at once. She'd never met anyone who made her feel anxious and thrilled at the same time. It was as if his presence made her senses go haywire.

She tried to judge his intent and failed, losing herself in those fathomless blue eyes. He was so effortlessly appealing, but terrifying too. She couldn't decide if she should run from him or to him.

She took a step in his direction. Unlike humans, she listened to her instincts, and they told her not to be trapped between escape and this Halfling. But there was another instinct, a deeper, more disquieting urging that she did not care to scrutinize as she glided forward.

His eyes dared her to cross. His smile relayed his eagerness for the sport. Was this a game to him? Why was she willing to play?

Samantha tried not to show her nervousness as she took another step forward, but now her knees felt stiff and her gait awkward. He maintained his position, head bowed, one arm extended toward freedom. His devilish smile encouraged, and the predatory glint in his eyes warned her to be cautious.

She almost made it past him before he lunged forward. She did not have time to escape or defend. An instant later she found herself with both hands trapped behind her back as he used his body to push her to the opposite side of the frame. Her body twitched with the shock of all that male flesh pressed to hers.

"What upsets you, Samantha?"

"Besides you?"

He grinned, flashing strong white teeth, and her stomach dropped. Why did his nearness do that to her?

She knew who he was and *what* he was. This son of her enemy was just like the horde that attacked her family. And yet…

"Tell me," he coaxed.

She gazed up into those entrancing blue eyes. Was that why she reacted to him, because he did not look like those others? Her mind knew what he was, but her body seemed fooled by the masquerade. He had two forms, and this one was the most dangerous because she could not defend against his appeal.

"Let me go," she said, just managing the words through clenched teeth. Her control slipped and she leaned forward instead of away.

He noticed, judging from the roguish smile full of male confidence. The urge to head-butt him was easier to resist than the impulse to lay her cheek on the hollow between his strong neck and wide shoulders. She came so close she could feel the heat of his skin on her face. His voice rumbled from his chest and she felt the vibrations on his skin.

"Do you have word from your family? Is that why you were unhappy?" He released her wrists with no fanfare. Now his hands gently stroked her back in a way that might have been comforting but instead set every nerve beneath the thin fabric of her shirt tingling with pleasure. Somehow he still captured her, but now he did it only with his touch.

Breathe. Answer the question. Step away. Put your arms about his neck.

Clearly she didn't know her own mind.

"My brother has reached his destination."

"That's good, isn't it?"

She sagged against him, unsure why her lip was trembling. The tears already burned her throat, but she held them off.

"How did you know where Blake went?"

"Your father would send him to the wolf or the buffalo. Those are his closest friends. But Chien is his oldest friend, and Blake, is it? Blake is his oldest son."

Handsome and smart. A double threat, thought Samantha.

"So why does the news of your brother's safe arrival upset you?"

She glanced away and managed to take her hands from his strong arms. The emotions she felt over her brother's success did not do her credit.

Alon's palms still danced rhythmically up and down the long column of her back.

"Will you tell me?"

She stared up at him. What gave him the right to pry, when he wouldn't answer her questions?

His eyes narrowed on her and the feathery touches ceased as if he sensed her change of mood. But that was impossible.

She stepped away and continued until she stood before the French doors that led out to a gigantic multilevel deck with a starlit view of the meadow and tall trees beyond. Her night vision was better than a human's and she saw the world beyond the window in shades of gray. The urge to return to him and nestle in his arms tugged at her.

No, you don't. You are not falling for that pretty face, those soothing words or those skillful fingers. Remember what he is.

Alon exited the pantry a moment later, and she realized he had read Blake's letter.

"So your father wants Blake to join the Niyanoka.

But he sent you here. Odd. What is your mission, little shifter?"

He came to stand beside her, a little too close, a little too tempting.

"Alon, we were attacked by your kind." She nearly told him it was her fault but stopped herself. "They tried to kill us. You are one of them. Why would I tell you anything?"

"Because I can help you."

She shook her head. "You want to help? Stay away from me."

"I thought you wanted to find my mother?"

She released a long breath. It was what her dad wanted. Find Bess. Ask her to join the cause and…and… She tried to remember his words. *None know the Toe Taggers better than Bess. Learn what you can.*

She fixed her eyes on Alon.

He folded one arm across his chest, using it as a rest for his other elbow. He studied her as if she were some problem he had to work out.

"My mother says that people distrust what they don't understand. If I tell you something about my family, how we came here and why we are different from those others who attacked your family, would that assuage you?"

"Assuage? Are you for real?"

"My parents are both over one hundred. I learned speech from them." He shrugged as if that explained all. Then he opened the door to the deck and stepped outside, then moved aside to let her pass. This time he stood well back and made no move to hinder her. She felt disappointed, and that realization made her heart sink even more.

Above them the stars wheeled in a perfect clear sky. Her vision was adequate enough for her to see him in shades of gray. In the night his aura became unmistakable and most definitely gray—bluish-gray, like the smoke from a rifle. It flared from the crown of his head like a halo.

He took a seat on the long built-in bench and motioned for her to join him. No way was she sitting that close. She moved upwind, so she couldn't smell the masculine scent, choosing to lean against the rail. She tried for a relaxed posture, certain that he could see her as clearly as she could see him. For them, the night masked nothing.

She gazed out at the inviting lawn, dew already glistening on the soft grass. From here she could jump to the ground and dash to the forest. But now she knew that he could also outrun her. Damn, she hated his advantage.

Alon settled back, secure in his superiority, she assumed, and then began the telling that was supposed to magically change her from enemy to friend. Yeah, right!

"My sister and I are the first of the Ghostlings to be adopted by my parents. My father found my sister and me in a Dumpster on Fisherman's Wharf in San Francisco. I was naked, afraid and starving."

She wanted to ask why none of their mothers survived, but that would imply an interest.

"He brought us here and gave us clothing, food, a home and a purpose." He met her eye. "To protect the Balance and to protect Mankind."

She cocked her head. His adoptive parents had combined each of their purposes. Bess, a Skinwalker, protected the Balance of Nature. Her husband, a Spirit Child, was charged with the care of all Mankind.

"But the two aims often run in opposition."

"True."

"*Is* that your purpose?"

"I accept the need to protect men and the need to guard nature. But I do not know if it is *my* purpose."

She sensed the honesty of his answer, and that surprised her. It would perhaps have been wiser to lie. She started to tell him that she knew her purpose, but that she had never been able to use her abilities because of Nagi. In the end she said nothing about that and instead asked another question.

"So they adopted you?"

"Yes. All of us. They teach us in that school." He pointed to the building to the right. "My sister, Aldara, is very good at finding newborns and bringing them here. Our parents have never turned away a set of twins."

"What happened to your real mother?"

He glanced away, hoping to hide the rush of shame. "Died giving birth. She was human. I don't remember her." He cleared his throat, but the emotion lodged there like a chicken bone. "We have forty-eight twins now, but six are under one year."

Her eyes rounded at the number.

"Why are there so many orphans?"

He held her gaze even as the guilt consumed him like a forest fire. "All humans die giving birth to my kind."

She gasped. "All?"

He nodded and dropped his gaze to his folded hands.

She could see the anguish on his face. His eyes pinched shut. All traces of the calm self-assurance vanished, and she felt that she was seeing him for the first time. The rawness of his pain stirred an ache deep inside her. She had believed that his handsome veneer was a mask. Now she wondered if his confident air was a facade, as well.

His birth caused his mother's death. What a terrible burden to bear. This was too awful to be a lie. Her instincts told her that his words were true and his pain genuine. She did not know whom she felt most sorry for, Alon, never knowing his birth mother, or the humans, used by Nagi and discarded like old wrapping paper.

She didn't remember crossing to him or sitting next to him, but there she was at his side, taking one of his hands in both of hers. Suddenly the grief drenched her until she swam in it like a river. He glanced up at her now, the pain still glittering like shards of glass in his pale eyes.

"I'm sorry for your loss, Alon."

"I didn't know her," he whispered.

"That only makes it a greater loss."

He nodded and his Adam's apple bobbed. Why had she assumed that he was incapable of feeling pain? He wasn't. He was a Halfling like her, and that meant he was half human.

The other half was Nagi. She slipped her hands back to her own lap. He let her go but stared at her hand as he struggled to gain control of his ragged breathing.

"My parents know Nagi is hunting us. They are trying to find a safe place for our family. I wanted to accompany them, to protect them, but she bade me to protect the young ones. They cannot yet reason and do not understand the need to flee. But there have been ghosts here, scouts of Nagi. I know he will find us sooner or later. We must be gone before he comes for us."

She reached for him again and checked herself. "Protect them? How does one protect against an immortal?"

"We have had this discussion many times. I do not know how to stop him, but I can stop his ghosts and I can stop the Ghostlings who have joined him."

His own siblings, she realized, half brothers and half

sisters. She shuddered. He caught her physical display of aversion and narrowed his eyes on her.

"I would prefer to fight than run."

"Just the opposite of me."

"You are a good runner. But it is not your nature."

She threw up her arms, flapping them uselessly at her sides. "Oh, you're wrong. I've been running my entire life. Hiding, pretending I have no powers." She stared at him, feeling a connection that was not there before. "All I want in this world is to use my powers to protect the Balance and keep men safe from Nagi. Do you know what it is like to have the powers to help, to save lives, and never be able to use them? I want my family safe, but sometimes…"

There was that protective wall again. What had she been about to say?

"Sometimes?"

She cradled her forehead in her hands. "It's not me. I want to be useful, but I also need my family safe. I just wish I could figure out a way to do both."

Alon stared at the woman at his side. This conversing was difficult, like a dance they had been taught. Two steps forward, two steps back and swing. Still he felt more comfortable with Samantha than he did with any other except his twin. Why was that?

Certainly he had never told a living soul what he had shared with her. She had the power to use that information to hurt him. Did she realize the risk he had taken to earn her trust? If it helped him protect her, it would be worth the hazard of laying himself bare before her.

"I have the opposite trouble. I want to find a place where I won't ever need to use my powers. I do not wish to steal away souls."

She wondered if that was why he had said he wanted to be left alone.

"You are lucky to have a gift that is of some benefit. Mine is a curse."

"But you can return souls to the body. That's positive."

He made a sound that seemed a growl. "Rarely. When a soul escapes it is because the body can no longer hold it. It seeps away like rain into sand. I put it back and it only bleeds away again." He turned his gaze on her, and the look was one of exquisite sorrow. "I would need someone who could heal the body before I could return the soul."

She looked quickly away. He was right. With her healing skills and his ability to retrieve a soul, they could save many who would otherwise be lost. The prospect both terrified and thrilled.

Was it right to save one whose soul had already begun its journey to the Way of Souls? She didn't know.

"I fear the day Nagi finds us. But even more I fear leaving the Gamma Pack behind."

"Because they would die without you?"

He lifted his face to the night sky as if choosing his words with care. At last he spoke. "We can survive without any assistance from birth. I am not afraid *for* them. I am afraid *of* them. Without guidance they could easily join Nagi, and then I would have to kill them."

"He would take newborns?"

"Yes." He scrubbed his palms over his cheeks as if the topic exhausted him. "It is one of the reasons my mother asked my sister and me to stay behind. If we are not found within the first year it is much more difficult to civilize us. Any we have not found will likely join Nagi. They will become like the ones who attacked your family. A new deadly race."

Instead of the fury she expected, she felt sorrow. These infants were born with no one to protect them or raise them. Only Bess Suncatcher and Cesar Garza gave a damn about them.

She sat up straight and stared at Alon as she felt the sensation of icy fingers creeping over her skin. He had done it. Somehow in the course of a simple conversation he had made her feel sorry for those hideous monsters that had attacked her family.

At last she said, "Your parents are very wise."

Chapter 6

Alon sat beside Samantha on the bench.

A quarter-moon crept over the tall trees, the silvery beams pouring between the mighty trunks. It was not enough to illuminate the dark places on the forest floor.

All that he had told her had made a difference. She still saw the Ghostlings as enemy, but now she also saw them as something more than feral, evil interlopers. Could they also be victims of Nagi's reckless need to control the Living World?

She didn't like to think of them that way. It would make it harder to kill them when the time came, and she would need to kill them when the fighting began.

Samantha glanced at Alon. Which side would he take—that of his adoptive parents or that of his real father?

She rose and walked to the rail of the balcony. The

chorus of peepers filled the air and leather-winged bats darted through moonbeams in pursuit of their next meal.

He followed her, standing close enough so she could detect his presence, but not so close that she could feel his heat. Her aura flared at his proximity, shining violet and cinnamon. She did not think he could see auras, for he never glanced to the place where one would find them.

His fair hair seemed to glow as pale as spun silver in the moonlight. She glanced toward him and then forced her gaze away and then finally gave up the battle and turned so her hip rested against the rail and her eyes rested on him.

The disturbance he caused her had changed from fear to something more troubling. Now she felt him on her skin like the wind before a storm. She breathed in his scent and found herself hungry for more. He was invading her senses as surely as his kind had invaded her world.

She wouldn't have it. She would not be controlled like a human possessed by some evil ghost. Her heart went cold. Was that what he was doing, some sort of possession? Samantha gripped the rail until her fingers ached.

The dampness of her skin and the heat of her face worried her. She met his steady gaze, refusing to be the first to look away, knowing the wise thing was to break this spell.

Alon moved closer and Samantha resisted the urge to step back. Why was she always running?

"It's late," she said, or she'd meant to say it. Instead her words were a low, hushed murmur, as if she feared to wake some sleeping tiger between them.

Alon was more dangerous than all that. She knew it. He was the stronger and he compelled her in some way that she did not understand. He made her breathless with only a look, and she wanted to touch the intriguing planes of his cheeks. But that was only one of his faces, she reminded herself.

Instead she pressed back to the rail, holding on with both hands as her control thinned until she feared a single breath might break it. She looked away. It wasn't a retreat, exactly, just a moment without looking into his blue eyes. Her attention fixed on the false security of the bedroom she had chosen on the second floor. Poised between the unfamiliar woods and the unfamiliar home, she felt lost.

She turned again to Alon and found him a step closer. She never heard him move. Her skin prickled a warning. He reached, and she leaned away in a halfhearted effort to evade. A moment later he had captured her just above the elbows. Her gauzy shirt did not cover her arms, and she felt the heat of his hands on her bare skin. His earthy scent intoxicated. She rolled her weight to the balls of her feet, knowing she appeared too eager but unable to hold herself back.

Dangerous and alluring all at once, she decided.

"I have to go," he said.

She nodded, wanting him to go and wanting him to pull her near. The urge to press herself to him beat in her with the rapid pounding of her pulse. "Stay in the house," he ordered. His voice, now low and full of a gravely tenor, vibrated through her deliciously.

She shivered and pressed closer.

Alon glanced toward the bedroom above, glowing now with the soft artificial light she'd left on. She followed his gaze.

"Is that the room you have selected?"

She nodded.

"Interesting that of all the rooms in this house, you have chosen the one that I once occupied."

His room? She had picked his bedroom.

Samantha couldn't breathe. She couldn't swallow.

She'd be sleeping in Alon's bed.

"You'll be safe here. My siblings know not to come into the house. Stay indoors until I come for you."

She wanted to tell him that she did not have to obey his orders. Instead she nodded her consent.

"How long?"

"Until morning."

He lifted a hand and stroked her head, running long pale fingers down her shoulder. When he reached the middle of her lower back, he eased her forward until their bodies met at the hip.

"Then you'll bring me to your mother?" she asked.

Alon did not answer. Instead he held her with one hand while the other gripped the rail, as if he needed it to stay upright.

"Will you?" she asked.

"Once I know where to find her, yes."

She reached for him now, eager to put her hands about his neck, angling her mouth to meet his. But he captured both her wrists, staying them for a moment until she realized what she was doing and had time to reconsider.

"Don't, Samantha. I'm not this face or this form. I have three shapes. This one is a lie. Think. Remember what I am."

Then he let her go.

What was she doing? This was no friend and certainly no lover. Alon was a Toe Tagger. The fact that she'd forgotten, even for an instant, only emphasized just how dangerous he was.

He nodded his approval. "Now go in the house and stay there."

She backed toward the French doors, wanting to run and wanting to object all at the same time. He was treating her like a child, treating her just as her parents had done. She didn't like it. Samantha's shoulders sagged as she realized she was still acting like a child.

When she bumped the glass, she fumbled for the handle. Samantha gripped it as she looked to Alon, but he was gone and all that remained was a pile of discarded clothing. How had he vanished like that?

She made it inside and locked the door, knowing the ridiculousness of that as a method to keep Alon out. If he chose, he could break any lock more easily than she could.

It was a long time before she left the window, before her heart returned to a normal rate, before her skin lost its tingle.

Samantha made her way upstairs and prepared for bed as if this was any normal night, but nothing was normal. She checked her email again and discovered that her mother had arrived safely in New York and had already met with the chief of the Northeastern Council. Blake's second email said that Chien's father-in-law, a Peacemaker, would bring him to meet the chief of the Northwestern Council in Spokane, Washington, tomorrow. There was still no word from her dad. But Nicholas Chien was tracking him. That gave her reason for hope.

Samantha slept restlessly. She woke with a start to find the room bathed in sunlight and Alon standing at the foot of her bed. Or was it his bed?

She startled up and back, hitting her head on the wooden headboard.

"Are you trying to scare me to death?"

"I just have that effect on people."

"I'm not people."

"Right." He lifted a mug. "Coffee?"

She extended her hand in acceptance, using the other to cover herself. She had fashioned her cloak into a cotton shift on the chance that something like this might happen, but it was short and sleeveless and Alon had a way of making her feel exposed even when she was fully dressed.

Alon backed away and Samantha took a sip. The coffee was black and sweet.

"How did you know I take sugar?" she asked.

"I could smell it in the mug you used downstairs."

"I washed that mug."

He shrugged. He was more handsome today than she remembered. The dove-gray shirt and darker gray trousers made his eyes seem bluer than she recalled.

"How long have you been standing there?"

"Only a moment, unfortunately."

She drew up her knees and used both hands to embrace the mug. Should she order him out or ask him to sit?

"You should have knocked."

"Why?"

"Because it's impolite to enter a woman's room without permission."

"It's my room and you are not a woman."

She narrowed her eyes. "But I am still your guest. Or am I a prisoner?"

"I have no hold on you. I only try to keep you safe out of respect for my mother. But you interfere with my work."

She leaned back against the headboard, took another sip of coffee and then cradled the mug between her hands.

"But you'd rather be left alone?"

"Yes. It would have been better for me and for you if the Great Birds had not carried you to me."

On that, at least, they agreed.

"How did you disappear like that last night?"

"My second form is a kind of vapor that resembles smoke or mist."

He could turn into smoke? "Is that how you caught me in the forest?"

"Yes, but I could have run you down."

"You said second form. How many do you have?"

"Three. The one that you saw at your home, the vapor and this." He waved a hand over the front of his body. "Our final form."

He rubbed the back of his neck and glanced toward the balcony as if planning his escape.

"I heard from my mother," she said.

"Is she well?"

"Yes."

"But you have not heard from your father, the great bear. And so you are worried." Alon looked away.

She knew what he thought. But he was wrong. Her dad wasn't dead. He couldn't be.

"When can we go find Bess?"

"Perhaps tomorrow."

She slammed the mug on the side table, threw back the covers and slipped from the bed. Only when she noted him staring at her legs did she remember she was not well dressed for a fight. Or perhaps she was perfectly dressed. He was obviously distracted.

"I can't sit around the house doing nothing."

"I have already written to my mother of your arrival. She has yet to reply."

"Tell me which way she went and I'll find her myself."

"Much as I would like that, I must bring you."

Had she really almost kissed him last night? She couldn't believe her own stupidity. Frustration seethed within her and she lashed out.

"My dad needs help. He wants your mother to join us. I need to bring her his words."

His voice fairly dripped with scorn. "Why would she join you?"

She lost it. "Because she's a Skinwalker and because the Toe Taggers attacked my dad!"

At the phrase *Toe Tagger,* Alon's face went stormy. He glared at her with such loathing that she drew up short. An instant later she recognized what she had said, and regret pooled in her belly. "I'm sorry, Alon."

He headed for the door and she followed, matching his quick stride. "I forgot, Alon. I said I was sorry."

He spun on the stairs. The muscles of his jaw bunched and his mouth tipped down at both corners, and still he was the handsomest man she had ever seen.

When he spoke, it was through gritted teeth. "Don't forget. Don't ever forget for a second what I am."

He continued down the stairs at a lope.

"Alon, don't you dare leave me here again."

But he was already in the foyer and out the door.

Fine. The Thunderbirds might have dropped her here, but that didn't mean she had to stay. Nicholas Chien was not the only one who knew how to track someone.

Samantha followed the long driveway that wound through the woods. She only had to find civilization to access her accounts and get the money needed to go anywhere she pleased. She'd consult with her mother just as soon as she got clear of this compound. A familiar scent reached her. She paused, debating between following Alon and getting clear of this place.

The hell with him, she decided and continued, stopping again when she found his clothing, folded and stashed in the crotch of a tree. His scent now became more difficult to trace. It hovered in the air, but she could not find it on the ground. Likely he had turned to smoke. She shook her head and returned to the road. Sooner or later that would lead her to people.

She'd try to stay out of any large communities. The bigger the population the more chance she'd see ghosts. She didn't need one of Nagi's spies finding her before she could find her family.

Aldara had found the trail of the Beta Pack last night and reported their whereabouts to Alon before returning to them while he continued to hunt for the Gammas. The ten sets of Beta twins were old enough to understand and obey the rules their parents set out for them. His parents had left him and his sister in charge of their siblings. That meant guarding against vigilante Skinwalkers and Nagi's ghosts. His mother long suspected that Nagi used the evil ghosts to find his kind. Samantha's arrival required that they notify the packs not to attack her. It had taken half the night, but he and Aldara had finally located both the Deltas' and Gammas' trails. She'd taken the Gammas.

That left him the Delta Pack, youngest and most difficult. They still struggled with control. They had no natural enemies, so the concept of danger was as foreign to them as it was to a shark. Six twins all under two, feral and deadly as loaded weapons. The Delta Pack could not yet reason, could barely speak and were ruled by a voracious appetite that made it dangerous even for him to seek them out. He didn't know if he could make them understand that Samantha was not here to kill them. But he had to try. Damn her for coming here. His parents had drilled into his and his sister's heads that Skinwalkers were dangerous, especially if they traveled in packs. They'd known for years that vigilantes had been hunting the newborns. It was a miracle he didn't kill Samantha the instant he recognized her for what she was, Skinwalker, hunter, killer of infants. Only she wasn't like them any more than he was like Nagi's Ghostlings.

The sooner he got her out of here the better. But he couldn't leave the others unguarded. He needed to take the Beta, Gamma and Delta packs to the only mother they'd ever known while keeping them from killing Samantha. It seemed impossible.

The Delta Pack knew to stay away from the house and somehow recognized their parents as other than food. But would the house protect Samantha once they scented her? He didn't know.

He had to hurry.

His mother's information had been right. Since his parents' departure, some ten days ago, Aldara had seen evil ghosts drifting in the woods. If they had not located any of the three packs yet, it was only a matter of time. He and Aldara were in a battle against Nagi's lust for his children to join his cause.

Something moved behind him. He changed to his fighting form and reversed course. Was it a vigilante? Was it one of Nagi's Ghost Children? Was this the day that Nagi's vanguard found their hiding place?

Alon did not get far before he scented Samantha.

Damn her for not staying put. He wheeled and followed her trail.

He should have explained the danger. He had not, for to do so was to reveal completely what he had been. Still was. Always would be.

He'd been too weak to let her see his true self, and now she was here. He scented the air to assure himself that the Gamma and Delta packs were not near. When he closed on her position, he shifted from his flying form, moving swiftly to one of the many caches of clothing he had about these woods. In a few moments he wore the damp gray sweater and black jeans.

Then he changed course again, running to intercept her and bring her back to the house. The fear for her safety bolted through him like a thunderstorm. He had always felt protective of his family and responsible for the actions of the others. But this was something new, because until this minute he had never been afraid.

Samantha made him afraid.

Why should he care?

He didn't understand it. But since the moment she had appeared from that storm, she had consumed him. He craved contact of her flesh to his and longed for that trembling emotion that he felt vibrate through her each time he pressed his body to hers. She knew what he was, but she could not know what he was capable of. If she did, she never would have stayed the night.

Somehow he had kept away. But each time he saw her, the urge to have her grew stronger. He wanted to devour her. Taste her skin on his tongue and feel his body joining with hers.

Samantha exposed his weakness and his corporal need.

Anticipation and worry beat in his chest. He would

find her, ensure her safety and then…Alon's speed quickened.

He found her a moment later hurrying along the foot-path his Alphas used to run their territory. The trail ran parallel to the curving drive that led to the highway.

"What are you doing here?"

Samantha startled. The thick rope braid swung over her shoulder and settled between her breasts. Today she was dressed for the woods in a scooped-neck shirt and light fleece vest that hugged her bosom. His skin itched as he looked at the generous curve of her hips empha-sized by her tight jeans.

"I…I…"

"Go back."

She recovered quickly. Color still flooded her pretty face, but now she was scowling at him. It didn't help. He still wanted her. His attention fixed on her raspberry-colored lips. What would it feel like to brush his mouth to hers, press her soft curves to his hard ones and meld together like hot metal?

"You are not my keeper." She managed the words with just the right amount of indignation.

"Obviously, or I would have locked you up."

She gasped at that. He smiled, picturing her locked in the bedroom he once occupied, waiting for him there in that short little cotton nightie.

He moved closer. The lecture he had given himself, the knowledge that his very presence here endangered her, was not enough to stop him. Not enough to drown out the roar of need she roused in him.

He captured her easily, so easily that if he did not know better he would almost guess that she came here only for this.

Then he recalled that she had never seen his fighting form. He should show her now. No. He never would.

Samantha would know only the handsome, virile form that drew human females like nectar draws bees. She would know only the lie. He could take her if he wanted, and she'd let him unless she discovered what he was inside. Then she'd run screaming. He drew her closer.

Someday she'd realize what he was. Then he'd let her go. But for now he was just selfish enough to take what she offered—consequences be damned.

Chapter 7

Alon tilted his head. Samantha gazed up at him, her eyes half-closed as if she were caught on the edge of a dream. Her lips parted and she lifted her chin, as the appeal of his third form drew her to him, making her eager now for what he would give her.

He couldn't. Taking a woman would cause the cycle to begin again. If his kind reproduced, the Living World would never be rid of them. Alon's convictions collided hard with his desires.

She brought a hand to his cheek, and his craving for this woman drowned all his high-minded philosophy and notions of selfless sacrifice. His desire pounded and poured like floodwaters, sweeping away all objections.

She was his woman. He needed her and she was willing. That was enough.

Samantha made no objections. Was the attraction so all-consuming that she could not think at all?

She was on her toes now, and her arms encircled his neck as if she were capturing him.

Their mouths met, firm, eager, greedy.

Alon deepened the kiss, holding the little Skinwalker tight to his body. Did she know she played with fire?

Strong emotions brought the change. With the thinning of his control the demon inside took over. He feared that side and still he let her kiss him deep and hard, their tongues stroking and sparing.

He relished each small quavering sound of need that now emanated from her throat. She tightened her arms about his neck, trying to hold him. If she knew what was inside him she'd be fighting for escape.

Alon threaded his fingers in her thick dark hair, cradling her head, controlling her in a way that both thrilled and terrified. Her lips were velvet and her mouth hot and wet. He thought of that sweet mouth, that strong tongue working on another part of him, and his body hardened with need. Here was a woman who wanted him and whom he wanted. And one strong enough to take all he would give her. A Skinwalker. A great grizzly bear.

He growled as his skin tingled, signaling the beginning of his change. She'd made a mistake letting him touch her, because now he was never going to let her go.

She made another sound that might have been alarm, and he feared she would draw back. No, he wouldn't let her. But she didn't. Instead, she delved her fingers into his hair, tucking herself beneath his arm, lifting a warm thigh to his hip and using her heel to pull herself even closer to him.

He could take her beneath this very tree. He felt his nails extend and harden into the claws that were as vicious as knife blades. His mouth widened, stretching to accommodate the teeth poised to jut from his gums.

Alon tore away.

Samantha rocked forward, catching herself on the trunk of a tree on one extended arm, her expression momentarily dazed, her sweet pink mouth parted and her cheeks flushed with desire. He'd never forget that dreamy expression. He paused to drink her in, mouth open, panting and her lips swollen from his kisses. Before she could focus her eyes upon him, he shifted, soaring upward into the trees like the exhaust from a rocket. Just one more second and she would have seen him as he was born.

He'd been right to fear his control. A single kiss and he'd nearly let her see.

Alon dived and darted through the forest, surging away from Samantha as fast as he could.

Until today he'd shifted into his fighting form only when angry. But he'd been right to fear Samantha. His excitement for her was new, strong and dangerous.

He'd almost turned into his fighting form right in front of her. His monster form, that was more accurate. The form he could not bear to look at even himself. But it was a shape that was strong and deadly and thus far unmatched.

What would Samantha have done, he wondered, had she seen the rows of teeth snarling and snapping? Run? Scream? Turn away in disgust?

A fresh wave of shame broke inside him. He was born of the dead. He knew it was true. She'd been right to call his kind Toe Taggers, for it highlighted all he was in just two little words. Was he part of this Living World as his parents insisted, or was it as he feared—that he belonged to the world of ghosts?

He rocketed forward, fleeing, flying from the pretty

little temptation. If she had any sense she would run in the opposite direction.

His willingness to compromise everything in which he believed in the heat of lust only proved that he had been right. Since he was old enough to understand what he was and where he had come from, he had known that he was a threat to the Balance, to everything good and pure in this living world. He knew it, felt it in his beating heart. And he had nearly hurt the only good thing that had ever come his way. He did not belong in this living world. He belonged with the dead and the evil and the dark.

Would she forgive him?

If he had any pity, any shred of humanity, he would leave her behind and never return. As he flew from her, he pictured her in his mind, the pretty dark brown hair caught in a long ropelike braid, healthy skin the color of a walnut shell. He found her full lips enticing. Her eyes were cinnamon brown with golden flecks near the iris, and the corners of her lids sloped upward, slightly giving her a smoldering look that kicked him in the stomach whenever she stared at him. He liked that and he liked her curvy shape and full breasts. What would she look like naked?

He recalled their kiss. Why had his flesh tingled when she touched him? He had never experienced anything like that before.

Alon's distraction prevented him from immediately perceiving several of his kind moving in the forest.

Yearlings hunting in a pack. The Deltas moving fast along the forest floor. He'd found them.

Alon stopped. Fear, cold as the blade of a knife, stabbed deep into him. How could he have left her?

The Delta Pack was too young to understand that Samantha was not an animal, not prey.

Alon turned back. He had to reach her before they did.

Samantha scrambled after Alon as he evaporated before her. She stifled a scream as his body became clear as water and then turned to smoke. An instant later he billowed upward like a storm cloud, leaving her earth-bound and craning her neck to watch him disappear into the new green leaves above her. His clothing fluttered down to earth as if blown from a laundry line high in the treetops.

So this was his second form. Of course he had outdistanced her yesterday. He could fly like a storm cloud, a fierce dark storm cloud.

He was Naginoka, Ghost Child, a real living, breathing Toe Tagger. She realized she knew nothing about him except what he had allowed her to see.

If he was born of Nagi, how could Alon be so attractive? And then she realized what had to be the truth. Alon had told her that he had three forms. She knew what they were—smoke, handsome and hideous.

She'd seen the first two. If she was right, his natural form was as much a part of him as her bear form was a part of her. Had he run to keep her from seeing him as he was born?

She should know better than to kiss her enemy, yet just the memory excited her. Was it his immense power, the danger that hung about him like a mantle, or the loneliness she could taste on his tongue? Samantha had never met anything that was stronger than she, except her dad, of course. And there were precious few creatures that could outrun a grizzly. Alon had done it without breaking a sweat.

She pressed a hand to her heart as it pounded painfully against her ribs. Fast, as if she had been running instead of standing in his arms.

Her initial spark of excitement had ignited like dry tinder, burning her up inside. She had kissed Alon, the son of her most bitter enemy.

Samantha's neck ached from staring past the mighty pines and through the limbs to the blue skies beyond. Where had he gone?

She glanced to the ground at his clothing, a gray sweater that smelled of pine and damp black jeans, scattered about.

He couldn't carry them with him. That meant that yesterday he had run her down and still had time to change into something else before intercepting her. She found that disconcerting and irritating. Did he have little stashes of garments tucked in the trees, hidden in caches like a squirrel hides seeds? She gathered his belongings, folded them and then hugged them to her chest. She inhaled his scent of autumn leaves and freshly turned soil. Alon smelled of the earth.

She tried to understand what was happening. She would have guessed something had frightened him, but she knew that was impossible. He could remove the soul from a living body and he could fly. What did he have to fear?

And then his words came back to her.

These woods are not like the ones you have known. It is not safe for you.

Samantha sat down hard, clutching his folded pile of clothing as if it were a pillow.

Her fingers tingled and it took a moment to realize

that something was coming, something fast. She faced this new threat. It came from upwind as if it had no reason to shield its approach. She inhaled the strange sweet scent that reminded her of Alon, but was not exactly his.

They came at her in a pack, using the ground cover to circle her like wolves, giving her only flashes of vision. The silver of fur, the gleam of a deadly ridge of quills. Samantha roared. Still in human form, the sound was more a shout.

Pale flesh flashed through the undergrowth, so fast it was only a blur. One came at her from behind and she whirled, seeing the little ghostly gray Halfling, scrambling on all fours like a chimpanzee, teeth snapping, trying for her Achilles tendon. She swung a foot but the thing was too fast, reversing direction and scampering away as one landed on her back. Sharp teeth scored her shoulder before she could throw her new attacker aside.

She needed to change but knew she would be powerless for just a moment during her transformation. That instant might be all they needed to end her life. These Toe Taggers were pale as corpses and fast as ferrets, she thought, throwing another from her arm.

Samantha's shoulder burned. A glance told her that she bled from several gashes. She pressed a hand to her shoulder and concentrated, sending healing energy to the wound. It would do to stanch some of the blood until she had time for a proper healing ceremony.

Something swooped from above her. She leaped back to see the petroleum-black smoke materializing, taking shape. Alon now stood naked with his back to her, facing the little Halflings who emerged from the underbrush to circle them, standing erect, long hairy arms relaxed so the vicious claws grazed the ground. Samantha gasped. There were so many. Six, and even though they stood only three feet high, their numbers made her throat close as if someone squeezed her windpipe. Too many to defeat, she knew.

She inched closer to Alon, hating herself for having to depend on him to protect her. But she saw no gap in the attacking circle, no spot where she might break free, and she already knew how fast they could move. Would Alon fight with her or just hand her over?

"This one is mine," he said to the horde, who all stared up at them with the biopic focus of all predators.

His? No. She was not. Not now or ever. She would never give herself to the enemy of her people.

She recalled their kiss and her ears went hot.

"Mine," he said again.

Samantha turned to stare at Alon, joining the rest as stunned silence filled the clearing where she thought to meet her end.

"She is under my protection."

The tallest pointed at Samantha and made a guttural, tortured sound.

"No," roared Alon. He took a threatening step forward, the muscles of his back bunching. The challenger retreated to join the others. "She is *not* enemy! She is *my* woman."

The largest snarled and made a gurgling sound, then nodded. The others nodded, as well. The leader made a series of sounds, its long tongue lolling and then twisting, darting from behind the rows of sharp teeth in a tortured gesture. What was it doing? To Samantha, the movement looked both obscene and mocking.

Samantha glanced to Alon for understanding.

"Yes, like mother. Skinwalker. But not enemy. She is our guest."

Speech. Was the thing trying to speak? Samantha

listened harder and this time she thought she heard the word *guest* amid the snapping and snarling.

"A guest is a welcome visitor, an honored visitor. Not food."

They bobbed their heads.

"Mother wants you all to come with me. This territory is no longer safe for you."

The pack shook their heads and disappeared into the underbrush. She listened to their retreat. Her shoulder began to throb like a persistent toothache. Blood ran from the wound. She pressed a hand over the injury, sending healing energy to slow the bleeding. She needed a circle to properly heal the gashes.

Alon still had his attention on the retreating Delta Pack. "Damn it." At last he turned to her. "I can't get them to come, and I can't leave them to bring you to her."

She didn't like either of those options.

"Are they… Are they…?" she asked, feeling sure she knew since they were like the ones who attacked her dad, only smaller.

"My kin," he confirmed. "The youngest. That's the Delta Pack, each set of twins born of other human mothers and Nagi. We are always born in twins."

Where was his twin?

He broke eye contact, staring away in the direction they had gone as if he could not meet her gaze. His translucent skin flushed. He glanced at the clothing, some folded beside the tree.

He slipped into his jeans then dragged on his gray sweater. It took him several minutes to locate his loafers. Once he had removed all that rippling male flesh from her sight, she found her thoughts were easier to gather.

"Those are the creatures that attacked my family.

Only they were bigger." She pointed in the direction the Deltas had gone.

"Nagi's recruits. That's why my family has been so busy. It's a race to find more of my kind before Nagi does. They won't come to Skinwalkers or Spirit Children. That's why my parents brought most of the Alpha Pack with them. If they locate any newborns, the Alphas will be there."

"I didn't understand. It's important."

She said so only because she knew her family would have to face any Ghostling that they didn't find first. He shouldn't care what she thought, but her understanding mattered to him.

"That's why Aldara and I need to bring the Beta, Gamma and Delta packs north. If we leave them they will be recruited or killed."

Samantha rolled her shoulder and grimaced, then pressed a hand to it. An icy tingle slithered down his spine.

"What are you doing?" He had not meant for his words to sound so harsh.

She startled and stared with those lovely cinnamon brown eyes of hers.

"Let me see," he ordered.

"It's nothing."

He extended his hand and she lifted hers. Samantha's palm was crimson with fresh blood. Alon's stomach pitched. He'd seen blood on prey, of course, but this was different, so different. The sight made him ill, when he'd never been ill a day in his life.

He leaped at her and she startled, but allowed him to turn her so he could see her injuries.

Claw marks, four deep lacerations, as if cut by four scalpels. He recognized them instantly and from the size knew it was one of the yearlings. One of them had harmed her. Which one? His anger boiled inside him like lava. Which one had dared to touch her?

"It's nothing. I'll finish healing it later." She lifted her injured arm and winced but still stroked his cheek. "Don't look so fierce, Alon. I'm fine."

He captured her hand, trapped it against his cheek and felt the soothing calm fill him. He met her gaze, and the tightness across his chest eased. She was a healer. He'd seen her repair that rabbit's spine. He released her hand, and the worry crept back into his heart.

He glanced at her hand. Blood now dripped from her fingertips in a steady beat.

"I'm not leaving you injured and alone." He recalled the ceremony for the rabbit. "You need the stones."

She nodded. "I can work more quickly if you could find me a feather."

He drew her to a seat beneath one of the towering pines and glanced up at the canopy, where two crows peered down at them.

"Any particular kind?"

"Bigger is better, but any sort will work." She was glancing about on the forest floor when he streaked into the air. The crows were no match for his flying ability, and he quickly plucked a feather from the slower one's tail then returned the way he had come.

He held out the feather, stained red at the tip from the extraction.

She frowned as she took it. "I generally use found feathers, not ones still in use."

He lifted his brows. "Will it still work?"

She nodded. "Will the crow still work?"

Was she teasing him? No one ever did that.

"Yes."

She smiled. He felt his mouth twitch at the corners in return.

"Then all I need is a stone circle. Sage and tobacco help sanctify, but I can do without them for such a small injury."

Blood dripped between her fingers, spurring him to action. He dressed again and then gathered stones, dug stones, unearthed stones. He set them in a circle as she had done and helped her sit within. Then he paced as she began to chant. Finally, he stood with his arms folded across his chest as he rocked, restless as the March wind.

He circled and watched in fascination as the blood ceased and her flesh knit. Even her blouse mended. But she was a Skinwalker, he reminded himself. This was not really clothing. It was a part of her, her magical animal hide that appeared at puberty and which she could reform to suit her needs.

"There," she said, favoring him with a lovely smile. "All done."

He offered his hand, certain she would not take it. She hesitated a moment but then allowed him to assist her to her feet. The electric tingle at the pressing of palms sent a thrill through him. He'd never experienced anything like it, and he craved more.

"Can you heal anything?" he asked.

"Yes, my dad taught me the prayers."

Samantha stepped from the circle and withdrew her hand from his. He allowed it then felt a tinge of melancholy as she moved away.

"Thank you, Alon, for rescuing me. I've been needing a lot of that lately."

She didn't move away. He thought about kissing her again then remembered the change that had occurred the last time. His desire died in a rush of shame. She cocked her head to look at him and then leaned in to brush her lips across his cheek. He closed his eyes to savor the tenderness of her gentle kiss and then felt the jolt of desire make him hard. Her sweetness was no match for his lust.

His skin tingled. He stepped away. "We best go."

Samantha carried the feather along. Better to keep it with her. If she used part of her coat to tie it in her hair, if she wasn't too rough in her bear form, the feather might stay with her.

Something caught his attention, and he turned to glance behind them. She followed the direction of his gaze at some undergrowth, finding no sign of the others.

"More Halflings?" she whispered.

"Just one, I think," he said and then raised his voice to be heard. "Aldara?"

A moment later a woman darted from behind a tree dressed in only a simple formfitting sky-blue T-shirt and tight denim shorts. They had a keen resemblance. Aldara's waist-length straight blond hair was similar. Her skin tone was even paler than Alon's as if she were Scandinavian, rather than Native, with only the barest blush of pink on her cheeks. Nearly albino, except for those eyes, Samantha thought. His sister was shorter than Alon by more than a foot, athletic, slim, but still curvy.

"Samantha Proud, let me introduce my younger sister, Aldara."

Aldara narrowed her blue-gray eyes on Samantha and glared. She seemed like a wild little animal, and Samantha didn't know if she should extend her hand or run.

Chapter 8

Aldara's gaze flicked over Samantha and then returned to her brother as if dismissing her as unimportant.

"The Beta Pack is on their way back and I located the Gammas. They're close. I see you found the Deltas."

"Yes, but they won't go and they attacked Samantha," said Alon.

This news did not seem to surprise or concern Aldara in the least. She shrugged. "Small wonder."

"We can't go without the Gammas."

"Together we can make them understand. The Betas and Gammas can help us. I saw another ghost. We need to go."

The look on Alon's face had Samantha hugging herself. Nagi's scouts, she realized. Alon had told her so.

"I have to take Samantha to the house. Then we'll go after the Gammas again."

Now Samantha had Aldara's attention. She turned

her flashing eyes on Samantha and curled back her lip to show strong white teeth. "Didn't you tell it to remain there? I thought animals could follow simple directions like 'sit' and 'stay.'"

"Aldara." Alon's voice held a warning.

"*She's* one of them."

"None of her family has ever attacked our kind."

Aldara folded her arms and glanced away.

"She is our guest," said Alon.

"An uninvited guest," Aldara objected.

"My guest," insisted Alon, his voice holding unmistakable menace.

Aldara threw up her hands as if conceding the point. "Well, it's taking too much of your time. We need to move them now. The Beta say they spotted two just east of us. They could be here anytime."

Alon grabbed Samantha by the elbow. "I'll catch up."

He turned and marched Samantha away. Behind them, Aldara growled.

Alon guided Samantha along the worn animal trail that he knew as well as his own face, faces, oh, hell. She'd seen them, the young ones in their natural form, the shape in which all born of Nagi began their lives. Changing to smoke came next, almost as soon as they were born. Why couldn't they change to smoke to be born and keep their birth mothers from dying in labor? It was one of many questions to which he could find no answer.

At puberty they turned handsome, losing the gray cast to their skin, learning to transform quills to the fine pale hair. This was the same time the Ianoka, born of Tob Tob, assumed their animal form, according to his mother, Bess.

Did Samantha find them horrible? Of course she did. They *were* horrible, hideous, the stuff of nightmares. Walking, talking monsters.

She would now find him repellent. It hurt him to think of her rejection, even though he had not yet experienced it. But he would. Surely he would.

He glanced back, making certain that Aldara didn't come at Samantha from behind. He and Aldara had argued last night. She favored bringing the young ones to safety as soon as they gathered them all and letting Samantha fend for herself. He didn't think Samantha would survive the hunting ghosts or Nagi's marauding Ghostlings without their protection. Aldara did not think Samantha was their problem regardless of her father's connection to their mother. But Alon could not leave Samantha.

Aldara needed him. Samantha needed him. He felt torn in two.

He brought her within sight of the house and left her there.

"Is it safe here?" she asked.

He knew nowhere was safe any longer.

"Our packs will not intrude here." But any outsider would look there first.

"Nagi's ghosts?"

He hesitated, not wishing to lie to her. He needed to follow Aldara and gather the packs.

"They are still to the east." He left her, feeling her gaze upon him. Wishing he could stay with her and knowing he could not.

Samantha watched him go, her senses prickling on alert. Nagi's army was about, as were his ghosts. She shivered as she recalled their attack on her dad.

Should she sit alone in that big log target and wait for
Alon, or should she follow him? She knew that he was
her best defense. And the Delta Pack understood she was
under his protection. At least they seemed to understand.

Samantha hesitated, weighing her options. She didn't
want to die. Perhaps if she kept him in sight she might
stay alive long enough to find his mother.

Her dad's words came to her again. *Learn what you
can.*

Samantha shifted to her bear form and followed
Alon's scent trail.

Alon found his sister with little difficulty. Aldara met
him in her fighting form. Not a good sign.

"Maybe the ghosts are after her."

It was a possibility he already considered. Samantha's
arrival might threaten them all.

"We need to get rid of her."

"If you mean kill her, I won't."

"They kill us."

Aldara changed back to her human shape. In this form
she was slim and curvy, with pale skin and long, cascading silver-blond hair that covered her naked breasts.

Alon looked away. Aldara was constantly losing her
garments and had little modesty. Alon tugged off his
sweater and handed it over.

Aldara drew on the soft cashmere, which reached her
midthigh. The sleeves fell well past her fingertips, but
she scrunched them up to her elbows as if preparing to
give him a thrashing. If anyone came close to succeed-
ing in that, it would be his twin. She was much tougher
than she looked in her petite human form.

Aldara snorted. "I can still smell her."

He changed the subject. "Any luck with the Gammas?"

"They agreed to come after they finish their kill."

She had done well.

"We'll bring the packs with us. Get Samantha to Mom. Then we can resume the search for strays."

"They're not strays. They're infants. Just like we were, alone and afraid. I hate the thought of leaving them behind."

He preferred it to trying to reason with the feral little monsters. He made a face. "I don't know how you can even bear to look at them."

Her scowl held this time, and she pressed her lips into a thin grim line. "How can you not?"

Aldara knew how ugly they were, but somehow she did not find them repugnant. She forgave them their appearance in a way that both shamed and humbled him.

But he didn't agree with her or his parents. The Ghost Children didn't belong here. That much he knew. The Naginoka upset the Balance. It was why he had vowed never to bring another of his kind into the world.

"Even if we convince them all to go, that Skinwalker can't fly. She'll hold us back."

She was right again. When he did not answer, Aldara snapped at him.

"Fine! I'll bring the packs to Mom and Dad while you babysit the little animal."

"I don't want you traveling with them alone. What if he finds you?"

"He might just as easily find you and the bear."

They stared at each other a moment as worry spiked in his belly, as sharp as a tack.

Aldara's shoulders sagged. "They must have brought her for a reason."

"I wish I knew what it was."

Aldara looked miserable. Tears trickled down her face, and she used the cuff of his sweater to sop up them up.

"I'm scared," she whispered.

"I know." He glanced back toward the house.

"Can you think of another way?" she asked.

"No."

"Then we separate. Perhaps we'll both make it."

She gazed up at him, her eyes no longer yellow but blue-gray, a shade much darker than his own. Her pretty face was contorted, her brow wrinkled, but in human form the words came easily now.

"I listen to the Niyanoka. I've been to their communities, attended their gatherings." She could, too. They'd never notice her, a little gray shadow, a hazy cloud of vapor clinging to the ceiling like blue smoke from a pipe. "They'd like us all dead."

Maybe we already are, he thought. *Half-dead at least.*

"They *know* that the Skinwalkers are hunting the babies, and they do nothing."

"What?" Shock struck him still.

"The Niyanoka chief said so. *Sanctioned* was the word they used."

Alon shook his head in denial, knowing in his heart that her words were true. "Does father know?"

"I don't have the heart to tell him. The Spirit Children say they will ignore the hunts. That way they can keep their hands clean, maintain their smug superiority and have the Skinwalkers remove the troublesome problem."

He pictured a pack of Skinwalker wolves finding his sister sleeping. The image iced his blood. He thought of their new guest and hardened his heart.

He had to keep Samantha safe and he had to keep Aldara safe.

"We're out of time," said Alon. "No more persuasion. We'll use the Beta and Gammas to force the Deltas to come with us."

"You kissed her."

He glared. "So?"

"There are plenty of girls back at the school. But you kissed a Skinwalker."

He snorted and then realized his mistake as Aldara's eyes narrowed. "Oh, right." She swept back her silvery hair and glared. "We're not good enough for you."

"I didn't say that."

"Your actions do. Her kind is killing our people. How could you…you…kiss a beast?" Her words turned into a series of snaps and growls as her mouth began to contort with the change again. She rounded on him. "She won't want you, you know?"

Her words hit him like a blow, echoing the truth he had already accepted. Samantha was not of his race, and some of her people were trying to exterminate his. How could she ever understand him, and why would she want to?

"For a moment I forgot what she was. A mistake. It won't happen again."

Samantha stood in bear form with her back pressed to the tree hidden just upwind of the place where Alon and Aldara spoke of Skinwalkers as the enemy.

Vigilantes. Could that be true? Did her dad know?

No wonder Aldara hated her on sight. Her people were hunting infants. It was too terrible.

Sebastian's instructions echoed in her mind. *If you*

see a Toe Tagger kill it, and she knew Aldara's words
were true.

She closed her eyes as his sister had called her a beast
and rather than defend her, he'd agreed. That hurt so
much she had to hug the tree for support.

Alon admitted that kissing her had been a mistake.
Her head drooped, suddenly too heavy for her to hold
upright. Her heart pulsed with her shame.

To know exactly what he thought of her was hard.
She understood that there were many who thought Skinwalkers less than human. It was what all the Niyanoka
believed. But to hear this from Alon's mouth somehow
felt like a slap across her face.

She winced. Letting him kiss her was nearly as stupid as sending that evil ghost for judgment.

Regret and shame rolled into an electric ball of anger
that rumbled through her like thunder. A Toe Tagger
calling her a beast. It wasn't as if he had a glowing lineage. His father was trying to take over the entire living world. She knew that and still she had been lured by
Alon's handsome face and raw sexuality.

What did she care if he belittled her? She knew what
she was and where she belonged. But her defense fell
flat. The truth was that she didn't know where she belonged or what she should do. Blake and his mother
were to rally the Niyanoka. Her dad would gather the
Skinwalkers into an army. And her job was to try not to
get eaten by yearling Toe Taggers and wait around for
Alon to have time to bring her to Bess. Her head sank
even lower as Alon's words echoed through her like an
emotional earthquake.

A mistake.

Yes, that it was. He made her ashamed of her weakness for him. Ashamed to let herself want a Halfling who found her attention a disgrace.

To the Toe Taggers she was a beast. Both the Dream Children and the Skinwalkers saw her as a half-breed born of the enemy race.

In her heart she was torn in two. Straddling two races, she felt wholly a part of neither.

Just then a feral scream came from a place beyond the clearing where Alon and Aldara stood.

"The babies," said Aldara, already turning toward the sound. "Something is attacking the babies!"

Samantha's heart pounded in fear as she peered around the mighty tree. There was a discharge of green light, and then Alon and Aldara stood eight feet tall in their third form. She shrank back at the sight. These were the creatures that attacked her dad. Long silvery hair, a ridge of spines down their backs, long apelike arms and vicious claws.

They charged toward the sound as more screams reached Samantha. She pressed a paw to her chest, trying to ease the pain of her pounding heart. Should she follow or run?

She turned to move in the opposite direction when something occurred to her. What if it wasn't Nagi or his Toe Tagger army? What if vigilante Skinwalkers were attacking the infants?

Samantha's scalp tingled. She couldn't let her own kind kill those little ones. It was wrong—so wrong.

She charged after Alon, following his scent as she plowed through the undergrowth toward the unknown.

Chapter 9

Samantha caught up with Alon and Aldara before they reached their objective. Alon turned to face the threat coming from behind and stopped the instant Samantha appeared.

Aldara bared her fangs. Samantha reared up to face this threat, but Alon extended a hand to stop Aldara. Samantha couldn't hide her distress. They faced her together with huge yellow eyes, gray, pointed, batlike leathery ears and those terrible spiny teeth. They were near identical except Alon was larger and Aldara had fur-covered breasts. They were the most frightening things she had ever seen, and her body began to tremble even as she reared to her hind legs, rising to her full nine feet.

"It's Samantha," he said, his words slurred by his fangs.

"She's a bear?" hissed Aldara.

"A healer, like her father. We might have need of her."

Is that why he stopped the attack? Because she might be useful?

Aldara lifted her chin as if listening. A moment later she shuddered.

"They're here. I can feel them on my skin," she whispered. "Nagi's forces."

Alon went still and then the skin on his shoulders quivered like a horse chasing off a fly. "Yes."

"What do we do?" Aldara's huge, bulbous eyes were wide with terror.

"Kill them before they can report back." His words were hushed, slurred and sinister. The harsh, guttural tone sent a shiver through Samantha.

"He'll know. He'll see them in the circle. They'll tell him where to find us." Her words were an urgent whisper.

Alon raked a hand through the long silvery fur on his head. It was so fine that the tracks of his fingers remained for a moment.

"Kill them quick. Get the Beta, Gamma and Delta packs and run." He turned to Samantha. "They will kill you if they see you. You can't defeat them alone. Your best chance is with us."

Best chance. Her ears began to buzz.

She growled in acknowledgment as she could not speak in this form.

Aldara leaped away, running on all fours like a baboon. Alon glanced back at Samantha and then raced after his sister.

Samantha dropped to all fours and charged after the twins, who left a wide path through the undergrowth. Before she reached them, the terrible howling erupted again and then a roar. She broke from cover to find two

Ghostlings locked together in combat. Alon, she realized, with an intruder.

Aldara scrambled from one small Ghostling to the next, stopping briefly to emit a high-pitched cry before moving on. Six small bodies littered the ground in bloody contortions. Four had been torn open in the middle and two had had their throats ripped out. The Delta Pack, Samantha realized.

She heaved with a wave of nausea at the carnage. Aldara finished her survey and roared. It was a sound that Samantha would never forget, full of pain and wrath and the need for revenge. Aldara leaped on the back of the intruder, heedless of the spines that punctured her, and sank her fangs deep into the juncture of its shoulder and neck. Alon released his foe, and Samantha now saw it was a female. The Toe Tagger twisted and howled in a vain effort to shake off her attacker. The Halfling's movements seemed to drive Aldara's fangs only deeper into the vessels and tissue at its throat. She could not shake Aldara off. Finally the Ghostling staggered and dropped to her knees. Only then did Aldara release it. Her bloody mouth gaped and she gnashed her teeth as she stood over her fallen foe.

Samantha caught movement from the corner of her eye. Alon and Aldara faced the female, so they did not see the second Halfling attacker streak from the cover of ferns. But Samantha did.

It came so fast she did not have time to think. Instead, she charged, meeting the thing in midair as it tried to tackle Alon. Her block drove it off course, and they both hit the ground.

The ease with which it knocked Samantha down both shocked and terrified her. The male Ghostling raised a claw that glistened with the blood of the Delta Pack.

But his blow never landed. Alon grabbed its raised arm and sank his long, spearlike talons deep between the male's ribs.

Her attacker gasped as he sank to his knees. Alon withdrew his talons, and red, frothy blood bubbled from the Ghostling's mouth. It fell forward and lay still.

Alon glanced at Samantha and then turned back to Aldara, who tried and failed to rise as she gripped her chest and abdomen. Blood seeped between her fingers.

Samantha bellowed.

"They're gone," Aldara said to Alon. "Their souls have already fled!"

His gaze darted here and there, sweeping the ground. Did he search for the souls of the young ones? The fur on Samantha's neck lifted as she watched him hunt for what she could not see. She could see ghosts, but not the escaping souls. What was the difference?

She placed her paw over her heart, closed her eyes and concentrated. An instant later she felt the flash of energy and the zip of power as she shifted forms. For one moment she stood naked in her long bearskin cape. She stroked her shoulder, summoning another flash of light. Now she stood dressed in sneakers, jeans and a clean white T-shirt.

Alon did not shift. Neither did Aldara. But Aldara did topple sideways before Samantha could reach her.

Alon charged away. He returned a moment later with a pile of stones.

"I have to check for other intruders," he growled and was gone again.

Samantha placed the stones in a circle and motioned Aldara to the center.

Samantha tugged the crow feather free from her hair. Aldara closed her eyes as Samantha began to chant.

The wounds healed from the inside out. First the blood ceased and finally the tissue knit. She finished her work and discovered Alon there guarding them both. Still in his third form, he now seemed more imposing than terrifying, and the sight gave her an unexpected sense of ease.

"No others," he said.

"None of the souls can be saved?" she asked.

He shook his head.

Aldara curled into a ball and wept.

Alon knelt beside her, resting a hand on her silvery back.

"Aldara. We need to find the Beta and Gamma packs and we need to run."

She lifted her damp face. "What about them? We have to bury them."

"I'll do it," said Samantha. In her bear form the digging would be no trouble.

They both stared at her with those terrifying jaundice eyes. She nearly succeeded in repressing a shiver.

"You both go after the others. I'll bury them and meet you at the house."

Alon shook his head. "We can't leave her."

"You said there were no more intruders," reminded Samantha.

"Bury them, please," said Aldara. She staggered to her feet.

Samantha knew that Aldara would feel dizzy and weak after the healing. But still Alon's sister dropped to her knees and began to dig. Her long talons tore through the packed soil like steel through sand.

Samantha shifted and joined Aldara. A moment later Alon added his efforts. The result was one long deep grave for the six twins to rest side by side. Aldara made a bed of ferns and blanketed their desecrated bodies with the same. Together they filled the grave, covering the little twins who had not survived their first year. This was what Nagi did to his own kind.

She stilled as she realized this was also what her kind were doing, hunting the infants. Killing them while they were small. Samantha felt sick and ashamed. No wonder Alon and Aldara both hated her.

Samantha shifted back to human form to say a blessing.

"We have to find the rest," said Aldara.

They did not have far to look. The Gamma Pack had also sensed the intruders. Samantha did not understand it. Alon said they could feel others of their kind on their skin just as they could feel ghosts.

The group of twenty all hid in the cover of thick fern and brush. Alon sensed them first. Aldara met them with open arms.

It took a moment for Samantha to realize that the yipping and snarling was weeping. The Gamma Pack members were mourning for their lost siblings.

Samantha wept, as well.

She felt Alon squat beside her and glanced down to see his elongated foot covered with silvery-blond fur, the nails just as terrible as a grizzly's claws.

"Are you surprised to see that we can feel?" he asked in that strange guttural voice.

"No," she said, her denial quick and defensive. She let her shoulders droop. "Yes," she whispered. "You aren't what I was taught to expect."

He left her there and joined his sister, who was trying to explain what had happened to the youngsters. They could not understand why two of their own kind would attack them. Every adult Ghost Child they had ever met had been kind and nurturing.

These Ghostlings were bigger, nearly half Aldara's size, and imposing in such a large group. Still Samantha did not feel afraid. She listened when Aldara explained about her but could not really understand what was said.

"They know where the Betas are," said Aldara. "And they've agreed to leave with me. To find our parents."

Samantha glanced to him and found his gaze pinned on her.

"I can't leave her," he said, speaking to Aldara while looking at Samantha.

And then she understood. Aldara and Alon, even these little ones, could all fly. She was holding them back and endangering them all.

"But there may be more of them," said Aldara.

"More reason to stay."

Aldara glanced from her brother to Samantha and sighed. "You will follow?"

He nodded. "As quickly as we can."

"We'll go to the Beta Pack first. Then find our parents."

She stepped forward to hug her brother and then turned to face Samantha. "Thank you for healing my wounds. I owe you a favor, but if you get my brother killed you answer to me."

With that mixed message delivered, Aldara made a clicking sound in her throat. The Gamma Pack gathered about her. She pointed to the sky. They nodded their understanding.

Then, right before her eyes, Aldara evaporated into billowing gray smoke and rocketed into the blue. Each of the Gammas poofed into smoke and followed their half sister.

Samantha gaped in wonder as she witnessed their retreat. They could fly!

Alon watched them until they disappeared.

"I'm sorry," Samantha said.

"We have to hurry," he said.

How long until the souls of the Ghostlings walked the Spirit Road and reached Nagi in his shadowy realm?

How long until her enemy found her?

Alon wasted no time getting Samantha back to the house. Fifteen minutes later he was back in human form, dressed in boots, creased trousers and a gray pinstriped shirt with cuffs rolled to the elbow. His mussed hair and untucked shirttails spoke of his rush. He hustled her out to the garage and threw a small duffel into the bed of a red Ford pickup truck. She strapped on her shoulder restraint and he led them out of the mountains, driving as fast as the twisting switchbacks would allow. Samantha had never learned to drive and was relieved that Alon had.

Twilight painted the sky purple. Samantha held on to the armrest and braced her feet on the floor, trying unsuccessfully to keep from banging into the door frame. Many switchbacks later, the road, and Samantha's stomach, leveled on the valley floor and the sky opened above them, giving her a view of the stars emerging one by one. First the Holy Star, Venus, twinkled bright and then Winter Maker, the cluster called Orion by many, appeared, still clinging to his place in the heavens.

As Alon drove, Samantha told herself to keep her attention out the window, but she could not resist snatching quick glances at him. He was handsome again. She could not get her mind around the reality that this stunning, sexy man was that terrifying, vicious creature who had so effectively used his claws to puncture the heart and lungs of his challenger.

His third form called to mind the ones who had attacked her family. It was a comparison that lifted the hairs on her neck. Had they done the same to her father? Alon thought so.

He wasn't one of them. This was Alon. Still she inched farther from him and clung to the armrest.

He had been right not to show her his third form. How had she ever kissed him? How could she have fallen for his looks when she knew what he was inside? He'd been born that way. This, what she now saw, was not his natural form. She, on the other hand, had been born human and only later grew into her second shape.

Her entire life had been filled with the terror of being found by Nagi. Always she feared his ghosts and lately his evil monsters. Alon was one of them.

She had not always balanced her fear for her family's safety and the urging of her heart to do what she was meant to do. What would Alon do with her if he knew that she was also a Seer, one of the three Halflings whom Nagi most wanted dead?

She shivered.

"Cold?" he asked and fiddled with the air system.

She was cold right through to her heart. What did she do now?

She closed her eyes and wished for the kind of life many took for granted, one of peace, security and purpose. Would she ever have that?

When she opened her eyes it was to find Alon casting worried glances at her. Her vision worked well in near darkness and she could see his features clearly, even with only the dashboard as illumination. His ghostly gray aura provided even more light as it stretched toward her. She pressed her back against the door.

When he spoke, the strain in his voice caught her in the chest. "I didn't want you to see me like that."

She knew what he meant. "It's what you are. As much a part of you as my human form is to me."

His fingers clenched the wheel, constricting with the relentlessness of a boa constrictor.

"My mother calls it my fighting form."

"The shape in which you were born," she whispered, her words an accusation.

He stared out the windshield. "Yes."

Alon's aura glowed bright and unnatural in the cab, flaring to the roof the color of pewter. No, that wasn't quite right, more silver, capped with inky black. Black, she knew, was the color of death, and being born of Nagi that did make sense. But what about the silver?

"Why didn't you want me to see?"

His eyebrows tented and he gave her a long look. "Because I'm hideous."

She gasped. Did he think so, too? How terrible. Her unease shifted to empathy. Alon hated his original form, and yet it was a part of him.

"I'm sorry."

"I don't want your pity. I want…" His words dropped away.

She folded her hands in her lap, resisting the urge to reach out to him.

His aura flared and arched toward her again, but this time her rust-and-gold-capped aura also stretched toward his. She drew a quick intake of breath.

Electricity charged the air.

Samantha recoiled and banged against the door. He shot her a look.

She'd witnessed something similar before between her parents. Her neck prickled. No, that wasn't it. It couldn't be. Simply impossible.

"Am I that repugnant?" he growled.

"Did you see it?"

He swung his gaze about, hunching over the wheel as he scanned their surroundings. "Ghosts?"

She shook her head. "That aura."

He exhaled his relief and straightened behind the wheel. "I can't see auras."

He lifted a brow as if waiting for her to elaborate. Damned if she would. Letting him know *she* could see them was a mistake. Only Niyanoka saw auras. He must suspect now that she had another gift. Would he still protect her if he knew she was the one Nagi sought?

In the darkness, his eyes glowed bright as any predator, only not the normal green of an animal caught in the high beams, but orange like hot embers.

"How is it that a Skinwalker can see them?" he asked.

She dropped her gaze, knowing she was a terrible liar. When she looked back it was to find him still staring, his gaze flicking from the road to her and back.

"You saved me today," he said.

She had, too, or at least gave him the time he needed to save himself. Samantha glanced away, staring at the yellow lines that divided the narrow highway.

"And you healed Aldara. You buried our dead."

"Well, don't make it out to be more than it is. I need you to get to Bess."

"No." He kept his eyes on the road. "It was more."

"Why did they kill them?"

"Join or die. Only they were too young to even understand the question." Alon's grip tightened dangerously on the steering wheel and she saw it bend. He extended his fingers then gingerly returned his hands to the wheel.

Would he ever face that choice?

Someone had to stop Nagi. Could that someone be Alon?

She swallowed back her uncertainty and cleared her throat. "Alon, if he finds you. Would you join?"

His look was incredulous, as if he did not understand how she could even ask. His conviction shone in his crystal eyes. "I fight against Nagi. I fight for the Balance."

"You would fight against your father?"

"My father is a Soul Whisperer."

"Nagi sired you. You are a part of him." She said this aloud for herself. She needed to remember what he truly was.

"A curse I face every damned day." He glared through the windshield, not looking at her as he spoke. "Nagi threatens the Balance. I will never side with him."

She exhaled her relief and realized she believed him.

"But neither will I fight with those who hunt my kind."

Samantha's brow knit. "You mean the Ghostlings who have joined Nagi?"

He cast her an incredulous glance, and in that instant she understood that he meant the Skinwalkers, the ones his sister had spoken of. The realization made it impossible to hold his gaze. Silence stretched. "You didn't know?"

She shook her head, already feeling stupid. Her stomach knotted as she prepared to admit she had been spying on him. "I didn't. Not until I overheard Aldara tell you in the woods. Vigilantes."

He scanned her face as if assessing her answer.

"That's right. They are hunting newborns. Only they do not give them a choice. They find them. They kill them."

Samantha shivered and then covered her face with her hands. "Why didn't you kill me when you found me in the forest?"

"I almost did, but the Skinwalkers come in packs. You were alone."

She kept her hands pressed to her eyes, as if this could block out the horror of his words. Here she thought she had reason to hate him. He also had reason to hate her. Enemies with only their parents' friendship to keep them from tearing each other to shreds.

"I am so sorry and so ashamed." Her words seemed hollow in the closed cab. She'd never felt more alone.

"Do you not think we deserve to die?" Something in his tone brought her to attention. His words were not delivered with sarcasm but something else, something more caustic. Was it self-loathing?

"Of course not. I'll admit to being terrified of you at first. But you are quite obviously not the nightmare I was led to believe."

"In what way?"

"You can think, for one, and feel, for another. You are loyal to your sister and your family. You protect the children."

"I *failed* to protect them."

She continued as if he had not interrupted. "You saved me from attack and you rescued the soul of an innocent creature."

"I also killed one of my own kind."

"Self-defense. He attacked you."

The silence returned, filling up the cab until Samantha could not breathe in the gloom that surrounded him. Even his aura was growing darker by the minute.

"Alon, he is hunting your kind. He is killing mine. We can't let that happen."

He snorted.

"We have to bring your Ghost Children into the fight."

He gave a quick dismissing shake of his head. "We? There's no *we*."

"There could be."

"You're a runner, little rabbit. Running all your life, you said. Now you wish to turn and fight?"

And suddenly she understood why the Thunderbirds had dropped her here with him. It wasn't Bess she needed to find. It wasn't to learn all she could about their enemy. It was to find Alon. Alon, the Naginoka who refused to join Nagi.

She sat back as the realization jelled in her mind. This Ghostling fought for the Balance and for Mankind. Maybe others would, as well.

He glanced at her sitting frozen against the seat.

"What's the matter with you?"

"I—I'm not sure." She felt nauseous as the shock and fear collided with the certainty of her realization.

He glanced out the windshield, his aura now glowing a pure silver. "Do you sense some danger?"

She shook her head.

"I won't leave you unguarded. Not until I know you are safe."

She knew he wouldn't. He was a magnificent protector. The Thunderbirds could not have done better.

But his allegiance to her was transient. Would he leave her with his mother, or could she convince him to extend his protection to the impending battle?

"My family is trying to bring the Skinwalkers and Spirit Children into an alliance to stop Nagi." She held her breath, waiting for his reply.

His laugh held no mirth. "They hate each other."

"They hate Nagi more."

That wiped away his sarcastic grin. "Perhaps. 'The enemy of my enemy is my friend.'"

Sun Tzu, she realized, *The Art of War.* How perfect that he knew the strategies of so great a military commander.

She glanced at Alon as he drove in silence, the bunching of his jaw muscles the only indication of unrest.

"Even if you defeated his Ghostling army," he said, "you can't defeat his ghosts. Once they take possession of a human, even I can't get them out. Not without killing the host, that is."

She could. But if she told him then he would know she was a Seer. She wanted to trust Alon with her secret, but she had kept it so long, run so far. It was hard to release it to him.

"And Nagi is immortal. You can't kill him."

"I know it."

"Then he'll kill you, too. He kills anyone who tries to stop him."

She held fast to a bravado she did not feel, lifting her chin in defiance, disregarding the worry that gnawed at her belly. "Then he'll have to kill us all."

"Yes. I'm sure he's looking forward to that."

Samantha stared at Alon, trying to decide what to do. If she told him that she was a Seer, he might abandon her or turn her over to his sire. But there was a third possibility flickering in her heart like a tiny, fragile flame. If she told him she could rescue possessed humans, heal all wounds and cast evil ghosts to the Way of Souls, could she convince him to join their cause?

Chapter 10

The ring of the incoming call made both Alon and Samantha jump. Alon glanced at the display, saw his mother's name and number and pressed the button on the steering wheel to connect.

"Mom?"

"Alon?" It was his father's voice. "Thank goodness. I tried the house and your cell."

"I forgot it."

"It only just occurred to us to try Aldara's number in the truck. She said she left her phone in the glove box."

Samantha flipped open the door and held up the phone.

"Has she arrived?" Alon asked.

"Yes. Safe and sound with the Beta and Gamma packs." There was a long pause. When he spoke again his voice was a whisper. "She told us about the Deltas."

"I'm sorry, Dad. I couldn't stop them in time."

"I know, son." There was a pause and then his father cleared his throat. When he spoke again his voice held strain. "How's Samantha?"

"Here with me. You're on speaker."

"Hello, Samantha. I'm looking forward to your arrival. Alon, we're outside of Calgary at the Kootenay National Park."

"Got it."

"Samantha? I've had word from both your brother and your mother. They say that your father is alive. He's safe."

Samantha covered her mouth, stifling the little cry of relief. Tears sprang to her eyes.

"Samantha?" his father asked.

"She hears you, Dad."

Samantha released the safety belt and tilted sideways, resting her head on Alon's shoulder as she cried. He wrapped one arm about her and tucked her tight to his side.

"Oh, good," said his father. "Nicholas located him. The Thunderbirds took him pretty far north. They're on their way back. He was injured, but he's all right now. I'll let him tell you the rest. The Skinwalkers are meeting in Montana at the site of the Greasy Grass Fight," said his father, using the old name for the Battle of Little Bighorn. "Samantha? Your brother has become a member of the Niyanoka community. He will ask to be appointed War Chief at the next council meeting. I think his chances are good. I'll admit that I never expected them to accept him so readily. Bess says his gifts make him invaluable enough to overlook the Skinwalker half."

What gifts did he have? wondered Alon. Was he a healer like Samantha, or was there something more?

Samantha dashed at the tears. "Thank you, Mr. Garza. Thank you so much."

"Alon? Stay off the main roads. Keep out of the cities or anywhere a ghost might see Samantha. There is less risk driving than flying, I think. Get here as soon as you can. We're safer together." His father gave him directions for their meeting place and said goodbye.

Samantha moved back to her side of the cab, huddling now against the door. He waited for her to speak, but when she did not he asked the question.

"I thought Nagi hunted your mother. Why did my father caution me to keep you clear of ghosts?"

She drew a long breath and let it go. Then she faced him. Everything about her radiated the importance of what she would say. He gripped the wheel as anxiety snaked through him.

"What?" he asked.

"Do you remember when you said that Nagi would defeat us because of his ghosts, that once they take possession of a human even you can't get them out?"

He nodded as understanding dawned. "But you can because…"

"I'm a Seer." She wrapped her arms about herself as if huddling in a snowstorm. "I meant to tell you. But you are one of them. One of the ones hunting my family, and I was afraid."

And the pieces fell into place. Why her parents had sent the Seers in different directions. Why the Niyanoka would accept a leader who was half Skinwalker. Why she could see auras. Why his father had warned him to keep Samantha clear of ghosts. And why the Thunderbirds had brought her to him.

He could protect her. At least he was a better choice than his mom. He could see ghosts. He could kill ghosts.

The realization rocked him. He couldn't leave Samantha with his parents. He couldn't ever let her go. Not until Nagi was defeated or they were all dead.

Now he understood why she'd spent her entire life on the run. His sire had sent every ghost and every Ghostling he could recruit to find the Seers and kill them because once they were dead, there would be no one to stop his possessed army.

Alon gripped the wheel. No wonder she hated him. He was one of the creatures who stalked her family.

"I didn't know," he whispered, reaching for her.

She leaned away and he drew back his hand.

"What are you going to do?" she asked.

He wasn't certain. The responsibility was daunting. But the Thunderbirds thought him capable or perhaps the best of many bad choices. "I'm going to try to keep you alive."

"And leave me with your mother?"

He couldn't. Even if he wanted to do so. She needed a Ghostling to keep her safe. He should tell her, but he could not bear to see the disappointment when she realized she was stuck with him. So he said, "That was your father's wish."

She expelled a breath and then covered her face in her hands. "I thought you might…"

"What?"

"I was afraid you might turn me over to Nagi."

He glowered at her. "Then you don't know me at all."

Still it was a reasonable worry. What reward would the Ruler of Ghosts give for the deliverance of one of the three Niyanoka who could defeat his ghosts? Samantha and her brother and her mother were the only living things that could remove a ghost who possessed a human.

No wonder the Niyanoka wanted her brother as their War Chief. They'd be fools not to take him.

"You can defeat his ghosts," he said.

"I can."

"But to do that, you'll have to stay alive." Alon pressed the gas pedal to the floor.

Suddenly he felt a spark of hope. With three Seers, an army might be able to defeat Nagi's forces. His brothers and sisters could take Nagi's Ghostlings if they were not outnumbered. They'd have the Skinwalkers' help, and the Seers could take the possessed fighters.

But who could stop Nagi?

His thoughts turned dark again. There was no way to kill a Superior Spirit. He gripped the wheel and glanced at Samantha, wishing to discuss his thoughts.

But her chin was making a slow descent to her chest and her eyes drifted shut. Samantha began to doze. Her head lolled and she jolted awake. He watched this repeat several times until he could stand it no more. Finally he reached for her and dragged her beside him on the wide single seat. Her head lifted for a moment and he pushed it against his shoulder. She gripped his arm and cuddled close to him. He growled deep in the back of his throat, and the sensation of well-being returned to him again. For someone who was trying to avoid his company, she certainly spent a lot of time pressed up against him.

Because she needed his protection. Nothing more. Remember that and you might get out of this alive.

Samantha scooted closer, hugging his biceps as if it were her teddy bear. His heart began to squeeze in his chest and his ribs ached. Just her nearness did this to him. He had never experienced anything like his physical reaction to Samantha.

She slipped downward until she rested her head on

his thigh like a pillow. None who knew what he was ever got so close to him, not even the others of his kind. Only Bess, Cesar and Aldara ever willingly touched him. He glanced at her dark head, her closed eyes, the peaceful expression. In sleep she trusted him. He released the wheel and stretched his fingers, his breath catching at what he wished to do. Gradually he lowered his hand until his palm rested on her glossy hair. Then he petted her in long, even strokes. She allowed it. Samantha's mouth turned up in a smile and she sighed.

A wave of peace and a feeling of contentment resounded through him like a shout in an empty cave. Why did touching her make his chest ache?

Alon drove to the closest place of safety he could think of. He and his sister had purchased a series of isolated homes throughout the mountains of California because this was the area where they had located many of Nagi's offspring. Aldara was a whiz at getting twins to come with them.

There had been no other sightings in the United States, Canada or Mexico until word of the group outside Calgary.

When they left the road, Samantha roused from slumber. She asked few questions, but he provided what assurance he could. They would eat, sleep and continue tomorrow morning. The ride was another eighteen hours yet, and he had to rest.

They paused at the high wrought-iron gate as he entered the security code. The house came into sight as they crested the hill. Bathed in moonlight, the glass and steel construction glinted and winked. The structure most resembled some modern sculptured cubes sitting in a mowed meadow. The isolated house seemed as out of place in this clearing as he was. The fenced perimeter and security system assisted in his need for privacy, though they would not deter ghosts.

Only the lawn crew and his human housekeeper entered this sanctuary. His housekeeper kept the place in order and the kitchen stocked with the peculiar foodstuffs he requested. He and Aldara preferred rare meat, and the large freezer in the garage kept them fed.

He recalled finding two of the Delta twins in this area and felt sad all over again. The anger followed on its heels, and he realized he wanted a chance to settle with his sire for all the pain he caused.

If not for the Ruler of Ghosts, the Deltas would be alive, Samantha would be with her family and Alon would not have had to kill his own kin. If not for the ambitions of Nagi, Alon and all his siblings would never be here to infest this lovely world like some new and deadly plague.

Everything began and ended with Nagi.

Alon ushered Samantha in, saw her fed and showed her about the place. It wasn't much, just two bedrooms upstairs with an adjoining bath. Downstairs had everything one would expect, except the touches that made a house a home. She stood at the sliding doors, looking out at the woods behind the house glowing blue in the moonlight.

"I've never seen a ghost here," he said.

She slipped out to the deck and he followed, standing beside her as she gazed up at the night sky.

"Beautiful," she sighed.

He made a sound of concurrence and stretched his neck to stare at the heavens.

"I tried to follow my mother to the Way of Souls once." He lifted his hand and pointed at the Milky Way.

"I watched her disappear through the veil, but I couldn't find the way."

"You're not a raven. We only get to travel that road once."

"Some of us not even once."

Her attention shifted, meeting his troubled gaze.

"What do you mean?"

"I'm born of the Ruler of Ghosts. Where do you suppose I will go when I pass from this living world?"

She never considered it. "I don't know."

He expelled a long breath. "Neither do I."

She did not try to reassure or change the subject to something more pleasant. He appreciated that.

"None of us know that, Alon. It's why we must walk the Red Road while we live."

That wasn't what he meant. He was not speaking of living an upright life so he could one day reach the Spirit World. If it were only so simple.

He felt the urge to tell her what he believed. That it would make no difference what he did because his lineage would bar him from entrance to the Spirit World. But when he looked down into her sweet face and saw the earnestness of her expression, he could not do it. He forced a smile and she returned it.

Something shimmered between them. He glanced away, checking to be certain it was no ghost.

"What was that?"

"You saw it?" She smiled up at him. "It's our auras. Sometimes they are bright enough for anyone to see."

"I can't see it now."

"I can. Yours is silver. Mine is mostly violet with some deep blue, gold and brown. A Niyanoka's aura is capped with gold, and all Skinwalkers have some brown. It's how the Niyanoka can so easily spot us."

"But you are also Niyanoka."

"Yes, both and neither."

It was the first time he thought to consider that she was a mix of two races. How much more difficult must that be for her?

Samantha turned away so that her back now rested on the rail. He gripped the wooden banister to squash the urge to reach for her and felt his fingers sink into the hard wood.

"Is that a hot tub?" she asked.

It was. Suddenly Alon's mind was not full of the threat of ghosts but the threat of seeing Samantha naked in that hot, pulsing water.

He invited her to use the Jacuzzi before bed. She hesitated, glancing toward him in silence. Did she think he meant to use this as some opportunity to seduce her?

The notion sent a hot, tingling wave of desire. It was what he wanted to do. But he couldn't. There were so many reasons why he couldn't. Not the least of which was his conviction never to bring another of his kind to this world. They didn't belong here, and he would not bring one more unwanted Halfling into this joyless existence.

But oh, how he wanted Samantha.

Her look was inscrutable. Did she want him to make some advance, or did she hesitate out of fear he might do so.

He recalled her drawing away from him in the truck and felt he had the answer. But she had slept on his lap like a beloved pet.

How could he even dream that someone as lovely, powerful and necessary as this Seer of Souls could ever want a misshapen monstrosity such as him?

She couldn't. Wouldn't. Didn't.

"I need to scout for any threat. I'll be gone at least an hour."

The urge to touch her gripped him. He told himself to step away and found himself stepping closer.

"I want to kiss you," he said.

He'd given her fair warning. Why didn't she run away or tell him no? And then he saw it, the slight turning of her head. Oh no, he thought, and ceased his advance.

But she wasn't shaking her head, he realized. She was gazing up as if there were something between them, something he could not see. Their auras again? he wondered. Did they beat between them with the urgent desire that grew like a living thing? He wished he could see them.

Finally her gaze met his and she took a step forward, looping her arms about his neck.

He thought of the day they met. How his need for her had brought on the change, bringing forth that feral monster locked inside him. What if he changed again?

He could feel her heat, sense the opening of the tiny capillaries in her skin. Her scent filled the air. He breathed in her fragrance, summer flowers mixed with Samantha's rising arousal.

He did this to her. A terrible realization hit. It wasn't really him. It was this last form, this mask that drew her. He was the orchid luring the moth, fooling it into seeing a kindred species instead of the lie.

She pressed her body to his and suddenly he was lost. Lost in her scent. Lost in his need. Lost in the glittering desire of her dark eyes.

He rubbed his muscular chest against the soft cushion of her breasts. She sucked in a breath, closing her eyes as her head dropped back, exposing her neck to him. Need now beat within him, pulsing with his heart. He didn't care if he deceived her, if only she would let him hold her a moment longer.

Her sweet breath fanned hot across his cheek as he leaned in to take what she offered.

He dipped his head. She turned away and he captured her earlobe between his teeth, sucking the soft, sensitive nub of flesh, and was rewarded by the sound of her satisfaction rumbling deep in her throat.

His tongue traced the shell of her ear and then darted inside. She arched against him and he slid his hand beneath the hem of her shirt and jacket, sliding upward over her taut skin, feeling the changing contours of her back and torso until his fingers splayed over the mound of one of her breasts. He rolled his palm in a circular motion, bringing a moan of pleasure from her throat. At his touch, her nipples tightened and she leaned forward, pressing one soft breast more firmly into his palm.

Samantha lifted her free hand, threaded her fingers through his hair and tugged. Soft little pants urged him on, and he walked her backward until she reached the hot tub, covered now with a soft, padded top. The odor of chlorine rose to greet them as he stretched her out on that cushion. His mouth found hers. Her lips parted as she gave him access. Her hot tongue darted against his. He growled as he forced one knee between her thighs, nudging her legs apart, making room for himself.

And then her clothing was gone. Alon paused in astonishment. She had removed every barrier that separated them. He wanted to howl in triumph, tear his own clothing to ribbons and thrust inside her. Bury himself deep.

He fumbled with the fastening of his trousers, freeing himself from the confinement. Samantha's hand encircled him, her cool fingers dancing over his engorged flesh. The flames of need consumed him.

He pressed forward, sliding his erection along the wet folds of her cleft. Just another moment and she would be his.

She was ready and willing to accept him. Because she didn't remember what he was.

He drew back, positioning himself to take her. But he wanted to see her expression, look into her eyes when he thrust home. Alon lifted his head and gazed down at Samantha's lovely face.

Her skin shown pale as starlight and she blinked up at him in a daze, drunk from the passion they shared. She writhed her hips beneath him, eager for what they would share, and he could see clearly for one moment that she had also lost her mind.

Whatever this was between them was strong enough to make him forget everything he ever wanted or ever believed. Strong enough to make Samantha surrender herself to the likes of him. Strong enough to kill them both.

She lay naked and vulnerable, eager for the death he would bring.

It was enough to snap him to his senses. He drew away. She clung. He pulled her arms away from his neck and staggered back, drawing up his trousers. She propped herself up on both elbows.

"Alon?" The note of concern hit him hard. He didn't mean to hurt her pride, but taking her might hurt her in other ways.

She was breathing in short little pants. Her brow knit and he saw the shame first. A moment later the realization struck. She covered her mouth with one hand and her breasts with the other.

"I'm sorry," he said. He'd never keep her. Not when just one night together might be enough to tear her from him forever.

A cold panic washed down his body.

No female was strong enough to bring his kind into this world. He had wanted her to feel only pleasure. Instead he had nearly brought her death.

Samantha was like a gemstone, sparkling with hope and promise. He couldn't resist bringing her into his dark world. But she didn't belong with him. No one did.

He hated his weakness for her. Hated what he was. Hated his father for what he did to his mother.

"Alon, please." Her gentle touch spoke of yearning. He could almost feel the pulse of her desire. She made it so difficult to stop himself.

"No, Samantha. No. Never. We can't." And then he told her. He spoke of his greatest shame. Of how his kind was born, in blood and death. All their mothers dead. All. The pain and the guilt tore through him like a knife blade, and the words poured from him like seawater from a drowning man.

Samantha stared in horror.

"It's why I never took a woman. Never will take one. I couldn't bear it. You have to remember my words."

"But they were human, your mothers. I'm not human."

"It will make no difference."

"How do you know?"

He raised his voice. "I won't gamble with your life." She reached for him and he drew back. She wasn't thinking and neither was he. To protect her, he needed to go.

She stroked his cheek and he closed his eyes. So tempted. His control frayed.

Alon shifted so quickly some of his clothing tangled with his swirling form, flying out and away before fall-

ing back to earth. He needed to get as far from her as
possible for his sake as well as hers.

Samantha lay on her back on the padded hot tub cover
bereft of his wonderful heat as the overwhelming need
beat insistently in her. She was so crazed by need that
she tried to follow him. It was not until she discovered
herself standing in the dewy grass, naked and alone,
that her blood cooled enough for her to recognize what
she had almost done.

She staggered and then dropped to one knee to keep
from falling. It seemed the earth heaved beneath her
and she clung, digging both hands into the soft tufts of
grass to anchor herself.

Was he right?

She was a Skinwalker and a damned strong one. And
she was a powerful healer. Was it arrogance to think that
what befell his mother would not happen to her, or was
it the need speaking?

Samantha toppled, falling to the grass, squeezing
her eyes shut as her mind and body battled. Her desire
roared, pulsed, demanded. Her thoughts raced, stumbled and swayed.

Hadn't she seen their auras leap and dance, rising like
twin flares against the night sky? Even Alon had seen
them. And she knew that her parents' auras danced in
that same way. She also knew what this might mean.

Soul mates.

No. That was not possible. Alon was a Toe Tagger,
the child of her enemy. What would her family say if
she were to bring home a Ghost Child?

She wrapped her arms about her knees and stifled
a sob. She didn't want to bring him home. She only
wanted to sleep with him. Just to feel him inside her.

That might douse this unmanageable need. If it was just some lust that roared between them then a single coupling might satisfy their desires. Why wouldn't he take her—just once?

Perhaps if she explained. But what if she was wrong? What if the connection ran deeper? What if she couldn't manage it? What if she was never rid of this wanting? The hairs on her head rose up and she shivered with dread.

He was like Pandora's box, enticing but dangerous, and once opened there would be no easy way to shut that lid. She sensed it in the same place that urged her on against all reason. She should be grateful one of them showed some sense.

But she wasn't grateful. She was cold and covered with dew and shamed by her need.

Worse than that, she respected him. He did the honorable thing. He had taken her in even knowing what some of her people were doing to his, and he had kept her safe. He was a magnificent fighter.

Samantha pressed her forehead to her knees. She rocked back and forth at the horror of her thoughts.

What if Alon was truly her soul mate?

She wouldn't tell him. He couldn't see the aura. She'd just pretend it was a mistake. Well, wasn't it? Yes, the worst mistake she had ever made. Rivaled only by her stupidly removing that evil ghost from that little boy. This mistake, at least, did not endanger her family.

But it threatened everything she ever believed was true.

How often had she dreamed of finding her soul mate? But never in her wildest imaginings was he a fearsome Ghostling who could steal her soul as easily as kiss her.

Samantha pressed the heels of her hands to her eyes,

but still the images of Alon hungry and wanting flashed before her.

Even without him here, even without that electric attraction that came with each touch, she still wanted him.

Gradually she became aware of the breeze cooling her skin and the damp ground drawing away her heat. She dragged herself up and dragged off the Jacuzzi cover. Sinking down in the hot water and warm jets relaxed her tense muscles but left her skin smelling of chlorine.

She headed toward the house.

By the time Samantha showered and found a suitable bed in the upstairs of Alon's home, she had nearly convinced herself that the flare of auras she had seen was nothing more than a roaring physical attraction manifested in a blaze of light. She burned hot for him, and that she could not deny. But that was *all* it was.

With that settled in her mind, she crawled beneath the covers. Tomorrow she must convince Bess Suncatcher to bring her children into the battle against Nagi.

Her dad said that Bess was fierce and opinionated. Would she be willing to endanger her children to protect the Balance?

Chapter 11

Alon had made a full search of the perimeter, flying low through the pines and finding nothing but the expected game in the woods. A few elk and one less mule deer now that he had eaten. With his belly full and his patrol ended, he returned to the house.

The need to see her beat inside him like a drum. Letting her out of his sight was harder than he expected. The urge to protect her grew stronger by the minute. It made no sense to him. It didn't seem to matter that she loathed his kind or that she belonged to a race of sneaky child killers. He billowed in disgust. She mixed him all up inside. All he knew for certain was that sleeping with her would make everything worse.

In the blackest, longest part of the night, Alon flew around the exterior searching for ghosts.

He hovered before Samantha's second-story window. None of the windows in this place had curtains. There was no need for there was nothing to look through the windows to see until now.

She had left hers open to the night and lay in a tangle of bedding, her dark hair fanning the white cotton sheets. Now he knew how thick and silky her hair was and how soft and warm her skin was and how absolutely perfectly she fit against his body.

Alon billowed through the window, under her locked door and down the hall to his own room. Once there he transformed to his final form, the one that so aroused Samantha. The one that was a lie.

He lay in bed naked, knowing he must sleep but not knowing how to put his need for her out of his mind when she was within his grasp.

Samantha had wanted him. He'd made that happen and could do it again. He could make her forget what he was, at least temporarily.

He'd been willing to let her pretend that he was a handsome lover there to meet her every need, instead of a harbinger of death.

Perhaps that was where the name Toe Tagger came from, for certainly none who lay with one avoided a toe tag. Alon rolled to his side and thumped the pillow. Yet he still wanted to have sex with Samantha. That only made him more of a monster.

Avoiding her would be more difficult now because he had seen her, felt her, tasted her.

Alon groaned and closed his eyes. Images of Samantha filled his mind. His body grew hard with need.

Nagi wanted her and *he* wanted her. Who was the bigger threat?

He placed his hand on his needy flesh, wishing her hand was there instead. Perhaps this would satisfy the relentless thirst to taste Samantha once more.

A familiar prickling began at his neck and spread rapidly over his flesh. He bolted up, knowing what it meant.

A ghost.

Alon was on his feet when Samantha's scream tore through the darkest part of the night.

Halfway down the hall he recalled he was naked. He changed to his fighting form as he kicked open her door.

His vision penetrated the blackness of the interior, turning the low light to shades of gray. Samantha sat upright pressed against the headboard, clutching the bedsheets to her chest. Her pale nightie twisted about her, showing her long, toned legs drawn up as she huddled in the dark. Her gaze flashed to him and then back to something beside her bed. He had not seen it at first because the evil ghost sank half through the floor. Pure souls were as transparent as plastic wrap. A dull, sickly haze clung to this one like smoke from a cigarette. Wicked and likely one of Nagi's vanguard. Alon's hackles rose and a growl rumbled deep in the back of his throat.

"What is she?" asked the ghost.

Alon roared and charged toward the apparition. He lifted both hands, summoning the power that erupted as a bright green flash of light from each palm. Alon had meant to send it to judgment, but he couldn't control the rage that poured out of him at this thing who threatened Samantha. Something changed. The soul was not cast to the Ghost Road. Instead it writhed in torment before him. The hazy, diaphanous body turned to swirling particles of charred dust. Consumed like paper, still screaming in his head, the soul contorted once more as the last vestige of existence stubbed out.

Samantha clamped her hands over her ears. Could she hear it, too? The ash sizzled like a raw steak hitting a hot grill, and then came the echoing silence. The lifeless particles hung like dust motes in the cold morning air but the soul was no more.

Samantha hunched, bracing as one does when trying to avoid being hit with flying debris. Her hands slid from her ears but remained raised to shield her face. She straightened and turned to him, her eyes seeking answers to what she had witnessed. Now did she understand how wrong he was for her?

She could heal any injury. He could extinguish an immortal soul.

"It's terrible," she whispered.

"*I'm* terrible," he corrected. He stood in his fighting form, letting her witness what he was. Did she see the creatures that had attacked her family, mauled her father, hunted her even now? He was one of them, just as surely as she was a Skinwalker. It was there in the marrow of his bones, the viciousness and the danger. He needed her to see it and remember it, because he could not resist her any longer.

He would need her to resist him. He knew it and he feared for her. *Be strong, Samantha, and be wise. I am not for you. All I bring is death.*

At last she looked away, huddling against the headboard in the nightie that revealed clearly what he could never have.

"There may be more. Get dressed. We're leaving."

Samantha climbed into the truck as Alon tossed a cooler, duffel bag and a heavy sack in the truck bed. His shoes he threw behind his seat. Barefooted and hastily dressed in his favorite trousers and close-fitting dove-gray sweater, he looked tousled and appealing in his human form.

Appearances were deceiving, she remembered.

A moment later dirt and gravel spewed behind them as he fishtailed back out the driveway and through the opening gate.

Samantha peered behind them. "Are there more?"

"Didn't see any."

"Will it… It can't tell, can it?"

"It's gone, Samantha. I finished it."

She'd known it. Seen it. Understood even as her mind objected. Alon had not sent the soul to the Ghost Road. He had destroyed it.

"I thought souls were immortal. That they could never die."

He cast her an impatient look. "They die."

"Have you done that before?"

He glared out the window. "No."

And now he had because of her. Samantha realized she still wore her coat in the form of a flimsy pink nightshirt. She brushed her hand over the garment, focusing her energy on what she wanted. There was a crackling sound, like static discharging from warm, dry laundry, and then she sat in jeans, worn brown cowboy boots, a frilly flowered blouse and a faded denim jacket.

He lifted a brow at her transformation.

She folded her arms protectively across her body as the truck picked up speed.

"You want to talk about it?" she asked.

He hunched over the wheel. "Talk changes nothing."

His silence was more deafening than a steam whistle. Did he think he was the only one who carried regrets?

He stepped on the accelerator as if he could not reach his destination fast enough.

She closed her eyes and focused on her breathing, trying to calm the fear of seeing that ghost in her bedroom. Alon had saved her. He'd protected her again. Gradually the tension in her shoulders drained away and she opened her eyes to a light show of their auras.

His glimmering silver with flashes of bright blue sexual energy. It reached across the wide distance that separated them and hers stretched to meet his. They blended in a shimmering curtain of violet and gray punctuated with tiny pops of light, like the last bit of a sparkler burning bright on a warm July night.

She stared in slacked-mouth wonder. As he sat there, hunched over the wheel, eyes fixed on the road, some essential part of him reached for her. But it wasn't the soul mate connection. Or at least not like her parents' connection. Their auras never twinkled. Theirs simply found the other in a wash of light that reminded Samantha of a watercolor painter's palate. Her mother's a golden hue of all Spirit Children and the violet unique to Seers blending with her father's rich nutmeg brown and vivid navy blue. They came together in tones of copper and deep purple.

Samantha's aura crested most vividly with cinnamon tones in a gilded cap. Beneath them both the violet beamed close to her skin.

"What are you staring at?" he asked.

His voice startled her out of her trance.

"Our auras."

He growled. "What about them?"

She continued to watch the sparks. "They're dancing."

He glanced at her and then into what must seem to him empty space. Alon returned his attention to the highway before he spoke.

"What does that mean?"

She shook her head in bafflement. "I don't know."

Outside the truck the stars winked out and the trees that lined the highway appeared in silhouette. The sky turned deep blue as dawn approached. Samantha drifted between dreams and wakefulness. The hypnotic monotony of the road lulled. Her head lolled and she forced herself back awake. The dashboard clock read 5:00 a.m. When she opened her eyes again it read 7:32 a.m. The sun was well up and the truck rode half on the shoulder of the road.

"Alon!"

Alon's head snapped up. He gripped the wheel and steered them back onto the pavement as Samantha clutched the dashboard.

"You need to sleep," she said.

He nodded wearily. Samantha's eyes burned with fatigue and Alon blinked at her with red-rimmed eyes.

"I'll find a place to pull over."

According to Alon, his parents were traveling in a large RV with the Alpha Pack and possibly any twins they had located. Aldara was also there with the Beta and Gamma packs. If Alon was as weary as she was, they'd never make it.

It took another hour for Alon to find a suitably isolated spot on a long stretch of dirt road that seemed to lead nowhere. Once parked, he walked to the rear of the truck and removed his clothing. Samantha watched him in the rearview mirror, lapping up the sight of his bare chest and muscular shoulders.

"Stay near the truck. I'll make a quick pass to see if we are alone." He gestured toward the truck bed. "Eat something."

Before she could answer he was gone, billowing up into the sky. She left the truck to relieve herself then walked the kinks out of her muscles. Returning to the vehicle, she explored the cooler packed with nothing but bottled water. The sack held a neatly ordered variety of dehydrated food used for camping, canned food and prepackaged crackers and oatmeal. There was even a single-burner camp stove, two fuel cartridges, mess kits and a series of aluminum pots that stacked one inside the next.

She realized she was famished. After about twenty minutes, Samantha's stomach no longer grumbled and Alon returned. He approached from the direction of the truck, pulling on his sweater. She caught a glimpse of his ripped torso. The flash of pale skin and contracting muscle made her stomach flutter.

"I ate all the tuna," she confessed. And most of the crackers and all the diced ham. The water boiled and she added the oatmeal and stirred.

"The area seems clear of ghosts. Did you find the sleeping bags?"

"No."

"In the back container with the chairs and tents. Do you want a tent?"

She glanced up at the blue sky. "Seems unnecessary."

He retraced his path, returning with two tightly rolled bags.

"Do you camp often?" she asked.

"Aldara keeps this truck ready for extended outings. It gives us another base on our expeditions."

"When you search for other Ghostlings?"

He nodded and accepted a bowl of oatmeal. His pale skin revealed dark circles under his eyes. He ate quickly, blinking as if struggling to stay awake.

Surely that wasn't all he was going to eat. He'd provided the bounty. The least she could do was fix it for him. "Can I get you anything else?"

"I ate at the house. I just need a few hours' sleep."

She rolled out the bags and set them side by side with

a respectable distance between them. She'd be damned if she'd cross that distance again.

Alon crawled inside his bag. A moment later he pulled his trousers and sweater from beneath. Knowing he was naked and sheathed in only nylon and down batting did funny things to her insides. Samantha forced her hand away from her chest, where she had placed it to keep her heart from beating out of her ribs.

"Would you prefer I remain dressed?" he asked.

She shrugged. "What's that to me?"

"I don't know, but your pulse is rising and there is much color in your cheeks and neck." He pointed in a manner she found very rude.

Samantha thrust her legs into her sleeping bag and rolled to her opposite side.

"You really are the most disagreeable man."

He propped himself up on one elbow. "Not a man. It's why I sleep alone."

She found his tone condescending and annoying as hell.

"You've seen my true form, Samantha. You would do well to remember just what it is you almost took to your bed."

She thought of their dancing auras and feared that his words would not be enough to keep them apart. Whatever was between them, it was strong and growing stronger.

"All I want to do is get you to my mother."

"And be rid of me," she finished.

He said nothing to this.

She knew it was true and his refusal to say so only upset her further. How could she convince him to bring his family to fight with her father? How could she convince her father to allow the Naginoka to join him? Samantha knew what was needed. But she had no idea how to make it happen. With her mind spinning like a top, it took some time to relax enough to sleep.

He woke her at dusk.

"We're going," he said and left her there. She watched him return to the vehicle and replace his neatly rolled sleeping bag to the box in the truck bed.

She crawled out of the bag and sought a little privacy before returning to find Alon waiting in the driver's seat. She climbed in and swung the door shut. He handed her a box of granola bars and a bottle of water.

From there Alon stopped only for gas and food. The following morning, he pulled off the interstate just before the Canadian border.

"Can you make it across?" he asked, indicating the woods.

"Don't see why not."

"I'll meet you on the other side."

Samantha transformed and loped off into the forest. Her trek took a family of hikers by surprise but was otherwise uneventful. When she reached a paved road, she stopped. Alon descended in his vaporous form then transformed to human for the time it took to tell her where to meet him.

She made her way to the rendezvous thinking of little but how Alon looked naked. When she arrived it was to find him dressed and sitting in a cream-colored four-door Jeep.

She closed her eyes as the energy ripped through her, bringing her to her human form. A moment later she stepped into the Jeep in the same clothing she wore that morning.

They made it through Calgary and headed west on 93 and entered Kootenay National Park.

Samantha grew hopeful that they'd arrive soon, but it was another hour before she spotted the camping sign. They bounced over the gravel road at dusk and into the primitive camping ground. The sites were all empty except for one mammoth RV. A string of lights hung from the awning, casting bright light all about the camper like the perimeter of a high-security prison. Samantha wondered where the three packs might be and kept close to Alon.

The door to the bus slid open and a tall, handsome man stepped down. His jeans and button-up shirt were ordinary enough, but that was the only thing expected. His copper skin and dark eyes complemented the close-cropped cap of brown hair. His physique showed him to be fit and physically capable, and he moved with the grace of a Skinwalker, though his aura showed he was not. The jagged white spikes were tipped with black and crowned by the familiar gold of all Spirit Children. The odd mix of the purity of white and the deathly black was new to her. But she had never seen a Soul Whisperer before. Cesar could speak to the dead, and his wife could follow them to the Spirit World. Samantha repressed a shudder.

On reaching the ground he lifted a hand to assist his female companion down the steps. Samantha noted that the couple's auras blended naturally together, like colors of light merging in a rainbow. A fully formed soul mate bond, exactly like her parents, though Alon's father's aura was a more unsettling black and white.

"That's my mother," said Alon, extending a hand toward the woman.

Bess Suncatcher's aura was a familiar fawn brown surrounded with the white of a spiritual being. She did not have Samantha's height but was still unusually tall for a woman. Slim and reedy, Bess had long black hair that cascaded over the shoulder of a black tailored blouse cut to reveal her elegant neck and slender arms. The rest of her attire, also black, consisted of a sedate pair of formfitting pants tucked into stylish calf-high boots. So this was the Skinwalker who married a Soul Whisperer and adopted Nagi's ghastly offspring.

"Mother. Father." Alon extended his hand to Samantha. "This is—"

Before he could say her name, Bess repeated her given name, the one held secret to all but family and the closest of friends.

"Night Sky Woman."

Her smile was warm and welcoming, but her eyes held an intense scrutiny that disquieted.

Bess took Samantha up in her arms and hugged her tight.

"You've grown into a beauty just like your mother."

Bess released Samantha to greet her son with a kiss on each cheek. "Welcome home, Alon."

Alon did not look at home. In fact his rigid posture and strained expression told of his mood.

"I'm sorry I could not save them, Mother."

Bess's dark eyes filled with tears that caught on her lower lashes. "If you could not then no one could."

Alon dipped his chin, breaking their eye contact. "It is the wish of Samantha's father that I bring her to you."

An instant later smoke billowed from the place he had stood and his clothing collapsed to the earth.

"Wait," called Bess, but her son was gone.

There was an unfamiliar sound like the fluttering of wings and many more billowing clouds escaped from the bus.

Bess rolled her eyes, glanced to her husband and then

back to Samantha. "The Alphas. Alon is their leader. They will want to know his plans. You wouldn't know them, would you?"

Chapter 12

She knew only that Alon wished to be done with her. Now he had his wish. His obligation was finished and she had reached her goal. Why then did her chest ache and her stomach twist?

Bess motioned to the picnic table and waited while Samantha sat before joining her on the long narrow bench. A larger cloud flew out the door.

"The Beta Pack," said Cesar. "Plus the ones we found here in the forest." There was another rushing sound like a sudden wind on a calm night. "Gammas." Cesar sighed and took a seat in one of the folding chairs. "Alone at last," he said.

Samantha turned to Bess. "Have you heard anything more from my family?"

"I have word from your brother. Blake has been elected War Chief of the Northwestern Council."

Samantha sank back against the connecting table.

He had done it. Blake was now in a position to speak before the other councils and convince them of the imperative of joining the Skinwalkers against Nagi. Their dad would be so proud.

Satisfaction buoyed her up. Then an arrow of self-doubt pierced her bubble of contentment. She'd been running and hiding and lusting after Alon while her brother had accomplished the impossible.

"None of mixed blood has ever reached such a position," said Bess. "Perhaps there is hope for those Spirit Children yet."

Samantha hunched and folded both arms across her middle. "Father will be pleased," she managed to whisper.

"Yes. He hopes to bring Skinwalker and Spirit Child together to fight. But old wounds heal very slowly."

Samantha assumed Bess referred to the wars between the Halflings. Both sides had endured heavy losses, but that was before her time. Had Bess fought the Spirit Children?

"Blake will convince them." If her dad wanted something, Blake would move heaven and earth to bring it to him. Her brother made everything look effortless. She released a long breath. Would she ever get a chance to make her dad proud?

Bess spoke softly. "I've known this day would come. Your father asked me long ago to protect you should the need arise, and you are welcome to remain as long as you wish. But…"

Her hesitation gave Samantha time to grow anxious.

"But?" she asked.

"But the Thunderbirds did not bring you to me. They brought you to Alon. I wonder if they think he is better suited to be your protector."

"He's happy to be rid of me."

"I know my son, and I can assure you he is not happy. Now, why is that?"

"He finds me a burden."

Bess glanced at Cesar, who shook his head. Then she directed her attention back to Samantha.

"What are your plans? Will you rejoin your father or your mother?"

Samantha felt her breath catch. But she needed to say aloud what was in her heart.

"Neither. Since my arrival I've seen many things. And I think…that is I believe that it is essential to include the Ghost Children in this fight."

Both Bess and Cesar rose to their feet. Samantha followed them, now feeling awkward and uncertain.

"Did your father send you here to ask us this?" asked Bess.

"No. He told me you had strange ideas and that there would be Toe Ta…Ghostlings about you. He told me that if I saw a Ghost Child, I was to run and if I could not run I was to kill it."

Bess threw up her hands. "He doesn't listen to me. I warned him of Nagi recruiting the lost children, but still he sees no difference between those Nagi has captured and those we have found." She pinned Samantha with a focused stare. "But you see. Don't you?"

"Yes."

"I believe you are right. Your father cannot win without the Ghost Children."

Samantha clasped her hands together before her heart. "Then you'll help me?"

Bess shook her head. "I am not their leader. Alon is. He has always been. If you wish them to fight, you must persuade him."

"How do I do that?"

"It will be difficult, as he hates the Skinwalkers, but the Thunderbirds brought you to him for a reason. Perhaps this is it."

"There is another reason," said Cesar, looking at Samantha. "Isn't there?"

She looked into the eyes of a Spirit Child, one who could see auras as clearly as she could. Her stomach dropped.

"And now, Samantha, you and I need to have a talk."

Aldara found him first, of course. She materialized in her fighting form. The other Alphas appeared a moment later.

"Alon, what is happening?"

In the course of a few moments the other twins from the Beta and Gamma packs took shape around him, and he was forced to change to his fighting form or stand naked before them all.

"I was scouting for ghosts."

"There are none," reported Bart. He and his sister, Bella, were the second twins found by their father. It was Cesar's idea to name them alphabetically. The Alpha Pack also consisted of Cody and Callie, Daniel and Darya and Evan and Elizabeth.

"Aldara said that she's a Skinwalker," said Callie, her speech much better than Cody's, whom Alon still could barely understand when in this form. "Why would you bring her here?"

"She is a Seer of Souls."

The gathering gasped.

"If he finds her, he finds us," said Darya, her yellow eyes huge and round.

There was nothing his siblings feared more than Nagi.

Samantha's arrival threatened them, and that put her at risk. He wondered if he should take her away.

"You said there are no ghosts here."

"Brother, there is a war coming," said Aldara. "Our parents speak of little else. What are we to do?"

"That is up to each of you to decide."

"No," said Bart. "You are the Alpha leader. You decide for all of us."

The honor swelled inside him. A moment later the responsibility dragged him down. He tried to think of someone better qualified. Aldara? She was as good a fighter but she lacked self-control. His sister was always ruled by her heart.

"Will we join the fight against Nagi?" His sister sounded so anxious to fight and die. Did she understand what they faced?

"Why should we fight with those who hunt our young?" asked Bella.

"Because Nagi is trying to upset the Balance," said Bart. "It is our duty to protect it."

"And Mankind," added Daniel, his words slurred and awkward.

They were willing to fight for a world that did not want them. Alon bowed his head in humility at the magnitude of their generosity.

Bess and Cesar would be proud.

When he lifted his head, it was with the conviction of his brothers and sisters.

He lifted his voice and spoke to the three packs. "We have not chosen war with Nagi. But he hunts us. From this moment on we will fight all who threaten us. It is better to die in the battle to be free than to be taken as a slave."

They cheered.

"We will fight to defend ourselves. But we will not join the Skinwalkers who hunt our babies or the Spirit Children who do nothing to stop them. They reject us so we reject them."

The assemblage nodded their approval of this.

"To defeat his army we will need more than bravery. Nagi will drag the humans into this fight. I would not kill innocents. That is why we must protect the Seers."

They cheered again.

"But the Seers are Spirit Children," said his sister.

"We cannot save the possessed humans without them."

She nodded her understanding of this. He wondered if she would be so understanding of his next order.

"Aldara, you will go to Samantha's brother, Blake Proud, and act as his bodyguard. Keep him safe from ghosts and any of Nagi's forces."

Aldara frothed at the mouth and gnashed her teeth. "I am a better fighter than any of them." She pointed an accusing finger at their siblings.

"It is why I send you. I know you will keep him safe."

"They are Niyanoka. Not our concern."

"Am I Alpha leader or am I not?"

Aldara hunched. "You are."

"Then you go."

She nodded her acceptance.

Alon turned to the next oldest. "Bella and Bart. You will guard Michaela Proud, Samantha's mother. Find out from our parents where she is. But do not let her see you unless it is to save her life." He turned to his sister. "Aldara, you go with them."

She scowled at him but did not argue. The three burst into their flying form and billowed away.

"Who will guard the last Seer?" asked Hamilton, the leader of the Beta Pack.

All eyes turned to him.

Alon knew he could not leave Samantha with his mother because only a Ghostling could protect her from her enemies. But it did not have to be him. Hamilton was a good fighter. Not as good as him, but still formidable. The hopeful expression on Hamilton's face made Alon seethe. No, he would not hand her over, even though it might be safer for Samantha if he did.

"I have taken her under my protection. She's mine."

Hamilton bowed his acceptance.

"The rest of you go back. I need to hunt and think. I will see you in the morning."

The packs dispersed. In a moment he was alone.

She's mine. But she wasn't. Never would be.

His heart beat painfully against his ribs. Until this was done, Samantha would be under his guard protection. He knew that it was only a matter of time before he lost control and took what he wanted.

Icy fear for Samantha crept through his blood like poison. With all his strength and power, he couldn't protect her from himself.

Cesar drew Samantha away from his wife, and Bess allowed it. He walked with her toward the riverbank beside the ribbon of water that still glinted bright against adjoining banks. Beyond, the tree line loomed darker against the midnight sky.

"Alon is quite protective of you," said Cesar.

He had stopped walking. She glanced above his head to where his black-and-white aura burned beneath a glittering gilded cap.

"You can see my aura," he said.

She nodded.

"And I can see yours. Yours and Alon's."

She knew it.

"Did you know I found Alon the day he was born, feeding in a Dumpster a few feet away from his dead mother?"

Samantha nodded.

"He told you? This surprises me." He paused to look out at the water. "He and Aldara. Bess was there and Tuff Jackson. But Alon came to me. He couldn't speak, but I could see his aura. He sought help. His sister was too afraid to come with us. But she followed. I released them in the woods. Both Tuff and Bess thought I was crazy. I tried to set them free, but Alon kept following me. I didn't adopt him. He adopted me."

"I thought it was Bess."

"Bess was rightly afraid of them at first. They smelled the animal part of her, and that meant food. A buffalo does not adopt a wolf pup or a raven foster an eagle. But that's what I asked her to do. And she did it for me. Now you could not find a fiercer defender of her Ghostlings."

"But they're so dangerous."

"That is part of what makes them wonderful. That viciousness brought under conscious control."

"No one can fully control their instincts."

"You do. Right now, when your instinct tells you to run. But here you are." He rubbed his palm over his jaw as he stared up at her aura. "Alon didn't bring you safely from Nagi's ghosts because of his love for his mother. He brought you here because of his love for you."

Samantha stepped away, the denial springing to her lips. "Love? He can't wait to get rid of me."

"Only because he is afraid of what you make him feel. Do you deny what you see?"

She dropped her gaze, unwilling to accept the truth reflected in his eyes. "It is not love. Just a physical attraction," she whispered.

"Yes. But it could be more."

She raised her gaze to his, her hands curled into fists. "No. It cannot be. Not with a..."

"Toe Tagger?" supplied Cesar. His mouth set in a grim line.

"Just like Bess. She couldn't see the beauty in them at first. She thought I was crazy. But she was willing to set aside her fear and loved them because she loved me."

"He doesn't want me. He's told me so."

"And you believed his words instead of your own eyes?"

Her heart beat so loud she felt sure Cesar could hear it dashing against her ribs. Alon's soul and her soul reaching... But they did not touch. They were not true soul mates. Yet.

"I didn't want to believe my own eyes because..." Her words fell off. When she spoke again it was only a whisper. "I don't want this. Not with him."

"But it is there, whether you want it or not."

"Is there some way to break it?" She didn't like the desperation in her voice.

"None that *I* know. You will always be connected in some way. What way is up to both of you."

"Will you tell him?"

Cesar shook his head. "That's not for me."

"I just want to go back to the way things were. Back to my family."

"Back to running? Back to never being allowed to be who and what you are? Is that what you really want, Night Sky Woman?"

She didn't. But neither did she want Alon. At least not as a soul mate.

She covered her face with her hands and hunched over as the sobs racked her. Cesar gathered her up in his arms and held her just as her own dad would have done.

"It can't be him."

Alon hung in the darkness in his flying form, watching his father embrace Samantha. His mother had tried to speak to him, but he would not leave Samantha alone with another man, even if that man was his own father.

Alon was there when she told him that she wanted her family. He had known that. But what did she see that he could not? What was the connection between them that she denied?

It can't be him, Samantha had said.

Alon's shape contracted at the agony in her tone. Her hurt and dread drove him wild. He did not pursue her, had not asked for her affection because he had known how it would end, and even knowing all that, he had allowed himself to grow fond of her. Now he must suffer the pain of her rejection.

Alon billowed away, scouring the forest for something he could kill and eat.

Whatever this connection was, she didn't want it. Of course she didn't. No one would want to be connected to him. Alon knew what he was. But it was hard to hear it from Samantha's lips.

If only he could be free of her. But to be free was to leave her unprotected, and that he could not do. He sank to the forest floor and hung there, blanketing the ground like a black fog.

Even if he left her, would he ever be rid of her?

You will always be connected in some way.

He did not understand this connection. But he felt it. It burned within him like molten lead eating him away from the inside.

Chapter 13

Alon woke in the forest and scented the air. The first rays of morning shot through the trees, bringing color back to his bleak world.

Hunger yawned and stretched in his empty belly. He ran through the woods, fast and fleet, bounding over the spongy ground beneath the trees. He had the scent of elk, and his hunger urged him on. One thing that he could not change about his existence was the hunger. The hungrier he grew, the harder it was to stay in his human form. Between his lust for Samantha and the knowledge of how she felt about him, he thought he might go mad. Now he was mad, raging down an animal path, knowing his prey was close. Knowing his quarry had no chance against him.

One, he told himself. He'd take only one. But upon seeing them he lost his mind, and when he came back to his senses he had broken the necks of two, a doe and a big buck. He started on the buck, ripping easily through the tough hide as a child might tear into a paper sack.

He devoured the thing, organs, viscera, meat and bone. He was about to crack open the skull when he saw something move. Something stupid. Something about to be dead. Not only was the urge to defend his kill nearly overwhelming, but he still felt the hunger. True, the impulse was now manageable, not the crazed gnawing want of a few moments ago. Now it was the greedy craving to binge. He needed the protein and fat if he was to stay strong to protect Samantha and if he was to stay strong enough to protect Samantha from himself.

Alon turned, claws raised, chest heaving, blood glistening on his face and hands and saw a familiar grizzly bear. The horror of her coming upon him while he ate nearly caused him to lose what he had put down.

"No," he gurgled. "Samantha?"

She nodded.

"Go away," he ordered, his voice harsh as the shame hardened cold inside him. How could he ever look at her again, now that she had seen him feeding on prey?

She shook her head and advanced on all fours, her nose raised as she breathed in the scent of his kill. What was she up to?

"Go away, I said," he tried again, but his voice had lost its authority and now held a definite note of desperation. It was best that she saw this. He knew it. But his vanity pricked and his heart grieved for what he could never have. He realized that he had enjoyed her touches and those adoring glances she cast. But that was all he would have of her.

She'd never willingly touch him again. Not after seeing this.

She walked slowly forward and then past him, brushing his thigh with her furry shoulder, like a cat rubbing up against an owner's leg.

Her touch had the same effect it always did. A prickling excitement began at the point of contact, tingled up and into his core, then, like a falling domino set off the next most obvious reaction.

Alon pressed his hands over his naked body, hiding the erection that lifted in her direction. It wasn't that he didn't want to see Samantha naked or that he didn't want to be naked himself, but when he imagined this in his mind, she was not in her bear form and he was not covered with blood and bits of torn flesh and viscera.

The humiliation seemed to stick with the blood. She sidled past him, right to his second kill, and used the claws of one of her massive forearms to tear open the hide covering the doe's shoulder.

He blinked in astonishment as she began to eat. No one but his sister had ever seen him feed, and he had never shared a kill with anyone until now. This privilege he did not afford even to Aldara, though they did hunt together. But Samantha was different, for he felt none of the familiar urges to defend his kill or the need to drive her away. Instead he was filled with a strange calm and pride at providing her with such a feast. He was not yet full, but still he wanted her to eat first. Some of his despair lifted.

She gave a huffing sound and then looked back at him, as if calling him to join her.

He did, approaching slowly. She allowed it. Somehow he thought that in most circumstances she would have chased off every challenger for this kill. Was this new territory for her, as well? He could not tell and, though he could ask her, she could not answer. Samantha sat gnawing away as if this were the most normal of all circumstances.

By slow degrees he became more comfortable beside her. Some faraway portion of his brain registered that this was how mates acted. The male offering his kill. The female accepting the tribute. Males of many species brought food to their mates in courtship. Was this *their* courtship?

Alon thought of the other reason for a male to bring food to his mate—when she raised their young. His stomach tightened and his heart ached at what he wanted so badly but could never have.

Children.

No. He would not bring more of his kind to a world where they were not wanted. He glanced at Samantha and felt his conviction weakening.

She needed him. But she did not want him. He heard her say so to Cesar. Why was the truth so hard to hear?

The ache in his chest spread until he could not breathe. His kind was too terrible. The earth would be better without them. The planet, in balance before their arrival, would recover more quickly once they had vanished back into the mist.

Samantha finished first, groaned and sidled back to one of the pines to scratch her back against the ridges of the trunk.

Alon was not full, but he was no longer weak from hunger. It seemed rude to eat without her, so he followed to where she rested beside the tree.

"You know I might have killed you," he said, trying for a chastening tone. He hated the slur and gurgle of his words. "My kind does not share."

She huffed and showed him her fangs.

"Will you change back?"

She shook her large head and patted her belly then groaned.

"Do you wish to return to my parents now?"

In answer she closed her eyes and then used a large paw to pull him against her warm, furry body.

Alon rested a clawed hand on her chest, stroking the thick, coarse fur. It was like snuggling up to a gigantic teddy bear. He hadn't meant to sleep, but his full stomach and the buzzing of insects lulled him and he dropped, like a stone, into slumber.

When he woke, low gray clouds swept across the sky. A storm was coming. How much time had passed? He glanced about him, recalling himself to his surroundings.

Where was Samantha?

He sat up, alert now as he sensed for ghosts and found no trace of their clammy presence on his skin.

He rose to follow the clear highway of her scent. It led toward the water he heard burbling a little way off. Was she bathing?

Alon broke into a run.

He slowed when he neared the churning river that bounced between rocky banks over ghost-gray rocks and swirled in quiet eddies among boulders. The water shone the strange azure blue of all glacier-fed rivers and must have been as cold as the melting ice that created it.

Naked in her human form, Samantha stood calf-deep in quiet water between two massive rocks that wore green caps of lodge pole pines, their branches sweeping and dancing in the rising wind. She dipped her cape into the azure river.

Alon drank in the sight. No one had ever accepted him in his fighting form before. No one except his family had ever seen him eat. Yet Samantha had done both and with an easy grace that made it seem as if what she had done was nothing at all. Yet it was everything.

He didn't know if she was blind or just crazy. What else could account for her holding him, nestling against him when he was so hideous?

His chest ached now and his throat felt raw, as if he had swallowed something scalding. Could she really not see him for what he was, or could she overlook it for the protection he provided?

"I may not have the gifts of a wolf," she said, casually, as if speaking to her bearskin, "but I can smell well enough to know when I'm being spied on."

She threw her bearskin cape over her shoulders, covering her form from shoulder to knee. The wind whipped her loose wet hair, lifting it in ropes.

He thought to change into his more human form, but seeing her nude had stirred the wanting again. The prospect of holding her in his arms scalded his skin and burned deep into his lungs and viscera.

He wanted to take her in every way a man takes a mate. But if he came to her naked and wanting, she might reject him. Rejection from Samantha was one defeat he could not bear. He knew it was impossible between them. But still he moved toward her.

He told himself that he *needed* her rejection. It was her only chance to escape him.

So he stepped out from cover still in his fighting form, walked to the water and waded in, quickly washing the blood from his body. Samantha slipped out of the water as he splashed in, but she did not go far enough. How could she sense his presence and not what he wanted from her?

"That was an excellent meal." Her smile was generous and bright. "Thank you."

She smoothed her cloak of glossy fur. There was a flash as if from a camera as her dark brown fur cape turned to a blur of pale purple.

She stood before him now, in a pretty lavender sundress that revealed her slim, muscular arms and hugged her lovely round breasts before cutting away to dance in the wind in waves of fabric about her cinnamon-brown legs. She was bare from midthigh to the straps of her wafer-thin sandals that crisscrossed her trim ankles. She had chosen this lovely vision for him. He felt a gratitude that struck bone deep.

I don't want this. Not with him.

Her words bounced up in his mind, smashing against the enticement she now presented. What was she doing?

Her smile was welcoming. "I have something to ask you. A request, really."

Her words confirmed his suspicion. This was why she offered herself in such a garment, to better her odds at getting what she wanted. He gave her another long look. Well, it was working.

She cocked her head. "Do you like it?"

"Very much."

Her smile radiated pleasure. He tucked the sight of her away in his memory, to be drawn on later when she was gone. She swished her skirts and pivoted from side to side, giving him an ever-changing view.

His lips tugged upward into a smile that he knew must be hideous. The blood pulsed to his sex. He lowered his chin, fighting the urge to capture her. Would it be better to remain in his fighting form or change into his third form to stand before her naked and fully aroused?

She took a step in his direction, the pretty smile still on her raspberry-colored lips. "Your parents told me that you lead them, all the others."

He nodded, apprehensive as to where this conversation was heading.

"And you told me that the Skinwalkers were no match for Nagi's army."

"Well?"

"We could be. If you all joined the alliance, we could win. And you'd be protecting the Balance and Mankind." She held her smile, but it seemed forced. She waited for his response.

His eyes narrowed upon her as she confirmed his suspicions. This was why she sought him out. Not to hunt with him or share a meal or sleep at his side. It was to make this proposal. He shifted, resting his weight on his knuckles, resisting the urge to growl. Had he actually let himself believe she sought his company? That she longed for him as much as he did her? The shame crept through him like crystals of ice.

He had protected her, guarded her from harm, and all the while she was scheming. He would have defended her with his own life.

"I'll bring you to them." Her voice held a forced enthusiasm.

She couldn't possibly be looking forward to introducing him to her family. But she was willing to do it for the cause. What else was she willing to do? How far would she go?

"I'll take you to them privately. Blake first then my dad."

"Privately." Of course.

"Yes. And I'll explain. They'll want your help. I know it."

"Have you already asked them?"

She glanced away. "Not yet." Her gaze sought his

again, and she placed one delicate hand on each of his hairy shoulders. "But I will."

Her scent surrounded him. The prickling heat of her touch tingled over his skin. She slid her hands about his thick, hairy neck. Alon knew he could break free, but somehow he couldn't. Her touch, her gaze, her heat all enthralled him.

When he spoke his voice held strain. "And what are you prepared to give me in return?"

Her hands slipped away. Her face registered surprise. Let's see what she did with his counteroffer.

"What do you want?"

Her question hit him in the chest like a dart. Did she know what she was doing?

"I want you," he whispered.

Her brow knit. "What?"

He summoned the energy, feeling it flash through him as he transformed into the lover she could accept. Her gaze flicked to his erection and her cheeks flushed.

Her ears pulled back and her eyes went cautious. She retreated a step. Too little too late, he thought.

The tension in her body and the scent of her blood pulsing through her told him she recognized danger.

"You don't have to, Samantha. You can just walk away. I'll understand. Your family would expect it. You'd be a fool not to."

Then he scented something else. Samantha's arousal came to him on the breeze as sweet and spicy as any exotic bloom.

Oh, no, he thought. *No. No. No. Run, you little fool.*

She seemed not to hear as she stared steadily at him. When she spoke, her words were a whisper, as if she spoke only to herself. "I have to know. This may be the only way."

He didn't understand her words and wondered briefly what she would know by lying with him. But he didn't care. He'd accept any excuse, any feeble rationalization on her part as long as it allowed him to touch her again.

Alon stalked forward in the form he knew she could not resist.

Chapter 14

Compelled by a force she could no longer deny, Samantha moved toward Alon until she stood so close she could feel the heat of his skin. Her aura pulled toward his, the smoky gray of his essence already blending with her violet, brown and gold.

She lowered her gaze to find his crystal-blue eyes locked on hers. His jaw muscles bulged as he set his mouth in a grim line. He looked like a man going to war. She swallowed back her fear, pressed down her uncertainty and ignored the warning of danger as she reached for him.

Samantha ran her fingers over the perfection of Alon's chest, savoring the texture of warm, yielding flesh over taut muscle. His third form, the one he called an illusion, was no illusion. Her fingers danced over his stomach, and his skin twitched as if in pain. His eyes spoke to her, begging her to turn back. But she couldn't. She glanced down at his sex, jutting toward her. She reached, taking hold of him, measuring the length of him with her two hands. His eyes closed, but not before she saw them change from blue to green.

She knew what it meant. Green was the blending of blue and yellow—his third form struggling to emerge.

His head dropped back and a growl of male yearning tore from his throat. His hands hung at his sides and he stood as if petrified, muscles taut, fully erect in her hands, neither welcoming her touch nor repelling it. He waged a battle against himself, suffering the call of desire and still refusing to yield. The dark clouds gave a gloom to the day, making it easier to see their auras. She glanced up, noting something new. There was a sparkling now, like dust motes dancing in sunlight.

What did it mean?

She needed his touch, yet still he denied her.

The urge to feel his flesh pressing to hers roared inside her. Suddenly the flimsy dress seemed far too confining. Nothing could stand between them now.

Samantha drew her hands reluctantly from his body and stepped back. His eyes snapped open, tracking her every movement. Did he think she had changed her mind? He watched her as if she belonged to him, as if he possessed her already. The intensity of his stare unnerved her.

He didn't want this. That much was clear from his expression. But it would happen, here and now, regardless of what they wanted. They both knew it because they'd already gone too far. She would satisfy this fascination for the forbidden, and no one need know.

She lifted a hand to the hem of her skirt and concentrated. The sheer fabric vanished in a flash of brilliant light as her clothing reformed into a simple necklace, a gold medicine wheel on a short chain. The wind blew cold over her heated flesh. Alon would warm her.

His gaze swept over her nude form, tracing her curves, lingering on her breasts, diving to stare at her sex.

She wished she were a Mindwalker or a Truth Seeker, so she could read Alon's thoughts. But he gave her nothing but the obvious excitement of his sex, the resistance of his body and the grave reservations in his eyes.

"Perhaps joining will make the hunger stop."

He shook his head, denying her childish fantasy that she could be as she was before. No matter what happened here, she would never be the same again. Alon had changed her.

"It will never stop." His words were like a deadly pronouncement.

She shivered in the rising wind, knowing it was true.

The realization frightened her enough to send her back a step. He captured her wrist. Their eyes met. She resisted, and he imprisoned her other wrist in a move so fast it was only a blur. His nostrils flared and his chest rose and fell in a rapid cadence too fast for a man standing still. His green irises had nearly disappeared, pushed back by the expanding black pupils that now looked like twin solar eclipses. She sucked in a breath.

For just a moment she thought he might use his superior strength to cast her aside. Instead he transferred both her wrists to one large hand.

He tugged her forward, compelling her with his gaze as he scowled down at her. He used his free hand, at the center of her back, to draw her forward until her hips collided with his.

She felt his shaft, now stiff and ready, pressed against

her stomach. The desire pumped through her, rocking Samantha on her feet. Yes, she wanted this.

When he spoke, it was through clenched teeth. "I might hurt you."

"You won't, Alon. I'm not human. Not fragile. You don't want me to forget your other form, but you keep forgetting mine. I'm a grizzly, and a damned big one. If that were not enough, I have the power to heal."

"You're not only a Skinwalker. You are Spirit Child. They are weak, fragile."

"I'm not."

"You don't know what I'm capable of."

"Let's find out."

She watched the tug-of-war play out on his features. Was it true? Shadow, sunshine and shadow again. And then she realized she was not only reading his expression. She felt his emotions as if they were her own. Hope. Dread. Acceptance.

She had won.

"Remember that I tried to prevent this."

He looked the picture of control, but there was wildness in his eyes and fever in his blood. The tight restraint of his body now seemed a coiling preparation. He was a seawall holding back the unstoppable ocean.

He dragged her arms about his neck, encircled her in his inescapable embrace and slanted his mouth to hers. The riotous kiss tipped her from her axis, and Samantha reeled off into space. His fingers coiled in her hair as he took possession of her in a fierce invasion of her mouth, his tongue sliding, stroking as he controlled her.

She leaned over his arm, yielding to his superior strength, allowing his ownership of her as anticipation fluttered inside her.

Samantha gripped his forearms as he lowered her to

the earth, and still her head spun. He kissed her throat, her neck and down along the line of her collarbone.

His tongue flicked out as he licked her skin, raising gooseflesh in his wake. The clouds sailed above them, billowing dark, but they did not match the storm within her.

Alon pinned her down with one leg as his hands swept up her torso to caress her aching breasts. She groaned and arched toward the sweet pressure of his skillful hands, her nipples tightening to hard knots in his palms.

He kept his gaze on her as he kneaded the sensitive flesh. She stretched her arms over her head to claw at the ground behind her and bucked her hips.

His mouth covered the tip of one breast, his tongue flicking over the taut nipple, thrilling her with tiny darts of pleasure. Her body had never been so ready, and still he did not take her. She writhed as he pinned her arms to the ground and then made his way leisurely down her belly, his teeth grazing and nipping at the sensitive skin.

He used one strong leg to nudge her thighs apart then took his place there. She opened her eyes to see him, poised between her legs, looking at her exposed flesh. The hunger in his eyes gave her chills. He dived and his lips danced over her sensitive flesh, parting the folds and driving her mad with each swirl of his tongue. Her breath caught in excitement. He grabbed her calves and pressed legs around his middle. She clamped her ankles across his back, digging her heels into the long, corded muscle as he mouthed her most sensitive flesh.

Her body pulsed and liquid heat made her slick and ready. He bumped against her with his mouth, his tongue entering her in an imitation of the sex act. She gasped and cried out, her skin tingling and her body aching for him to take her.

She needed him inside her. He was big, very big, and she wanted him to drive into her with everything he had.

"You're so wet," he whispered, his breath warm against the moisture on her thigh.

He lifted his head. His eyes were a ghostly yellow. Alon grasped her hips and dragged her beneath him. She saw the claws emerging from his hands.

She shivered in alarm and delight.

He knelt between her spread thighs, sliding his hands up her body, finally planting them on each side of her head and extending his arms. He used his knee to spread her legs wider. Samantha pressed her feet flat to the earth and lifted herself to meet him.

He growled and then bucked, sheathing himself fully inside her with one thrust. Samantha gasped at the arousing friction. Even as wet as she was, her body struggled to accommodate him, stretching as he pushed deeper, stopping only when he met the opening of her womb.

His eyes blazed with possession as he withdrew and thrust again. He pumped again and again. His expression might have been need or hatred. The hairs on her neck lifted even as her body reeled with the passion he stirred.

Her climax built, rising so quickly that she cried out in surprise as she clung to him. He delved into her again and again. She was so close. She needed only a few more of those perfect thrusts and…

Alon cried out and for a moment she thought he had come, but this was a different kind of release. This was a fracturing of his control. He grasped her hips and lifted her off the ground, holding her open to each hard thrust. Each slide was a perfect gift, each withdrawal a tiny tragedy. He was rough and she liked it. She closed her eyes to savor this wild joining, her head rolling to the side as the first orgasm burst inside her. A long, tortured cry of release tore from her lips and was met with one of his.

Exquisite waves of delight rolled outward from her core. Samantha threw her hands out, clawing at the earth, panting and shaking her head from side to side as the zing of excitement sped all the way to her fingers and toes. And still he thrust. One hand captured her neck.

His eyes brilliant yellow, his face flushed and his mouth open. Behind him storm clouds swept across the dark sky. She'd never seen anything more beautiful.

His expression seemed one of agony, but she recognized it as just the opposite. His eyelids fluttered closed as he made his final thrust, pinning her to the earth. Something rocked her. It surged with his release and stole her breath. She arched as she experienced the intense pleasure of her contractions like a blow. He held her, controlled her, as his body jerked and pulsed deep inside her. Her eyes widened at this new rush of pleasure. This was not from her. It was his release, but she felt it inside herself, curling her toes and sending her eyes rolling back in her head. The sensation triggered another orgasm, this one a slow, steady roll of liquid pleasure, squeezing him and taking the last he had to offer for her own.

What was that?

She went limp then. Her eyes dropped closed and she breathed deeply of the cold, damp air. The wind still rushed through the treetops as the storm closed in. Yet she could not recall when she had felt more relaxed, content and replete. His warm body kept off the chill.

Something glowed above them. At first she thought it was blowing debris from the impending storm. But then her vision came into focus and she recognized her aura and Alon's merging, her violet, brown and gold turning his gray into a rich maroon glow.

Cesar had been right. There was no denying it now. Her wild, wonderful tumble with Alon had not broken the connection. It had fused it. She stared up in horror at her soul mate and saw her horror reflected back in his eyes.

Alon rolled to his back beside her. She roused enough to reach for his hand. When she clasped it, a wave of anguish punched her in the gut. She released him and the feeling ebbed.

That was his emotion. He despaired over their joining, as if it were the most tragic occurrence in the world.

Was it? A mistake, surely. She blinked up at the angry sky. The treetops swayed and the cold wind held the scent of rain.

Their connection had increased. She saw it. But Alon felt it and it grieved him. She turned her worried eyes upon him.

"Do you know what could result from this union? You could be pregnant. Is the alliance really worth your death?" he asked in a flat, defeated tone that prickled a warning on her skin.

Of all the worries, that one had never crossed her mind. She feared the connection might grow stronger. She feared her parents might find out. But she had not thought of an unplanned pregnancy. Samantha recalled all that he had told her about how Naginoka were born, and a shiver shook her.

"It's unlikely. And if it happens, I'm a healer. I'm a Halfling. Surely I can survive it."

"A gamble, then. The alliance against the chance you

might die. Is that how you framed it?" He lifted up on one elbow and scowled at her.

"I wasn't thinking straight. I just wanted."

"Yes. And you got it. Here in the woods where no one need know. Secret, private. Did I scratch that itch, Samantha, or only make it more insistent?"

She looked away.

He used both hands to sweep the hair from his face and then laced his fingers behind his head. The lust had cooled now and the regrets poured in, filling him up like a cistern.

Shame burned against the first icy drops of rain. "Do you know how it feels to know you slept with me only out of duty to your family and your alliance?"

Her hand slid away and she stared at him but not before he felt her self-reproach. Guilt, he felt the emotion flash from her to him. She'd sacrificed herself to the big bad wolf. There was some honor in that.

"I won't tell anyone, Samantha. The truth is I already decided to fight Nagi. Fighting is the only way for my siblings to have any chance of peace. So it was all for nothing. You didn't need to sleep with me. I should have told you instead of taking what you offered."

Her eyes were wide and glassy, as if the truth might bring her to tears. His pride stung too much to comfort her, and he knew if he touched her now they might just do that again. He wanted to. Wanted her.

"I didn't do it for the alliance. I mean, I want you to fight with us, but I did it because… Oh, Alon, I can see our auras. I can see them. And…and we're soul mates." She blew out a breath as if relieved to get the words out.

Was she crazy? He stared in silence, waiting for the punch line, for surely this must be some kind of joke. But she said nothing more. The droplets pattered on her dark head and washed the tears from her cheeks. To the north a heavy curtain of rain approached.

He drew her up and led her to the relative shelter of the trees as the sky opened and water poured down.

Alon stopped under the outstretched branches of a large cedar tree and turned to Samantha. She trembled and he resisted the urge to draw her into the heat of his embrace. Instead he faced her head-on.

"Was that a joke?"

"No. It's true."

"I'm not your soul mate, Samantha."

"But our auras…"

"Trust me. It's some kind of trick, like this face and form." He swept a hand over his body. "I can't be your soul mate, Samantha."

Her brow knit in confusion. "You can't?"

"No. It's not possible."

She pulled her cloak more tightly about her shoulders and hunched against the rain that trickled from the bough above them. "I was so certain."

"You should have asked me first. Sleeping with me was a terrible mistake."

The rain soaked him, plastering his hair to his head and making his skin slippery. He didn't feel the chill but noted Samantha shivering. Somehow he thought she wasn't cold either, at least not on the outside. She stared up at him with wide, earnest eyes, and he felt his resolve weaken.

"It didn't feel like a mistake."

"It was. It was my job to protect you. Your family gave you to the Thunderbirds, and they gave you to me. But I failed."

"You didn't. I'm alive because of you." She placed

a gentle hand on his shoulder. He read the concern in that touch.

He curled his fingers into fists as the weight of responsibility pressed down.

"With or without the other Halflings, the Ghost Children will battle, for we fight for our lives."

Her hand slid down his arm. "Will you come with me?"

"I said I would fight. I did not say we would join your alliance. Even if I did agree, they will not accept our help."

She stared up at him, fearing he was right. Hoping he was wrong.

Alon drew a long breath and then let it go. "Is this what you wish?"

She nodded.

"Then for you I will go."

She bowed her head and he felt her relief wash through him, sweet and clear. He sighed, knowing he had more to tell her.

"I do not expect to survive this war, and Nagi will certainly not let you or the other Seers live. The choice will be only how we die."

He had a choice. But by sleeping with Samantha he might have stolen hers. Naginoka grew quickly. Only three months after conception they emerged from their mothers.

He didn't know which was worse: knowing that she might die in battle or knowing that she might die bringing his children.

Alon did all the talking. He spoke to his siblings, he spoke to his parents and finally he spoke to her. There was a formality in his voice that deadened her heart, as if what had happened by that riverside had only driven them further apart.

"My father's jet is waiting to take us to Blake," he said. "After we see your brother, I will bring you to your father."

Samantha's throat went dry as she realized that her brother and Alon would soon meet. Believing with all her heart that the Ghost Children must be included in the alliance was one thing. Trying to convince her family was quite another. She knew what they thought about Nagi's offspring, for she had once felt the same. The prospect of their next meeting filled her with dread.

Alon narrowed his eyes at her. "Have you changed your mind, then?"

"No." Her reply was too quick, too angry and too defensive.

He snorted.

"Did you tell your parents what happened between us?" she asked.

That brought him up short.

"No. I saw no reason to worry them further." Alon rubbed his neck as if it hurt. "But my father seemed to sense something."

His aura, Samantha realized. The storm had rolled past and dusk had crept in. The conditions were perfect to see auras. Had his father recognized the changes there?

"My parents will bring the others south because that is where your father is amassing the Skinwalkers. They are waiting to say their goodbyes. Are you ready?"

She nodded and they made their way to the truck through the muddy field. She walked stiffly beside him, out of sync now with his stride and his thoughts.

The open field was filled with Ghostling twins, all silent and serious. Most were dressed and in human form. But not the young ones. They stared out at Alon and Samantha with yellow golf-ball eyes, popping their jaws in distress. When she next saw them it would be on the battlefield. A shiver lifted the hairs on her neck. What would become of them all?

Samantha glanced to his parents, who waited beside the truck, standing with their hands looped about each other's waist. Cesar and Bess seemed so comfortable together, so much in love. Above them, their auras blended and glowed.

Could they feel each other's emotions, as well?

Samantha recalled experiencing Alon's pleasure and how it increased her own.

"Safe journey, Night Sky Woman," said Bess, and she kissed Samantha on both cheeks.

Cesar gave her a hug. He took the opportunity to whisper to her. "Stay with him. You both need each other now more than ever."

She drew back, feeling slightly sick to her stomach. She belonged with her own kind. Didn't she?

Or did she belong with her soul mate?

She looked to the truck, where Alon waited silently, hands gripping the wheel. He'd never looked more forbidding or more unhappy. Was that what this connection would bring them, duty and obligation instead of love?

Cesar and Bess saw them out and waved them away as they left the camp area and headed toward the closest airfield, where Cesar had sent one of his jets to meet them and fly them to Atlanta, Georgia. Her brother had finished up in Scottsdale, Arizona, with the Southwestern Council and was now off to persuade the Southeastern Territory to join the alliance.

Alon did not speak to her during the drive, but his

aura continued to reach toward hers until the interior of the cab glowed with a soft maroon light. Samantha folded her arms across her chest and sighed. It didn't feel like a trick.

The silence rang like a bell and filled the interior like heavy smoke. At the airfield they boarded the Falcon 900 and strapped themselves in.

Private jets were necessary for Cesar as he could not fly like his wife and children. Living a century made such luxuries possible and, according to her father, Alon's dad was a genius at growing money. Both his parents had life expectancies of three to four hundred years, barring accidents. But Alon was the first of his kind. How long would he live?

Alon closed his eyes and dozed. His sleep was restless and full of the scent of the woman at his side. He knew what kind of a reception awaited them, and still he went because she wished it. Finally the dreams ceased and he slept deeply.

A female voice came from behind them. "Mr. Garza. Final descent."

Samantha shifted, lifting her head from his shoulder and releasing his arm. She rubbed the sleep from her eyes.

"I wonder what kind of a welcome my brother will give us?"

He knew. "I only know that without us they will lose."

"Do you think Aldara has reached him yet?"

He had told her that he had sent bodyguards to her mother and his sister to Blake. He could not gauge if she was pleased or worried. Perhaps both, he mused.

"She's with him."

Samantha sat back in her seat as the engines roared, but he could hear her say, "I wonder how that's going."

"As well as our visit will go."

Samantha's brow furrowed.

"Are you sure about this?" he asked.

"More than I have ever been about anything in this world. I know the alliance needs you. We just have to convince them."

Alon wondered what it would be like to have a woman as brave and idealistic as Samantha forever at his side. When he was with her, he almost forgot what he was. He would be wise to recall that it was common interest that bound them and not love.

He stilled, recognizing what had happened with a rising sense of dread. Samantha did not love him, but against all his better judgment and best instincts, he had somehow fallen in love with her. How pathetic.

Alon's head dropped back against the high headrest as his eyes closed. He pinched the bridge of his nose with his thumb and forefinger, trying to control the panic bubbling up inside him like poison.

"Something wrong?" she asked, resting a hand over his and then quickly drawing it back as if scalded. What emotion had she read—his panic?

Oh, yes. Something was very badly wrong. Because he was either going to tell her the truth and watch her laugh in his face, or he was going to hide his love for her so deep in his heart he would never have to face the inevitable rejection.

"Alon?" she asked. "Are you ill?"

"Halflings don't get ill. You know that." But he felt ill. His skin went clammy and his stomach seemed to be knotted around his pounding heart like a python after a capybara.

"But you've gone pale."

"I'm always pale," he said impatiently. "I was thinking of the battle. Anxious for the fighting to start." He swung his gaze to hers and then let it bounce away again, unable to hold on.

"That isn't it. Tell me."

He wouldn't. Not ever. There was nothing so pathetic or cliché as his love for her.

She wasn't giving up. He knew her well enough to know when she dug in her heels.

"All right, then. I'm worried that you might be with child."

Her hands instinctively went to her middle, and for reasons he could not even begin to fathom, she smiled.

"If you are, I'll stay until your time comes. If not, I will go as soon as we have defeated Nagi." As if they could. He used his thumb and index finger to rub his tired eyes.

"Go? Go where?" Confusion wrinkled her brow.

"I promised to protect you, Samantha, until this is done. That time draws near. With it comes the breaking of our ties."

"But I thought… That is…" She stopped, clamping her mouth closed.

"You should be happy to be rid of me. We both know you only needed a protector. I'm willing to be that. The world needs Seers more than it needs one more Toe Tagger. When this is over you can stop pretending this is something more than what it is."

She drew her hand back and her eyes went as cold as obsidian. "And what is it exactly?"

He stared her down, but she held on, tenacious as a bear after a beehive.

"This again! Alon, I did not sleep with you as a way to get you to join my dad."

"No?"

"If you believe that, then you have a thicker skull than I do. When can we get off this plane?" She unclasped her belt and threw the two pieces in opposite directions. Then she stood, casting him a withering glare, and strode toward the back of the cabin.

When they touched down, she still hadn't returned. Only when the outer hatch was opened did she appear to try to walk past him to the door.

He clasped her arm, bringing her about.

"You're such an ass, Alon."

"You'll tell me if you're carrying our children."

She pushed him off with one hand. He allowed it.

"What will that matter if we all die in battle?"

Her words cut his heart like a razor blade. He couldn't let her die. Somehow he had to keep Samantha alive.

He watched her walk away, trying to convince himself that this was best. This way, at least, he retained his dignity and his autonomy. This way he… Alon sighed. He'd rather face Nagi's army single-handed than her scorn. And that was what surely awaited him if he had told her he loved her.

Chapter 15

Samantha arrived in Atlanta tired and rumpled from the two long flights and her unresolved feelings for Alon. A phone call to her mother had revealed where to find Blake. He had just finished with the Southeastern Council and had succeeded in bringing them to the alliance. That left just the Northeastern Council, and her mother assured her that she had convinced them. Blake's visit there would be more formality than necessity. All the Council Chiefs wanted a look at their new War Chief.

Her mother did not mention having two Ghostling twins as bodyguards, so Samantha assumed that they had stayed out of sight as Alon had ordered. Samantha did not tell her mother about the ghost attacks but did say she was traveling with the eldest son of Bess and Cesar and was on her way to Blake to discuss battle plans.

Samantha felt strongly that the conversation she

needed to have with Blake must be in person. What she was proposing would be unpopular at best.

They entered the lobby of the upscale Atlanta hotel in the heart of downtown, turning heads as they made their way to the elevator. It was Alon, she knew. He was striking with movie-star good looks that made both men and women double-take. Dressed today in a slate-gray suit, crisp white shirt and dove-gray tie, he looked like a runway model for designer men's wear. Her excellent hearing brought their comments to her.

"Who is that?"

"Isn't he an actor?"

"Look at that guy."

She clicked across the marble lobby on low heels, her tight plum-colored suit dress making long strides impossible. One foolish human stepped toward Alon.

Samantha looped her arm possessively through his and threw the woman a threatening look. Alon allowed her to cling as she glared at her competition.

"Don't worry, Samantha," he murmured low in her ear. "I don't go for humans."

He placed a hand casually over the one she looped through his elbow. His cool fingers stroked her skin, and her heart fluttered.

His breath brushed her ear as he spoke again. "Though *you* are no more human than I."

"That's true."

Hope fluttered within her for just a moment and then died as he glanced toward the female, who hesitated as they passed by.

He exhaled through his nose. "If they saw me for what I am they'd be screaming and running the other way."

She squeezed his arm. "I haven't."

He turned his head and held her gaze, and she thought

for a moment she saw tenderness in his eyes. But then they hardened to ice once more. "You should," he said and fixed his gaze on the closed elevator doors.

The bell chimed, the doors swept open and they stepped into the empty car.

She felt a momentary relief at being alone, away from the humans and thus far undetected by ghosts. Then she remembered that Blake would be able to see her aura. What would he say when he saw what had happened?

She shuddered and gripped Alon tighter.

"Samantha?" His brows lifted and his expression spoke of concern.

"I'm all right. Just, well…our auras. Blake will see them." Samantha released him and stepped away from Alon. He tracked her retreat with a steady gaze and the lifting of one elegant brow.

"Blake isn't going to like what you have to say, and I doubt he'll be happy to meet me. He's War Chief. That must be his prime concern."

"Your sister is already with him."

Alon watched the numbers ascend with their car. "Her text said that he has stopped trying to send her away."

"He's seen her? I thought she was going to stay hidden."

"Bart and Bella agreed to stay hidden. Aldara is less submissive. She often does as she pleases."

And it pleased her to show herself to her brother. Samantha scowled.

The doors slid open and they headed toward the suite of rooms rented by the Southeastern Council for their new War Chief. Her stride felt awkward and stiff. Suddenly Samantha was unsure what she was doing here. Neither her dad nor brother had asked her to bring the

Ghost Children to the alliance. Would he even want their help?

Was she doing the right thing?

Alon drew to an easy stop before the door marked Presidential Suite and folded his hands before him, standing with the reassuring calm of an undertaker at a wake. He waited, and when she did not lift her hand to knock he glanced down at her. If he was worried about meeting her big brother, he did not show any outward sign. Meanwhile her upper lip was sweating.

"I'm nervous," she whispered.

"I know," he said in a hushed voice that Blake still could here if he were listening. "I smell your fear."

That was enough to put some starch in her spine. She lifted her chin. "I'm *not* afraid of my brother."

"Uncertainty, then. Either you think the Ghost Children should fight or you do not."

"It's not that simple."

Alon's complexion darkened as clouds of discontent blew over his expression. "It is."

Samantha's chin sank to her chest. "You don't understand. Every time I have tried to do something other than what my family wanted, it has ended badly. I'm not sure I can trust my judgment. Nagi found us because of me. We've had to leave places that were safe because of me." She slipped a hand into his. "I believe this is right. That the alliance needs the Ghost Children to win, but I don't want to have to defy them again."

"Doing what you think is right is never easy."

"But what if I'm wrong?"

"What if you're right?" He kissed her knuckles.

"We need you. We need all of us in order to win," she whispered.

"You don't have to convince me." Alon motioned his head toward the closed door.

Samantha exhaled in a short blast, retrieved her hand from Alon and knocked.

Inside came the sound of her brother's footsteps padded by the carpet. A moment later the door opened and Blake filled the opening. Dressed in a sky-blue shirt with the top three buttons unfastened, black dress slacks and bare feet, he looked exactly the same but very different from the last time she saw him. He stood straighter, looked at her directly and carried himself with a new confidence. His smile seemed easy instead of tight. He opened his arms and she stepped into the warm familiarity of his embrace, breathing in the scent of home.

Blake lifted her off her feet as he always did, swinging her back and forth before returning her to the carpet. The awkwardness began upon his release. He stepped back and glanced past her. His smile vanished as he turned his attention to Alon.

Samantha stood between the two men as they sized each other up.

"Blake Proud," Samantha said formally, "this is Alon Garza, son of Bess Suncatcher and Cesar Garza."

Alon extended his hand. Samantha held her breath and waited. Blake glanced down the exterior hall as if making certain that no one saw them and then took Alon's offered hand. She had never expected Blake to accept the gesture, let alone reciprocate. Samantha expelled her breath.

The two performed a stiff handshake that established that they each had crushing grips and a high tolerance for pain.

Blake motioned them in. "Mom said you had company."

He stepped aside and then shut and locked the door behind them. Clearly he did not want to be seen with them.

"You have met my sister?" asked Alon.

Blake flushed and Alon's eyes narrowed. Samantha swallowed her dread. Blake hadn't thrown Aldara out, had he?

"She's here."

Samantha's shoulders sagged in relief until she recalled the flush of her brother's cheeks and thought to wonder what exactly had happened between Blake and his attractive female bodyguard.

Alon's stormy expression showed the same thing had occurred to him.

"She's in here," Blake said and led the way.

Samantha trailed him down the hall, wishing she could run in the opposite direction. She was a good runner. But today she would stand and fight.

"We are alone, except for Aldara," said Blake.

Samantha stepped into the suite, which included a full kitchen, all creamy marble and stainless steel, and a conference table large enough for all the members of the Southeastern Council to conduct business in private. Beyond sat a sleek, stylish living area with a sofa and recliners clustered about a square coffee table. The artwork consisted of an enormous television hanging on the wall parallel to the sofa. To the right and left were doors that Samantha fervently hoped led to separate bedrooms.

Every single light in the place was blazing. Samantha's eyes narrowed. That was a trick to hide auras. She spun on Blake, about to ask him what he was concealing, when she realized she also had something to hide. Calling Blake out would reveal her, as well. That made her hesitate, suspicion blooming with the anxiety. What would Blake do if he saw her aura blending with Alon's?

Aldara appeared a moment later but not from smoke. Instead she emerged from the bedroom wearing a white terry cloth robe bearing the hotel's insignia. Samantha's skin prickled a warning of impending doom.

His sister was absolutely stunning. Fine blond hair slid like silk over her shoulders. She looked tiny in the bulky robe that ended at her knees to reveal shapely calves and pale bare feet. Her eyes were grayer than Alon's, but the siblings shared the same wide, sensual mouth and straight nose. Unlike Alon, Aldara had a heart-shaped face and pointed chin that gave her a dainty, feminine beauty. Deceptive, thought Samantha, and easy to underestimate.

Her choice of attire was either unfortunate or calculated. Samantha did not know her well enough to understand which, so she glanced to Alon to find he had tucked his chin as if preparing to attack.

Aldara flashed a look to Blake. Had he ever seen her fighting form, or was she still hiding it from him?

Alon greeted his sister with a kiss on both cheeks.

"Have you seen any ghosts?" he asked his twin.

"Four," she answered.

Blake ran a hand through his glossy brown hair. He and Aldara exchanged a look.

"In the Sonora Desert," Blake said. "Aldara had been trailing me as smoke. I saw her but didn't know what she was until the attack."

Aldara inched closer to Blake and then hesitated, coming to a stop midway between her brother and Alon.

"I was going to send them for judgment when she changed form and blasted them." Blake turned to Alon. "That's some badass power, extinguishing souls."

Samantha wondered again at the responsibility of destroying the immortal essence and did not succeed in suppressing a shiver. Blake's acknowledgement of that power, however, might serve to help her argument.

"You did well," said Alon. If he felt any remorse, he did not show it. "We need the Seers. Without them we must kill all possessed humans."

Aldara moved to stand beside Blake, who gave her a tender smile.

"There have been no others since Scottsdale," she said.

Blake offered a recliner to Samantha then motioned Aldara to the couch. She settled beneath the bright side lamp. Alon took the chair opposite Samantha, beyond the coffee table, flanking his sister. His aura was slightly visible, a gray haze hanging about his head. Blake sat on the couch under the matching lamp, one seat cushion away from Aldara.

The silence grew uncomfortable as each sat stiffly, leaning slightly forward as if anxious to be somewhere else.

Blake spoke first, his voice seeming to boom into the void. "I want to thank you for protecting my sister, Alon, and for bringing her safely to her people."

Her people? They never had people except each other. Was he talking about the Niyanoka? Those whom she had never met or even seen during her entire childhood?

Alon nodded his acknowledgment to this and glanced to Samantha, deferring to her. It was her brother after all.

She cleared her throat and her first word still came out as a squeak. "Blake, the Thunderbirds brought me to Alon."

Her brother's eyes narrowed and flicked to Alon.

Sensing a fight brewing, she hurried on. "He brought me to his family. All of his siblings have been raised to respect the Balance and human life. After meeting them

it is my opinion that we need them. And you know yourself that they can defend against ghosts."

"I don't approve of killing souls. Even evil ones deserve judgment and to serve their time in the Circle,"
said Blake. "Some might one day be forgiven and reach
the Spirit World."

"They've avoided the call of the Ghost Road. Refused the natural order. They deserve no mercy," countered Alon.

"They can also force them to the Ghost Road," said
Samantha. Blake made no reply to this so she drew another breath and dived back in. "They are smart, protective, dedicated to preserving the Balance, and they
are excellent fighters."

Blake cast her an incredulous look. "Yes," he hissed.
"I remember. I learned this on the day they nearly killed
us all."

That made her squirm. Of course he remembered
the attack by Nagi's Ghost Children as well as she did.

"Yet you allow Aldara to protect you."

"I wouldn't call it that. She did not seek my permission, nor will she follow my direction. She is ever under
her own authority."

"I follow my brother's command. Not yours," said
Aldara.

When it suited her, thought Samantha, recalling Alon
complaining that Aldara tended to do as she pleased.
Samantha considered his sister. Why did it please her
to stay with Blake?

Blake did not notice Samantha's distraction as he continued. "She gave me no say. She wouldn't leave when
I ordered her to. She might be the first person I've ever
met who is more stubborn than you."

Samantha met the challenge in his gaze. "Alon sent her to protect you."

"It was a dangerous thing to do. If she had been seen…" His words fell off and he laced his fingers together as he rested both elbows on his thighs. He worried one thumb with the other for a moment and then glanced back at his sister. "She's got to go."

Aldara glared at Blake, her eyes now shining a brilliant mint-green. Samantha became more suspicious of just what was between them.

Blake would not look at her. "It took some doing, but I've succeeded with the Southeastern Council, Samantha. Mom is waiting for us in New York." He glared at Aldara. "Just us."

She felt a squeezing of dread in her gut. "Us?"

His dark eyes flicked back to his sister. "Yes. The Southeastern Council wanted reassurances that *all* the Seers will join their forces. They are afraid of the Skinwalkers having you or worse." He glanced at Alon. "It makes no sense to exile you among…" His eyes shifted between Alon and Aldara. It took a moment for him to reformulate his thoughts. "I spoke with both Mom and Dad and convinced them to let you join the Niyanoka."

"Let me?" Samantha snorted. "Well, thanks very much. And we will just deny that we are also Skinwalkers?"

"Samantha, you said you wanted to make a difference. You said you wanted to use your gifts. I'm offering you a chance to do both."

That had been what she had wanted. But not anymore.

Blake sensed her hesitance and continued on. "There are plenty of Grizzly Skinwalkers, but only three Seers."

She shook her head. This was going all wrong. She needed to steer the conversation back on course. She glanced at Alon, who kept his eyes on hers but lifted his chin toward Blake. The message was clear. *Tell him.*

She faced her brother. "But we fight better as Skinwalkers."

Blake pushed off his thighs, straightening in his seat. "Are you going to defy them again?"

And there it was. Her refusal to do as she was told. Her insistence on bucking authority. And woven through Blake's incredulous question like red yarn was the underlying condemnation he had served up on every occasion. Why was she always causing trouble?

Was that the real reason that she wanted the Ghost Children to fight with them? Just because she knew her family would object? The possibility made her hesitate, second-guess. What if she was wrong again?

Blake's tone turned gruff. "What the hell are you up to now?"

"I'm trying to help."

"By *not* joining the alliance?" Before she could answer, Blake fired another question at her like a barbed arrow. "Or do you plan to fight with the Skinwalkers?"

Alon lifted one finger and Blake turned.

"Maybe you should let her finish."

Samantha glanced from one to the other. Blake's flush made it clear that he objected to Alon's interference. Alon's locked jaw relayed that he didn't give a damn. In another minute they'd be at each other. A glance in Aldara's direction showed her body tensing as she eased forward, preparing to act. Which side would she take?

It was all going just as Alon had predicted, and she had not even made her proposal yet. Samantha spoke in a rush now. "Blake, listen. Nagi has recruited at least twenty Ghost Children fighters already. The Spirit Children can't stop them. You can't and I can't. I know. I've seen them fight, and I'm not sure the Skinwalkers can, either."

Blake rose slowly to his feet. A moment later they all stood.

"We'll take out the ghosts and possessed humans," he said. "And Father's forces will stop the rest," said Blake, full of the bravado of a Halfling who had never seen his enemy in action.

"What if he can't?"

Blake glared.

"What if the Skinwalkers fall? Who will stop Nagi's forces then? The Clairvoyants? The Peacemakers? Nagi's Ghost Children will shred them like tissue paper."

Blake scrubbed his palm over his mouth and jaw, his expression dark. "What exactly are you proposing, Sammy?"

"We have thirty-four Naginoka who are loyal to the Balance, all raised by Bess Suncatcher and Cesar Garza. Alon is their Alpha leader, their War Chief, and he has agreed to lead them against Nagi. He's come to join the alliance."

"Join the… Are you out of your mind? They tried to kill us."

"They did not. Those were Nagi's fighters."

"You heard Dad. Bring the Niyanoka by *any* means necessary. That's what he said." He pointed at Alon. "If I'm even seen with that, it's over."

"What about her?" asked Samantha, thumbing over her shoulder at Aldara, who growled in reply, her eyes more yellow than green. Samantha knew what came next. Did Blake?

"She stays out of sight."

Samantha felt her fury peak. "How convenient for you both."

Blake ignored her jibe. "It's also for her protection. If the Niyanoka see her, they might try to kill her."

"They wouldn't succeed," said Samantha.

"You'd be wiser to worry about the lives of any foolish enough to try," added Alon, his voice no more than a mutter, but Blake heard the remark.

"Skinwalkers have succeeded in killing your kind," said Blake, speaking as if the vigilante death packs were some source of pride instead of an abomination.

Alon stepped forward to accept that gauntlet, and Samantha found herself between them once more. But Aldara chose this moment to speak.

"They succeeded because they hunt babies." Her speech was already slurring, and her mouth was now full of elongating sharp white teeth.

Blake stared at her. She held his gaze as Blake blew out a breath.

"I'm sorry," he said to Aldara.

She nodded her acceptance of this but stood tense, and her breathing came in angry blasts. Had her brother just apologized to a Ghost Child? Samantha's concern deepened.

Blake turned to Alon. "I can't return those souls who have already flown."

"You could ban such hunts," said Alon.

"My dad is in charge of the Skinwalkers."

Samantha felt sick with guilt at being a Skinwalker. Did her dad really condone those hunts? Before she met Alon, she had thought much the same way as Blake. If given the chance, would she have killed a Halfling child?

"In any case, I cannot bring the Ghost Children into

this alliance," said Blake. "The Niyanoka will never accept them."

"Then I will go to dad and offer our services to him."

Blake shook his head. "Don't. He won't accept them. The Ghostlings are his enemy. But even if we *did* accept, how could we tell one from the other? No, Sammy. It's impossible."

"Your chances would be better if all the Halflings fought together. The Spirit Children are poor fighters," said Samantha.

"Not true. They can turn minds, change thoughts, bring confusion to the enemy, foster errors. We can cast ghosts from human bodies and heal the injured. We need the Niyanoka to win."

She waved an arm at Aldara and Alon. "You need them, too."

He lowered his voice to a growl. "What I need is to bring the Niyanoka to the alliance. That's what Father asked for, and that's what I'll do."

"But he doesn't know they're willing to fight with us."

"He wants this alliance. Why is this so difficult for you to understand?"

"As War Chief you act in the best interest of the Spirit Children. This is not their best interest," said Samantha.

"If I do what you ask, they'll replace me and lose. It's impossible."

"But, Blake—"

He lifted a hand to stop her. "You've brought me a proposal. I've listened. I've rejected it."

For the first time, Samantha saw that she must walk a different path from her brother. She loved him. But he was wrong.

"Please tell your Councils that I decline their offer to join the Niyanoka," she said. "I fight with the Ghost Children."

"What? Wait. You can't! Sammy, you'll ruin everything again."

Again. The word hit her low and hard, but she recovered, drawing her shoulders back and raising her chin. Her body trembled as she stepped forward to kiss him goodbye. Blake must have seen it then, because he clamped his mouth shut and stood stiff, his muscles rigid, his jaw clenched as she kissed his cheek and then drew back.

"We will see you on the battlefield, brother."

Blake opened his mouth and then closed it again as he shook his head. "Why can't you, just once, do as you are told?"

"And why do you always let them make your decisions for you?"

His mouth dropped open at that.

Samantha moved to stand beside Alon. Aldara glanced from Blake to her brother, her brow knit in anxiety.

"Aldara? Are you coming?" asked Alon.

She shook her head. "He needs me."

"He has just said that he does not want our help."

"I know."

"Then why would you stay with him?"

Aldara lowered her gaze. "The world needs Seers."

But there was more. Samantha sensed it.

"You won't stay?" asked Blake to his sister.

"Only if the Ghost Children are permitted to join the alliance."

"I will bring your offer to father and I will ask the Northeastern Council. But I already know their answer."

Samantha nodded. "We await your word."

Chapter 16

Blake and Samantha already stood in the hall. Blake was no doubt certain the coast was clear.

Alon lingered to say farewell to Aldara.

"You're not just staying to protect him. I can see it in your eyes."

His sister's desolate expression tore at him. "He needs my protection."

"As Alpha leader, I could order you to come."

Her lip trembled. "Don't."

"Come with us," he whispered. Then his voice took on a chiding tone. "Do you think anything will change afterward?"

"I don't know."

"As a Niyanoka, he can't claim you, not without facing banishment like our father."

She stared at the carpet. "I know."

"Is that what you want? To force him to choose between you and his people? He's their War Chief, Aldara. He has a duty to his people."

Tears leaked from both eyes. "I know his duty and I know mine."

Alon nodded and kissed her goodbye.

The roar of the twin engines made the fuselage vibrate, filling the cabin with a constant rumble as they made their approach at the small private airport outside Butte, Montana. Alon and Samantha were on their way west to find his parents and the rest of his family. Back to join an alliance that did not want them.

Word had come from Blake before they even departed. Neither the Niyanoka nor the Ianoka would accept them in the alliance. If the Ghost Children fought, they would not recognize them as allies. And the Skinwalkers went one step further. Alon's forces would be treated no different than the enemy.

He wished Aldara had come with them, but she was as adamant about protecting Blake as he was about protecting Samantha so he did not force the issue.

Alon felt a piece of himself wither. It was a fantasy of Aldara's that once they learned to control their hunger and their shape, they might live among the human race, like wolves in sheep's clothing. Alon argued that they needed to live apart from humans for the safety of all.

She must know that the Niyanoka would instantly recognize her even if she took human form. She might hide among the Skinwalkers but never the Spirit Children. But she loved Blake Proud. He saw it in her eyes. She loved him and it was breaking her heart.

She chose to remain with a man who kept her hidden like a dirty secret. When this was over Blake would leave her behind.

Alon could hardly believe that he and Aldara were twins, they were of such different minds. Aldara wanted to save the world and every lonely orphan Ghostling in it, while Alon wanted to fight. Fight himself, fight his kind, fight his father. Yes, him especially.

He knew he'd leave Samantha, because that was what she wanted. She'd told him once that she wished to return to her family and be able to use her gifts. If she stayed with him, she'd be a banished Seer and an unwelcome healer.

He couldn't do that to her.

The wheels touched down and the fuselage bounced then settled into the fast deceleration that forced them forward from the seatbacks.

Cesar and Bess had moved the family a great distance in only a few days, all the way to Wyoming. The Skinwalkers assembled in Cody, Montana, and so Alon made that their destination. Both the Skinwalkers and the Spirit Children had always believed there would be another war. But neither had anticipated it would be against a common enemy. His siblings. Not the ones he knew but the ones they did not find in time. Brothers against brothers. Sisters against sisters. One more cruel blow in a cruel existence. Samantha had been the one bright spot in his life. Soon he must send her away.

The plane stopped and he heard the stairs placed against the exterior. A moment later fresh air and sunlight streamed in through the open door.

Alon followed Samantha down the narrow metal stairs toward a shiny black limo. His father was more than just a Soul Whisperer. He was also a Truth Seeker and a Memory Walker. As a Memory Walker, his father could remove painful memories, like all recollections of some traumatic event. The trouble was, once he did his work, all the reminiscences, good and bad, were forever lost.

So the question was, did Alon want to forget Samantha completely after she moved on or hold tight to the most precious memories of his life and live with the grief?

His father left the limo to greet Samantha. He kissed her cheeks and then his smile faded. He could have noticed Samantha's upset but likely he read it all in a touch.

"He knows you have feelings for him?" he asked.

Samantha seemed momentarily surprised by the question.

"Yes. But he doesn't believe it." She scooted past him and into the rear seat.

Alon stilled as he watched it happen. His father's hand trailed from Samantha's arm as his expression changed. He looked stunned. An instant later, he glanced at Alon. What truth had he read in that touch? Alon was burning to ask. Instead he opened his arms to his father, knowing his dad would soon know all his thoughts, as well.

"Samantha told you?" asked Alon.

"I read it in her thoughts. Our offer was rejected by both the Niyanoka and the Skinwalkers. Can't say I'm surprised."

Cesar opened his arms and Alon stepped into his father's embrace. Cesar clasped Alon to him. His father's hand pressed to the bare skin of Alon's neck. He needed this contact to receive answers. Alon knew it was not necessary for him to speak or for his father to ask a question. Could his father read the grief and longing or only Alon's thoughts?

"Both," said his father as he released Alon.

"Mom's with the others?"

"Mom's already joined the Skinwalkers in Cody. Flew

out yesterday. She'll speak to Sebastian. Try to convince him we are not his enemy."

Without a jet, Alon knew. Bess preferred her feathers to fuselages.

"We'll meet them soon." He turned to Samantha. "I'm proud that you have taken our side. I'm sorry they didn't accept our offer. People are often afraid of what they don't understand."

Samantha seemed momentarily surprised, but she nodded. It was hard to get used to how much his father could perceive in such a brief touch.

"I've sent all those under thirteen away with Cody and Callie. Don't worry. Those two will be here for the fight."

These were the third set of twins his father and mother had found. A good choice to protect the babies and young ones, Alon thought, since Bart and Bella were still with Michaela Proud, the first Seer.

"All the rest of our family is ready to fight."

"How many?" asked Alon.

"Including the ones who have been arriving each day, forty-nine."

Alon wondered how many Nagi had coerced into service.

"They've been coming in pairs and small groups, all fleeing the ghosts who have been stalking them. Even the wild ones seem to recognize that their place is with us."

"These new arrivals might attack the Skinwalkers or Spirit Children," Alon cautioned. "It's dangerous to include the feral ones."

"These are dangerous times." Cesar motioned to the open door. "Before leaving Bess spoke to a Puma Skinwalker. She said Nagi's Ghost army is amassing in the

Bighorn National Forest, west of Rapid City. Clearly he knows where to find us. She told Sebastian to move from Cody to intercept them there."

Alon stilled and stared at his father. Had Sebastian chosen his ground based on the mumbo jumbo of a lion?

His father must have seen his disbelief because he grinned. "Lions are never wrong, son. Not like Clairvoyants because they don't see possible futures. They only see what is happening at the present in a different location. Apparently she had her teeth on one of the Ghost Children who joined Nagi, but he got away. Now she can see him and he is with our enemy."

Alon climbed into the limo across from Samantha, who now stared intently out the window. They needed to speak about what had happened between them.

He wanted to reassure her that he would not try to trap her into a relationship that would cause her pain. He knew the soul mate connection troubled her. He could assure her if he only told her the truth—how could he be a soul mate when he had no soul?

If she knew, would it change her conviction to fight at his side? If they survived she would surely leave him after the battle was done.

The war with Nagi loomed, but somehow losing Samantha alarmed him more than losing his own life.

In the two weeks that followed, Alon organized the Ghost Children into a fighting force. The only thing he seemed to put more energy into was avoiding Samantha. She knew that by not telling him immediately of their connection she had hurt him badly. Her silence told him all he needed to know about her feelings—or lack of feelings—for him.

What he didn't understand was that her silence came

from fear. Fear of what she would lose if she chose him,
fear of admitting aloud what she already knew in her
heart. She didn't need the aura to tell her that Alon affected her like no one else or that she could feel what he
felt when they touched. But was that love?

Her parents could read each other's thoughts when
touching. But since Alon would not touch her, she did
not know if their lovemaking forged this new connection
or if that came only with the commitment of the heart.

Were her feelings strong enough for her to choose
banishment for him? And could she really love a man
who so hated himself?

Once upon a time she had known what she wanted: to
be free of Nagi and become a true Seer like her grand-
father, Michael Proud. She had longed to use her gifts
to help others. Now she faced a hard choice: Alon or her
dreams. For if she chose him, the Niyanoka would surely
banish her. Marrying a Ghost Child would be far more
grievous a breach than marrying a Skinwalker.

That was why she had remained silent. Not because
Alon was less than her or not worthy of her, but because
loving him would be costly.

Now she had another secret. She'd used a pregnancy
test and, though less than a month along, she knew that
she carried his twins. It was likely two, as twins ran in
both families.

This pregnancy would be Alon's greatest fear come
true. He had told her more than once that he would never
have offspring, as he called them. So this news would
be unwelcome.

As the battle approached, her anxiety grew. Tell him
or don't tell him? Explain or don't explain? Choose him
or leave him? One thing she knew was that when the
battle ended, so would his promise to protect her.

If any of them survived, Alon would return her to her family and he would go his separate way. And that frightened her most of all.

Samantha stayed with Bess and Cesar, who camped in the national forest outside Yellowstone National Park in Wyoming, in RVs and trailers and tents filled to bursting with their adopted children. More Ghostlings arrived every day, seeking out Alon and joining his ranks.

Reports from the Ghost Children scouts were that Nagi's army had twice their numbers and possessed hundreds of humans ready to act as shields.

Tomorrow they would join the others, interlopers fighting for a cause they believed in, in a place they were not welcome. Tomorrow they might all die. Alon knew it, just as she did. So tonight Alon would not avoid her. Tonight, at least, she might once again lie in his arms.

Blake finished his meeting between the Skinwalker leaders and his people. The battle plan was set. It was a historic day. But Blake's footsteps were slow and his heart heavy. He had tried to include the Ghost Children and his proposal had been soundly defeated.

Now he had to tell Aldara. True to her word, she had stayed with him, protected him and remained hidden from all but him. But now, as the battle loomed, he could feel the bond between them breaking.

Gradually Aldara had become his confidante, his adviser, his lover. He thought of his mother throwing away all ties to her people to have his father. But his mother had been raised by humans. She did not know her people. She was not War Chief. To claim Aldara was to leave the Niyanoka without a leader in the most important battle of their existence. To claim her was to destroy the alliance.

He glanced up and saw the mist that hovered at his

side. Blake veered from his course and away from the circle of tents, both the traditional conical tepees and their nylon counterparts. They had commandeered a camping area, with the help of the Peacemakers, who suggested to the humans that, for various reasons, they needed to move on sooner than expected.

When he was away from the lights, away from the responsibility, she came, transforming naked before him. He smiled and opened his arms, but she stepped back. He felt a punch in his gut. Was she leaving him?

"Is it done, then?" she asked.

He nodded.

"You brought the alliance. You should be proud."

Instead he felt ashamed. "I'm sorry I could not convince them to accept your people."

She lifted her face and he saw that her lovely blue-gray eyes were swimming in silver tears. They spilled down her face. "I would fight beside you, Blake, if you would permit it. I would protect you as I have done since we met."

"If they see you, they will kill you. You cannot fight beside me."

Her gaze lowered again to the grass brushing her hips, her cheeks flushed with the shame he caused her.

"Then I will join my brother. Tomorrow will be a terrible day for my people, for we will die on both sides of this war."

"Aldara, I don't want you to fight."

Her voice was fierce now. "That is not your choice."

"Afterward, will you come back to me?"

Her eyes shimmered like the ocean as she stared for a long, silent moment. "Come back to a man who is ashamed of me? No. I will not. Better to leave now and retain my pride."

He felt desperate to keep her and desperate to keep the alliance. "But we are soul mates."

She shook her head.

"Afterward we could move away from the others. No one would have to know and we'd be free."

"Free? Hiding away from your people as your mother has done? Hiding our powers. I have been hidden my entire life, for fear the humans might see me. Now I have my third form and still you ask me to hide. But I am done with hiding. Tomorrow I will stand in the sunlight in my first form and I will fight the sire to protect the Living World. I will do all this so all can see that *I* am not ashamed of what I am."

Bright green light flashed and Blake lifted his arm across his eyes. When he lowered it Aldara stood before him in her first form. Silvery hair covered her muscular body that now stood eight feet tall. Spines raised up on her head and her pointed teeth glistened. She stared out at him with yellow eyes, daring him to look away.

She garbled her words as if they were hard for her to form, but he understood her. "This is what I am."

With that Aldara vanished into a fast-moving cloud of mist.

Blake ran to the place where she had last stood. Her scent remained. He breathed deep, trying to hold this tiny scrap of her essence. If he could have flown after her, he surely would have.

Samantha glided across the meadow shrouded by the descending mist. Wet grass swept her calves as she paused at the entrance of the conical tent fashioned like the tepees once used by their ancestors. The flap was open, an indication that Alon welcomed visitors. Had he hoped that she would come?

"Alon?" she breathed his name like a sigh.

He was at her side in an instant. The breeze lifted the tails of his open white shirt, and his snug jeans were unfastened at the waist.

"You came," he said. He took her by the shoulders and lowered his forehead to hers, resting like that for a moment as if too weary to hold himself without her there.

At the touch she read his longing and his sorrow. Did he already anticipate the casualties that would come with the dawn?

Nagi was delayed by his human army, who walked slowly overland. They would be here tomorrow. Alon would not give them time to rest.

He guided her through the raised opening in the canvas tepee, past the symbols of green lightning someone had painted on the surface. He paused only to lower the ring of sticks that supported the flap, indicating that visitors were no longer welcome. They were alone and no one would disturb them.

A single kerosene lantern hung from a peg, the wick turned low so to cast a golden light. Woven rugs, pillows, blankets and soft furs circled the interior.

They stood with hands clasped in the center.

She read his need, he read her longing. Samantha pressed her body to his.

"I feared you would send me to my dad," she said.

"You are safer with us."

Samantha lifted one hand to his cheek and he pressed against her palm.

"It's dangerous for us to be together again."

"More dangerous than facing Nagi tomorrow?" she asked.

He shook his head.

"Then let us have tonight."

She placed one hand on each of her opposite shoulders and lowered her head to concentrate. The energy pulsed and her cloak transformed to a single golden rope that circled her neck. The medicine wheel glinted between her breasts. He lifted the symbol of her Seer power and kissed the center of the cross.

He gathered her gently in his arms. This meeting had none of the frantic fury or rush of their first joining. Instead he lingered, stroking her bare shoulders, caressing her neck as she used her fingernails to lightly rake his back. The groan that issued from his throat made her tingle in anticipation. He rubbed his muscular chest against the soft cushion of her breasts, and she closed her eyes at the sharp darts of delight. Need beat within her, building with each pulse of her heart.

His sweet breath fanned her cheek as he dipped his head, capturing her earlobe between his teeth and sucking the soft, sensitive nub of flesh until her head dropped back and she shivered in pleasure.

His tongue traced the shell of her ear and then darted inside. She pressed herself flat against him, savoring each hard edge as she rubbed her hips against the rigid evidence of his desire. His sharp teeth scored the arched column of her throat, and she moaned in longing. His hands slid down her back until he cupped her bottom, using his strong arms to bring her even tighter against him, and still it wasn't close enough.

Samantha lifted her hands, raked her fingers through the fine silk of his hair and tugged. Alon lifted his lips from her throat and stared into her eyes. His mouth glistened and his eyes glittered, the color changing from blue to green. The flush of his skin and the panting breaths aroused her until she quivered with anticipation. He was hers at last, and they had the entire night. After that, who could tell?

One night, a thousand. She knew it would never be enough.

His hands slid down the backs of her thighs until he had control of her. Then he lifted, spreading her legs to make room for him between them. For a moment she was high above him and his rough cheek was scoring the sensitive flesh of one breast, and then next he was lowering her inch by thrilling inch onto his erection. She stared at his wild green, unnatural, exciting eyes and knew that no moment would ever be so perfect.

He slid inside her gently, her body stretching to take inch after inch. She wanted to throw her head back and cry out in pleasure. She wanted to fall upon him in a hot, needy rush. But she kept her eyes locked on his as he drew her down until her bottom pressed tight to his hips.

Only then did she arch, using her legs to clamp onto him and pull him even deeper. He sucked in a breath and dropped to his knees. The jolt drove him still deeper and the fall brought her upright, clinging to his shoulders.

He chuckled and nestled his face between her breasts as he took her to her back. He withdrew and then paused, arms stiff, hands flanking her head, the veins of his arms and at his neck blue and pulsing beneath his pale skin. He wanted to move. She knew it.

Samantha opened her legs to him.

"Come on, then."

He drove forward but stopped there to kiss her hard and fast, his tongue darting into her mouth, thrusting against hers and leaving her gasping for breath. She lifted her hips and bucked, but he pressed her down with his weight and took one dark nipple in his mouth, sucking and licking until she tossed her head from side to side and made a kind of mewling sound deep in her throat.

Her orgasm built like a slow fire until it roared through her, burning her to ash. Alon drew back and closed his eyes as the waves of sensation pulsed down every nerve, and she knew he felt it, too.

She expected him to take her hard and fast, but he withdrew and dropped between her legs, holding her twin cheeks in each hand. He kissed and licked.

"So sweet," he murmured. "I love to taste you."

Her limbs were weak and trembling. She could not resist this new sensual assault, but she was so tired. Alon used his clever tongue. He flicked and circled the sensitive nub at her cleft until she was lifting her hips and bucking against his mouth. She was so close, so…

Samantha screamed his name as her pleasure broke. She arched and moaned as the waves spun out from her core.

She fell back, panting and quivering, her muscles spent. Her mind reeling. And then she felt him sliding into her again.

Now he would take his pleasure and she would feel it. He'd be fast, he'd be rough, just like she wanted.

Only he wasn't. He was slow, his hips undulating in a leisurely assault.

"Faster," she ordered.

His deliberate slide and draw remained unchanged.

She glanced up at him to find a devilish smile on his face, and she knew he would not be hurried.

Samantha groaned her frustration. She wanted… wanted. Oh, the tingling delight that came with each lovely, lingering glide. Her body rolled and surged in counterstroke to each measured thrust. Her body quickened again and she gasped with surprise and delight.

"Yes," he whispered. "Come for me again."

She moved faster and this time he relented, matching her frantic pace. She felt his release as a powerful, bursting wave of pleasure. An instant later the rippling contractions coursed through her.

They fell together onto the soft furs in a tangle of damp limbs. For several moments she drifted in the glow of her receding pleasure, breathing heavily, content and replete.

"Oh, Alon. That was perfect," she whispered, her eyes drifting closed.

"Yes. Perfect."

She felt his emotions again. Not just the sensations he experienced, but something new. She recognized his longing to keep her safe and the fear that he could not. His dread cut through him, bright and sharp as a knife blade. She stroked his shoulder and arm, offering silent reassurance. Gradually his restless mind calmed and he drifted to sleep.

Slumber then stole over her, and when she roused it was to the feel of Alon's erection, smooth and hard against her hip. She rolled on top of him, kissed his chest and stroked his pale skin as the dance began again. They would not waste a moment of this night, not when it might be their last.

Afterward, in their sanctuary, Alon held her close against his side. She nestled there in calm contentment, one leg thrown across his muscular thighs. She pressed her cheek upon his strong chest and felt the calm assurance of his steady heartbeat. Outside the world rested, still and dark.

From somewhere beyond the curtain of their shelter, the first lark began to sing.

Alon tensed.

Chapter 17

Samantha stood beside Alon in the gray gloom that preceded the dawn. Behind them the Ghost Children awaited Alon's order to attack.

She glanced at Alon, tall and imposing in his most lethal shape. He looked every inch the leader of his people. His fierce expression and the tension radiating from him sent a shiver down her spine. She was glad she would not face him in battle.

To the right in the wooded area by the river lay the army of Ghost Children who had been coerced into the service of Nagi.

Nagi was immortal. He could not be defeated, yet somehow, they must do just that.

To the east the sky brightened. It would not be long now. Across the open field the army of Skinwalkers assembled beside their new allies. To the left, before the hastily dug earthwork barriers, Blake and his Spirit Children waited. Nagi had the low ground. But he did not seem to care—perhaps because of his superior numbers. Samantha knew she, Blake and her mother could defeat the possessed humans by dispossessing the ghosts. It would be up to the others to keep the Seers alive so they could do their job.

How many of those below hidden in the woods would join their cause if given the chance? How many fought only because their backs were to the wall?

Waiting was torture. The worst that could happen unfolded like scenes in her mind. She did not believe that her brother would order his people to attack Alon. But she was not certain about her dad. He hated the Naginoka and was eager to kill as many as possible.

She felt responsible for them all, because it was she who convinced Alon, and Alon who convinced the others to fight.

The burden of responsibility pressed down on her. If Alon felt uncertain, he did not show it. She mirrored his calm, knowing it was a thin facade.

Behind them the sun broke, gilding the leaves of the cottonwood as it crested the hill behind the Spirit Children. Still the Ghost Children lay in shadow as they had lived their whole life. Today they stepped into the light and into history.

A flash of white light ignited beside Samantha as Bess flashed into her raven form and burst into the sky. She called her farewell, a cry that perfectly relayed the sorrow of the day. Samantha rested both hands high on her chest and drew a deep breath, feeling the energy surge through her body as she changed to her animal form, rising to nine feet. She looked at Alon, now anxious for the signal to fight.

It would have been wiser for their enemy to wait for

the Skinwalkers and Spirit Children to advance, forcing them to leave the hillside, rather than trying to take the high ground. But instead, Nagi's forces spilled from the wooded grove, charging uphill toward Blake and Sebastian's position. She could see both now, a huge bear standing before her brother, who was still in his human form. Blake stepped out from her dad's shadow to stand in the light, but did not change to his bear form. Instead he held his medicine wheel loosely at his side, ready to perform his work as a Seer expelling ghosts to the Way of Souls.

There beside them, low to the ground, Samantha saw Nicholas Chien, a wolf shifter and the leader of a pack of Skinwalker wolves. Beside that a pride of mountain lions waited the signal to attack.

His wife, Jessie, had done her work through the night with the other Dream Walkers, visiting the sleeping Ghost Children of Nagi's army, planting the seeds of descent against Nagi. Hawks, eagles, owls and even swans burst into the air, their beating wings carrying them skyward.

The Spirit Children stood upon the hill. Though their powers were impressive, Samantha considered them of little use in combat. The time for words had passed. Truth Seekers, Peacemakers and Clairvoyants would be needed afterward, if any survived. Still they stood with guns and swords like a ragtag postapocalyptic army of misfits, ready to do whatever they could. Samantha remembered her dad's words. If Alon fought, he would be treated no differently from the enemy. Would her father really follow through with that threat?

Her stomach twisted as anxiety roiled like acid.

Samantha looked at Alon, knowing that Nagi's forces

would rip the Spirit Children apart like wolves through a litter of newborn kittens if they gained the hilltop.

The Naginoka howled as they ran, their speed a wonder and a terror to behold. All about them, Alon's Ghost Children grew restless. What was Alon waiting for?

"They won't be able to tell us from them," he muttered. "To them, we all look the same."

She glanced back at the faces of the Ghost Children. Some looked eager but the expressions of many held apprehension. They did not look the same to her.

The wolves and lions surged down the hill, followed by a herd of buffalo. Samantha knew Tuff Jackson was leading them. Dust rose into the air in clouds behind the herd.

"Advance and intercept," he called to his followers.

Samantha charged with Alon guarding his flank.

The vanguard of the Skinwalkers raced down the hill, meeting Nagi's army head-on. Wolves circled the outskirts, looking to hamstring an opponent or rip into an exposed neck, but the Ghost Children's quills protected from such an attack. The buffalo plowed through the center, swinging their massive heads like wrecking balls, knocking their foes to the ground and trampling them with sharp hooves.

Samantha saw her dad rear up on hind legs, fourteen feet of muscle and power. He roared and met his foes, using his long, curved claws to slash deep as he took his opponents to the ground. Ghostlings fell before him.

Blake led the Niyanoka on the hill, directing the firing at the Ghostlings, who charged directly into the bullets. None reached the hill.

She bellowed and charged, unwilling to watch as the horde attacked her mother, father and brother. She was glad for the chance to stand between them and Nagi.

All about her the Ghost Children locked in individual battles. Blood sprayed across the grass and she charged on.

The blue smoke from the gunpowder hung in the air, casting the hilltop in a haze. Here in the field dust burned her eyes and stole her view of the field.

The buffalo ran through the middle of Nagi's forces like bulldozers, skewering those not quick enough to evade their horns. And the wolves were there, taking advantage of the panicked flight.

She heard the growl of the pumas, now just to her left. Samantha reared up to deflect the attack aimed at Alon. The lion veered away, choosing another target with supple grace.

In her momentary distraction, one of the enemies leaped and she braced, but Alon met the strike meant for her with one slashing blow of his claws. Her enemy fell, gouged across the face and neck. Blood sprayed from the great artery at his throat, but Samantha had no time to linger as she and Alon each met a new attacker.

Two drove into her at once, taking her to her back. Samantha lifted her rear feet, trying to disembowel the Ghostling on top of her before he could sink his claws into her chest.

Blake ordered the riflemen to shoot over the combatants at the reinforcements surging from the woods. Just the Ghostlings. The possessed humans were for him and for his mother. But the bullets did not stop them. They just kept coming.

From his vantage point on the hilltop he could see his father fighting paw to claw with Nagi's forces. His heart nearly stopped as his father fell, but a huge buffalo knocked away his attacker.

"Tuff Jackson," he murmured, sure he was right. "I'd bet my life on it."

Above them, hawks, eagles and ravens soared in circles, some darting away to return and report what they observed.

He could barely see now through the gun smoke and dust. The acrid scent of gunpowder burned his nostrils.

Beside him, a raven landed.

"Alon's fighting to your left. Tell your men not to fire at Ghost Children there unless they advance to the hill. Alon knows to stay below that mark unless you are overrun."

"How do you know Alon?" he asked the raven.

"I'm his mother. And I changed your diapers, Blake Proud, so do as I say."

"Bess?" he asked. But she had already taken to the air again. Alon had brought an army, despite Blake's instructions not to do so. Without Alon, Blake knew the Spirit Children's position would already be overrun. Now he had to keep his forces from killing the wrong Halflings.

"Cease fire!" he said.

The guns fell silent.

"To the left! Fire if they break through the Skinwalkers. Sharpshooters! Aim only for the ones actually engaging the Skinwalkers. And only if you have a clear shot."

This was more dangerous, for his sharpshooters might accidentally kill the Skinwalkers.

"He's sending humans now," called someone from the line. "To the west."

Blake swung his binoculars right and saw the humans, dressed in rags, hair a tangled nest of sticks and debris, as if they had walked for days and slept on the ground. Even through the smoke, he could see the tell-tale yellow eyes of possession.

"Mother!" he called.

Michaela was there beside him in an instant. Though his senior by more than two decades, she looked as if she might be his younger sister, for like all Niyanoka, she aged very slowly. If they survived the day, they might both enjoy another two hundred years.

"They're possessed," he said, pointing toward the mob now halfway across the field.

Neither the Ghostlings nor the Skinwalkers engaged them, letting them walk right by, like toddlers wandering on a battlefield. But these toddlers carried clubs and guns.

"There's so many," he said, as he and his mother rushed to the end of the earthen wall.

"Call the Memory Walkers and Peacemakers. They will need to revise the memories of the humans after we remove the ghosts."

"I'm not sending them down there until the fighting is done."

His mother nodded, her lips pressed into a grim line. "Very well."

She handed over one of the two medicine wheels that helped channel their Seer gifts. She had had hers since before his birth and had used it successfully the last time she faced Nagi's ghosts. That day there had been no Ghostling army, for the third Halfling race had not yet come into being.

His wheel was also made of cottonwood, bent into a circle. Two strips of wood bisected the center and crossed each other at right angles. Her wheel held one eagle feather at the center with her medicine bundle tied beneath. His bundle was likewise tied in the center, but he had also wrapped one feather on the bisection of each of the four directions using red trade cloth.

Together they ran toward the puppet army of humans.

"Wait until they are on the hill. Then we'll work together. Remember, just keep breathing and focus on the middle of their bodies, right above the navel."

His mother raised the medicine wheel to the sky. Blake lifted his as well and together they began to chant their prayers. His mother's high voice rang clear above the chaos, while his boomed in a deep bass. In unison the people halted, clamping their hands to their ears as if the Calling Prayer was some heinous wail. The entire mob dropped to their knees, still clutching their heads, and together collapsed on the ground.

All the humans lay in the same direction, heads pointed north, motionless, except for their breathing. Blake gave a shout of triumph. They had removed the ghost invaders. All of them and without harming a single human.

He hugged his mother and she patted his back.

"You did well," she said.

His elation died when he looked across the battlefield to see Nagi, billowing black and menacing at the tree line. He seemed to be looking directly at them.

Blake acted on instinct, dragging his mother to the ground as the killing blast ripped into the earthen embankment and shot above them into the sky.

"He's seen us," said Blake.

His mother lifted her head to peer across the battlefield. "He's coming."

Nagi billowed in delight. He had found two of the three Seers. Had the stupid Niyanoka actually brought them to the battlefield? The Seers were all that prevented him from enslaving the entire human race, so he would kill them first.

Where was the third? Nagi's gaze swept the hilltop, looking for the telltale aura of violet that was unique to those three Halflings.

His search kept him from noticing when the tide of the battle shifted until the nearest of his forces charged past him. Had he not made it clear that any retreating would die?

He zapped the first half-dozen deserters with one blast. They stood seized in the grip of his killing force. He let the energy course through them as they began to smoke, their flesh cooking from the inside out. When they burst into flames, those retreating behind them reversed direction to make another stand as the souls of those he had killed slipped quietly away.

"Very smart," he muttered. His children were fast, strong and deadly. But they lacked intellect. "Must get that from their mothers."

His gaze swept from the hilltop to the mayhem in the valley. The Skinwalkers again, he realized, shocked to see that they were defeating his children. His offspring were stronger. So was it cowardice?

And then he understood what was actually happening. Some of his own children were fighting *with* the Skinwalkers. Impossible. Yet there they were, shoulder to shoulder with bear and buffalo, engaging the dwindling numbers of his vanguard.

"Traitors!" he bellowed.

Nagi searched the field for the leader of these traitors and found the huge Ghost Child fighting beside a Skinwalker grizzly. That one, he decided. Then, he did a double-take, blinking away the film of smoke and grime in his eyes. This world was very dirty, he thought.

His second look confirmed the impossible, a violet aura glowing all about the bear that stood beside the biggest of his offspring.

The third Seer!

"Get her!" he screamed. "Kill that bear!"

The horde turned toward the Skinwalker grizzly. He did not need to win this battle. He only needed to kill the Seers to ensure victory.

Soon he recognized two things: his numbers were inadequate because of the traitors, and he would not reach any of the Seers. Nagi billowed with fury, unwilling to accept what he saw.

He had hoped to avoid this step. But really, how could he? The Seers were all within his sight. All he need do was remove their souls and, poof, problem solved. And while he was at it, why not take the souls of the traitors and of the rest of the fighters, alive and dying? Simple, clean, foolproof.

Such a blast would mean that his loyal children would also perish, but who had time to sort them out?

Nagi summoned all his powers to tear the living souls from their living bodies. He had never reaped so large a harvest, and he was not strictly allowed to take souls from the living, but once done, he'd control the Living World. Then he'd make his own rules.

Alon's fighters turned the battle. He sensed the malicious ghosts still hovering over the battlefield. The Seers had expelled them, but they waited for their hosts to recover to repossess them. His kind and the Seers still needed to send them to face their judgment.

But that must wait until after the last of Nagi's forces fell. Alon gave them opportunity to run, keeping his forces from pursuit, but it did not matter. Nagi forced them back into the fighting. They would die at the hands of their siblings or die at the hands of their father. The entire battle made Alon sick.

It would not be long now. The wolves and bears chased the last of the Ghostlings.

Beside him, Samantha, bloody and weary, engaged a female of his kind as two of his own leaped in unison at him.

His claws ripped into the torso of one, finding the soft cartilage between the ribs. His attacker crumbled. Alon turned, lifting his spines, and heard the scream as the second's soft underbelly contacted with Alon's hundreds of knifelike quills.

Alon found Samantha had defeated another challenger and now bled from a wound on her shoulder that was terrifyingly close to her jugular. Alon felt fear lance him once more. Samantha's injuries and the danger she faced overshadowed his own peril. He would give his life to save hers, even to get her to run. But she wouldn't. He was admiring and furious in equal measures.

"What's that?" asked Owen, one of his compatriots, a Beta twin just six years younger than himself.

Owen's twin, Ophelia, turned with him to look in the direction Owen indicated. Samantha reared up to look.

Before them, the Skinwalkers were falling, rolling backward, crumpling to the ground and cascading facedown.

Samantha bellowed and fell sideways. Alon caught her as she toppled, feeling the blast of invisible energy that passed through him an instant later. It took his wind, leaving him unable to draw breath for a moment. Samantha, unconscious, shifted into her human form, her upper body draped in the great bearskin cape.

Owen recovered first. "They're all changing back."

Alon scanned the field. The Skinwalkers dropped in human form. The wolf pack toppled, naked in their hunting formation, still as death, and the pride of lions crumpled in the grass, their lion skins spread out about them like tawny wings. Even the great herd of buffalo now lay naked, their pale limbs poking out in every direction from beneath the curly-haired buffalo robes. The Owl, Raven, Eagle and Hawk Skinwalkers began changing and falling from the sky.

"Catch them!" Alon cried.

His men rushed to snatch them from the sky. Alon spotted a woman falling. His mother. He changed to his ghost form and flew as fast as he ever had along the ground, reaching her in time to change back and catch her in his arms. He lay her beside the fallen buffalo shifters and ran back to Samantha, leaping over the prone bodies.

"The Spirit Children!" shouted Ophelia.

Alon retrieved Samantha, clasping her to his chest and holding her.

"They're dropping, too," cried Owen.

Alon patted Samantha's pale cheek. "Wake up, Sam. Please, wake up."

Instead he watched her soul seep from her body, like mist rising from a meadow.

"No!" he howled. Alon was on his feet in an instant. He knew now what had happened. Nagi had done this. He had broken every law in both worlds and harvested the souls of the living.

Nagi had gone too far. And he would pay for this outrage. But how to defeat one who is invulnerable? Now, there was the crux of it all.

"Look," said Ophelia. "Their souls are all escaping."

Before them a mist of souls slipped from the bodies of the fallen.

"Why aren't we dead?" asked Owen, patting his chest to assure himself that he was still corporeal.

"It doesn't work on us," growled Alon.

"Why not?" asked Owen.

"Don't know. Don't care. I'm going to kill him and then I'm going to retrieve their souls."

The twins spoke at once.

"All of them?" squeaked Ophelia.

"He's immortal," reminded Owen.

"He's already tried to kill us and failed. Maybe we don't die, either."

"We die," said Owen. "I witnessed our enemies kill Gail and Gregory. And I saw Nagi murder the deserters among his ranks. We die, Alon."

"How do we kill him?" asked Ophelia, ready to join Alon.

Alon was already flying across the distance that separated them. He summoned all his remaining energy, determined to take his father's soul—if he had one.

In the valley, Nagi's troops turned to watch him. The silence of the battlefield added to Alon's fury. Nagi would win. He knew it. Still he raced over the uneven ground, straight at the billowing rain cloud that was his sire.

So this was the great Nagi, Ruler of the Realm of Ghosts, stealer of innocent souls. This was the creature that had forced his essence on innocent humans and created him. This monster.

Alon struck at his sire with all the self-loathing in his heart. The energy that shot from Alon's fingers was strong enough to steal a mortal's soul. The power collided with Nagi's vaporous body.

He writhed and then turned his yellow eyes on Alon. "You dare attack me?"

In answer, Alon hit him again.

This time Alon saw a small wisp, a trace of Nagi's essence, leave his body and evaporate into the air. The mark, the tiny nick that was no bigger than the bite of a field mouse, quickly disappeared in the rolling smoke that was his father's earthly body. The similarity between Nagi's shape and Alon's flying form sickened Alon. He hit him again.

"Stop that!" said Nagi.

Had Alon actually caused this Spirit some discomfort? Had he caused harm? Alon felt a surging of hope. He hit him again.

Nagi flinched and then recovered.

"Does it hurt you, Father?"

"No more than a bee sting to a bear. You cannot harm me. Stop or I shall end you."

He didn't. Alon struck again. As his energy wave struck Nagi, one more hit landed from a different direction. He turned to see Aldara shocking Nagi from his right. Then more stings hit and more. His army had followed and all of the Ghost Children struck with their soul-harvesting force, the gift inherited from their sire, using his power against him.

"Stop!" Nagi bellowed. But he writhed now, billowing and contracting as the stings hit him, sending tiny traces of smoke hissing from him.

He was right. A single bee cannot stop a bear. But a nest of hornets will send any creature fleeing. Alon struck again. Beside him, Aldara attacked.

"You killed Blake! I hate you!"

"Kill them," cried Nagi to his dwindling troops.

But they did not move to stop Alon's army. Instead several rose cloudlike into the air and joined the attack.

"Traitors!" Nagi turned to retreat.

Alon pursued. The others followed.

"Run, Father! Run back to the Realm of Ghosts and know that if you come again your children will be waiting to send you home. This is the harvest you reap."

Nagi turned to face them once more. "You fools. We could have ruled them all. You are their masters. Instead you act as their slaves."

Alon hit him again. "This world is for the living."

Nagi writhed. "Who will harvest the evil ghosts without me?"

Alon spoke. "We will. We need you no longer."

The others roared their assent.

"Enough!" Nagi bellowed. "I go! But none of you will ever cross the Ghost Road. When you leave this world you come to me."

Alon knew it was true, and it only enraged him more. He struck again but Nagi was already gone.

"Hurry," cried Aldara. "Before their souls leave the Living World."

The Ghost Children raced back the way they had come. Upon reaching the battlefield they stopped in unison. Their spiny quills drooped in dismay at the multitude of drifting souls.

Below the souls the Skinwalkers lay strewn across the grass. Upon the hill the Spirit Children had crumpled. Nothing stirred but the souls of the dead, glowing brightly, hovering near their mortal forms, confused by the sudden severance between the body and spirit.

"There are so many," whispered Owen.

Alon felt a desperation creeping in to drown him. How could they return them all?

Chapter 18

Alon turned to his sister. "Aldara, take Nagi's forces to the Niyanoka. Return the souls to the Seers first, then the Dream Walkers, because they can heal the injured. Then see to the rest. Hurry."

Aldara pointed across the field. "Mom and Dad first. Promise."

"Samantha, then Mom and Dad."

"Yes. Hurry." Aldara shouted. "Nagi's forces to me. We will take the Spirit Children." She turned to smoke and shot off to the hilltop with Nagi's followers hurdling along behind her. An instant later they transformed to their human appearance on the hilltop, fanning out over the fallen.

"Owen, Ophelia. Take the older ones to the Buffalo Skinwalkers. Callie, to Mom near the largest buffalo. Cody, find Dad and then you have the bears. Restore the healers first, understand? Then work on the others."

"Nick and Norma, you two work on the ravens. If they are not injured, tell them to fly to the Spirit Road and turn the souls back so we can restore them. Daniel, Darya, you have the buffalo. Quick now."

Alon divided the others into quadrants. Then he returned to Samantha's body. Still in his fighting form, he lay her gently down upon the grass. Her naked shoulder showed ragged tears in her flesh, and blood matted her dark hair. Where was her soul?

He glanced about, finding her hovering above the head of her body, staring down at him. Samantha's soul sparkled as bright as a welder's torch and with the same brilliant white glow. This was a holy soul, one who walked the Red Road. She would find instant welcome into the Spirit World, while he was doomed to the Circle of Ghosts. They could not be soul mates, for they would never spend eternity together.

Alon seized her soul in his fist and plunged it deep into her injured body, sorry for the pain she endured but unwilling to let her find the peace and joy she had already earned.

Selfish, he knew, for if he really loved her, he would let her go.

He pressed his ear to her chest and listened. An instant later her heart began to beat, strong and steady.

Aldara knelt beside him in her fighting form, her claws digging into her fur as she pressed them to her knees and rocked.

He peered up at her, his vision blurry from the tears. "I sent you to the Niyanoka. The Seers, Michaela and Blake?"

"Done," she answered. "And Mom and Dad. Callie and Cody found them."

Alon stroked Samantha's hair with his big, hairy paw, praying for her return, but her eyes remained closed.

He turned to Aldara to ask her why Samantha would not wake and caught her removing her ghostly hands from Samantha's body.

"What are you doing?"

"Helping her."

He drew Samantha into his arms, holding her to his chest with a desperation that choked him. "Did I do something wrong?"

"No. Look. She's waking."

He glanced down to find Samantha's eyes fluttering.

"She's bleeding again," said his sister. "Get her to Blake. I've restored him and he's already organizing the healers."

Alon bounded up the hill to the headquarters of the Spirit Children, desperate to find Samantha's brother and see her restored. When he arrived, Blake was on his feet. Having suffered no injuries, he recovered quickly from the separation, as Aldara had said. Several Niya-noka were coming around, retrieving weapons, pointing them at him. Alon turned so they would not hit Saman-tha. He had to get her to Blake before she bled to death.

"Hold fire!" shouted Blake. "Hold!"

The Spirit Children did as their War Chief ordered, lowering their weapons but still clutching them in prepa-ration for new orders. All about them Ghost Children, in both fighting form and in the buff, were striding from corpse to corpse and thrusting ghostly hands into each. Fallen Spirit Children convulsed and roused, waking from the dead.

"Where shall I put her?" asked Alon.

"Is she…"

"No. Restored. She's hurt." He flipped back her cloak

to reveal the gashes on her shoulder and upper arm. The one on her neck was obvious.

Blake led him to a healing circle, set up, he suspected, prior to the conflict in preparation for the inevitable injuries. Alon laid her on a buffalo robe and stepped back.

"What happened to us?" asked Blake.

"Nagi tore the souls from your bodies. He tried the same on us but we are immune to his powers."

Blake adsorbed this.

"Because they have no souls," said a tall handsome man behind Blake.

"Quiet, Mr. Healy." He faced Alon again.

Healy? Could that be Jessica Healy Chien's father, the one who disowned his only child for marrying a Skinwalker? Alon wondered what fate awaited Samantha for fighting with the Toe Taggers.

"Nagi?" asked Blake.

"The Ghost Children defeated him."

"How?"

"Later. Your sister first." Alon turned to go. Blake's hand rested on his shoulder.

"Aldara?" he whispered.

"Working on the others. Many are injured."

"My father is still on the field."

"I'll find him."

"Your parents, Nicholas and Bess?"

"Restored."

Blake's shoulders sagged, but whether from news of Bess's recovery or that Aldara was safe, he was not certain.

Blake turned to stare down the hill to the valley. The fallen lay strewn before him like rag dolls. He covered his mouth in horror.

Jessie Healy Chien charged up to Alon and clutched

his arm. "Save him, quickly, before I lose him forever. My daughters! Quick!"

Beyond her, Alon saw the fallen wolves unattended. Alon turned to follow her.

"No," said Healy, clasping his daughter's shoulders. He swept an arm, indicating the fallen Niyanoka. "The Spirit Children first." He directed his next comment to Blake. "Order him to see to us before the Skinwalkers."

Had the man really just commanded that his son-in-law and grandchildren be left to die? Had he just given the War Chief of the Niyanoka an order?

Alon met Blake's troubled gaze. Blake could not really direct him to do anything, but Alon waited to see what he would do.

"Go," said Blake.

"Blake," cried Healy. "Our people first!"

Alon billowed down the hillside to find the wolves, lying neglected between the buffalo and the bear. Just as he had ordered, his troops restored the healers first.

Sebastian was already on his feet and healing the wounded alongside a gathering of buffalo. Alon materialized in fighting form. Sebastian called to him.

"You are Alon?"

He turned to face Sebastian, wishing he was in his human form for this first meeting, dressed in a sports coat instead of bloody, matted hair and bristling quills. Alon used both hands to try to smooth the fur at his temples. It was the best he could do.

"Yes."

"Where is my daughter?"

"With Blake. He is seeing to her injuries."

"My wife?"

"Is well." He wished his words were not garbled by his teeth. "I gave orders that the Seers be restored first to keep the souls from crossing to the Spirit World. Your son works on the injured Niyanoka above."

He nodded, then he glanced at the wolves, before returning his attention to Alon. "Tell your forces to carry the wounded here to us."

"Yes, sir."

Alon turned to go, distracted by the many souls trying to cling to the bodies they had once inhabited.

"Son?"

Alon hesitated, blinking in surprise as the greatest of the bears, the War Chief of the Skinwalkers and the father of the woman he loved, extended his hand.

Alon reached, saw his own clawlike appendage and flushed with shame, but he clasped Sebastian's forearm.

"You fought well."

Alon broke away with a murmured thanks. He had expected many things from the War Chief of the Skinwalkers, frontal attack being foremost. But he had not expected thanks.

Alon worked his way along the wolves, restoring souls first to the wounded and then the fallen. He restored the daughters of Jessie Healy Chien, but he could not find Nicholas Chien. One looked like another and he did not know which one was Jessie's husband.

Finally he reached the fallen body of a large gray timber wolf. Unlike the others, this one's soul did not stray from his body and in fact seemed to cling to it, as if trying to anchor itself to the carcass. Alon nodded at the shimmering essence that still held some resemblance of the handsome form of the body it had inhabited for over a century.

His thoughts came to Alon. *Jessie. Jessie. Katherine. Lauren.*

This was why he did not stray. He had ones here who

held him. His love for his wife and daughters was stronger than the call of the Spirit Road. Alon envied him that unwavering love.

"She's all right. So are your girls." Alon reached out and captured Nicholas's soul and plunged it back into his body. Nicholas convulsed, waking instantly. Another outward display of both his conviction and his strength. In a blink he was standing, his thick wolf pelt slung over one shoulder. He spotted his daughters, who charged to him, their wolf pelt cloaks flapping about their slim legs. They embraced and Nicholas closed his eyes an instant. Then he fixed them on Alon.

"Jessie," he said.

Alon pointed. "With Blake."

Nicholas charged away, already dressed in jeans, T-shirt and running shoes.

Alon envied the Skinwalkers their cloak. He'd very much like to take his human form instead of letting everyone see his most terrifying visage. But he did not want to appear naked before them all.

Cody loped toward Alon. "I can't find Dad."

"Aldara said you got him."

"No, just Mom. I've searched but I can't find him." The panic in his brother's words surged through Alon as he turned his head, frantically trying to recall his father's last position. *No. No. Not his dad.*

A raven circled him, then hovered. He recognized her instantly.

"Mom!" called Alon. "Where's Dad?"

Unlike other Skinwalkers, ravens could speak while in animal form, though her voice was high and raw. "I found him. Hurry!"

Alon turned to Cody. "Save the wolves."

Cody nodded and set to work as Alon ran across the

field, following their mother back to the position earlier held by their forces.

His mother hovered, flapping madly. "Here!"

Alon dropped to his knees beside his father's body. Bess transformed to her human form in a flash of light and then dropped down to hold her husband's head in her lap. His father's soul tried and failed to touch his wife, but Bess could not see or feel him.

"Is his soul still here? Hurry! Hurry!" said Bess. Her head swiveled madly, as she searched for what she could not see. "Is he still here? Has he crossed again?"

Again? thought Alon. When had his father crossed the Ghost Road, and how had he managed to come back?

"I can fly after him. I can stop him."

"He's here, Mom. Right beside you."

His mother sagged, covering her face with her hands as she wept.

Alon grasped their father's soul and gently returned it to his mortal body.

Cesar gasped and rose, like a man at the end of his endurance emerging from cold water. It frightened Alon, for he knew they were running out of time to save the others.

His mother threw herself against Cesar, wrapping him in her arms as she wept. His father hugged his wife as she babbled.

"You knew it from the start. You were right. They saved us all. Saved the Living World. We've won, Cesar. Our children defeated Nagi."

Cesar lifted his head to meet Alon's gaze.

"I'm so proud of you, son. I knew. I knew all along."

Alon felt his throat closing. How had he known? Why did his father have faith in him when every other member of Cesar's people found the Ghost Children disturbing and dangerous?

Alon rocked back on his heels, but before he could rise, his mother grabbed him in a fierce embrace. "Thank you for saving him. Thank you, son."

His father gently drew Bess back from Alon and smiled. "He has more to save, Mother. Let him go now."

His mother wiped her eyes. "I have to go, too. I have to fly to the Spirit World and turn back those who have not crossed."

His father helped his wife to her feet and waved goodbye as she shifted and flew straight up into the blue sky to join the other ravens.

Cesar placed a hand on Alon's shoulder. It was a trick of his father, to touch his neck while he asked a question. His father knew that Alon did not often say what was in his heart. But that never stopped his dad from knowing.

"Is Samantha all right?"

"Yes."

"How did you do it?"

Alon did not bother to answer, for his father need only ask to know. His dad's eyes widened.

"He can't kill you?"

Alon shrugged. "He can. But he can't tear out our souls."

"Why?"

"I do not know."

"And you can harm him?"

"A little."

Cesar looked across the field at the Ghostlings working furiously to retrieve lost souls. "His forces turned on him, as well. All of them?"

"All that lived," said Alon.

Cesar patted his son's shoulder. "You've done well.

But there is more to do. I've got to go help Blake. And you have more souls to capture. I'll bet they are dancing over the field like butterflies."

"Fireflies," Alon corrected.

"Don't forget the humans."

"He did not take their souls. They lie there," Alon pointed, "to the southwest."

Alon knew that his father could easily make the human victims of Nagi's ghosts forget the horrors they had endured. Would his banishment and the stigma associated with Soul Whisperers keep the Spirit Children from accepting his help?

He hoped not, for it would be their great loss.

Alon worked throughout the long afternoon with the others of his race. Some of the injured had died before Nagi's attack, and those souls could not be found. If they had crossed to the Spirit World, not even the ravens could turn them back.

Those who were seriously injured were taken to the buffalo and bears for healing, and the humans were separated to an area where the Memory Walkers and Peacemakers worked to reformulate plausible explanations in the human's memories. The Ghost Children finished with the souls turned back by the ravens and then gathered in the valley to count their dead. Tomorrow they would bury the fallen. As expected, the Ghost Children had suffered the greatest fatalities, though the Skinwalkers had lost many brave fighters. Only the Niyanoka were untouched by death this day.

Shortly before sunset, the first of the ravens returned. Alon tried not to feel hurt when they landed across the field to the north in the Skinwalkers' camp. All but one, which flew to them. His mother, he felt certain, seeking her husband.

Where was Samantha? Back with her father? With Blake and her mother? Alon had saved her. That should be enough. He did not expect her thanks. He only wanted her safe and happy. He knew that for her to have those things, he must leave her.

He had promised to protect her from Nagi. Nagi was gone. And Alon now understood his purpose. He was not destined to find lost or confused souls and help them cross to the Spirit World. That was the Seer's job. He was not created to defend the humans. That was the role of the Spirit Children. And the Skinwalkers protected the Balance. His purpose, the purpose of all Ghost Children, was to protect the living world from Nagi and his evil ghosts, and when he died, he would face that special circle his father had promised to reserve for his traitorous children. Well, if that was the price for saving this world, then he would pay it.

Until that day, he would hunt evil ghosts and force them to face the judgment they deserved, and he would seek others like him, for they must know how to defeat their father should he ever come again.

It might be true that Alon had no soul, but it did not mean that he did not love this world.

"Alon?"

He glanced up to find his sister, now in her human form and dressed in a black skirt and an elegant, flowing black top. This was their mother's signature color, so he did not have to ask where she had found clothing. She'd likely just returned to their parents' trailer.

"The others are all gathered. They say there is a Skinwalker wolf looking for you."

"Nicholas Chien?"

She nodded. "He is coming."

Did he carry some message from Samantha? Alon

tried not to let his heart leap with hope as he hurried along with Aldara.

"Are you going back to her?" asked Aldara.

Alon shook his head. "Are you going back to Blake?"

"He's ashamed of me." She glanced away, twisting her index finger absently. "I offered my love. He doesn't want it."

Alon glanced at her drawn face and then away again. His sister's pain only amplified his own.

"They are not for us. We are not like them," he said.

"But they are our soul mates."

His face felt tight as he held on through the gut punch of pain. He did not know how he managed the words, for they took more courage than the battle.

"They can't be. You heard Nagi. We'll never cross."

"You still believe that? But we *must* have souls." Her voice rang with pain and desperation.

"Then why could Nagi not harvest them?"

"But I saw some of our kind die today. We *do* die."

"Were any of the fallen restored?"

Her eyes went wide.

He hated what he had to say to her. "Did you see their souls?"

Aldara fell silent then gave a shake of her head. "But the smoke and the dust. Perhaps..." Her words fell away and they stared at one another. Aldara's pretty blue eyes filled with tears. "If we have no souls, then when we die, there will be nothing."

"Better that than the Circle."

"More reason to savor this Living World. More reason to seek some joy."

"Not if it keeps her from finding her true mate."

"But she fought beside you, right out in the open for everyone to see. She left her people to side with ours."

"She fought with us because she rightly believed that without our help the Skinwalkers and the Spirit Children would fail. She did not fight for us. She fought for the Balance."

"Are you sure?"

"Certain."

Samantha's body burned and her joints ached. Someone was carrying her. Then she was lying still on soft bedding, a blanket covering her. A kiss pressed to her forehead, his scent earthy and familiar.

Her eyelids were so heavy she could not open them. She let herself sink back into darkness, escaping the pain.

The chanting woke her. She knew the chant. Her father had taught her this one for the healing of wounds and fractures. She blinked her eyes open. Her head was turned to the side, so she saw the bloody gash on her shoulder closing. The battle came back to her in a rush. She sat up and found herself in the circle and Blake performing the healing ceremony.

She scrambled to her feet and touched her cloak, finding that the energy to change the skin into jeans and a blouse was so taxing she swayed and toppled.

Blake caught her elbow. "I told you to stay with our forces. God, Sammy, you almost bled to death."

Bled to death? She clutched her belly. The babies. Were they all right? She didn't know, but the fear chilled the marrow of her bone.

"Sammy? Lie down before you fall down. You look terrible!"

She'd know, wouldn't she, if she'd lost them? She crumpled back to the ground, dropping to her knees, one hand across her abdomen.

"Alon?" she asked.

"He dropped you here and went back to help the others. Retrieving souls." Blake gave a shiver of revulsion.

She rubbed her forehead, feeling dazed, as if she'd been roused from a deep sleep. "What happened?"

"Nagi almost won. Would have won if not for the Ghost Children. You were right, Sammy."

He told her all that had happened, assured her that their parents were safe. But many had died in the battle.

"Alon turned all of Nagi's forces to our side, and he and the others have worked all day to restore the lost souls, ours included. He even organized the order for restoration, commanding that the healers be saved first. Sammy, without him, we'd all be dead."

Samantha tried to take it in. She had known they couldn't beat Nagi without the Ghost Children. But she had no idea how important they would be after the battle.

Souls. She pressed a hand to her clammy forehead. Had he retrieved all the souls or just hers? Had he saved their babies or had their tiny spirits slipped away with the night mist?

Samantha heaved. Blake rested a hand on her shoulder. "I'd better get Mom."

"Where is Alon?"

"In the Ghostling camp."

She had to find him.

"Samantha, we need your help. The injured."

All she wanted was to see Alon, to be certain that this was not what she thought, that he had only brought her to her family to be healed. But her heart clenched with rising dread. Had he abandoned her?

"Dad sent Nicholas with an invitation to a treaty meeting. He has suggested that the three Halfling races sign an accord."

"The Spirit Children will never sign it," said Samantha.

"They might. They aren't feeling so superior today. The Ghost Children frightened them before. Now they are terrified that they will rip out their souls."

"I have to see him." She pushed off the ground, rising to her feet, but swayed and fell back down, her head spinning.

"Sammy?"

"Dizzy." She closed her eyes and still felt as if the ground were swaying.

"Because I can't restore the blood loss. I can only fix what you still have. The buffalo are caring for the most grievously injured. Rest a bit. When you feel up to it, join us on the battlefield." He released her hand and easily scooped her up, carrying her to a blanket beside rows of other Niyanoka. She closed her eyes against the dizziness and fear.

"Here's Mom," said Blake.

Samantha opened her eyes to see her mother striding toward her, looking exhausted, but her smile warmed Samantha to the core.

Her mother hugged Samantha and then pulled back to sit beside her in the flattened grass. Michaela Proud pushed an errant strand of hair from her child's face.

"I watched you and your father from the hilltop. You two are likely to frighten me to death."

"Are you okay?"

"Yes." Her mother narrowed her eyes on Samantha, giving her an assessing look. "Are you?"

Samantha nodded and looked away.

Should she tell her mother about the pregnancy? Somehow she knew that if she spoke her fears aloud, they would gobble her up. She pressed down the panic. But what if their souls were out there on the battlefield?

She had to go look. Maybe it was not too late. Maybe…

"There is much to do. The Naginoka have ceased retrieving souls. They say too much time has passed. The healers are working to save the injured, and your brother and I are seeing to the humans."

Samantha sank back to the blankets. *Too late. If they were out there they had already crossed.* Samantha began to cry.

Her mother nestled her against her breast. "Oh, child. I know you are weak, but there are those who need us. Some of Nagi's ghosts have taken possession of the wounded humans. We have to dispossess them."

Samantha had waited all her life to be able to use her gifts. Now here was the chance, and she was too weak and heartsick to sit up. "I'm coming."

She managed to sit up and swayed only slightly.

Her mother offered some water. Then she helped Samantha to her feet. Samantha, Blake and their mother headed for the battlefield.

"The buffalo are helping us but Sebastian called a halt. It is no longer safe, even for them. We have to accept that not all can be saved."

"Are any of the Ghost Children still finding souls?" She clung to unreasonable hope, holding it like a soap bubble.

"No. Trying to save them will only kill the buffalo. We must help them cross over."

Samantha walked unassisted to the battlefield and worked beside her mother, expelling evil ghosts with the help of her medicine wheel, which focused her dwindling energy.

"Like pulling dandelions," said her mother. "Some of them are stubborn."

Her mother's smile faded when she looked carefully at her daughter.

"We'll manage the rest," she said.

Samantha shook her head, too weary to argue.

"Go to bed, Samantha, before you fall over," her mother ordered, using the no-nonsense tone Samantha remembered well from childhood.

"I'm too old for you to order me to my room, Mother."

They continued on past sunset, the Ghost Children, the Seers and the owls. The Ghost Children were clearly better at expelling evil ghosts, but too impatient to deal with the confused souls whose bodies were beyond retrieval and who needed assistance to find the Spirit Road. Expelling Nagi's evil ghosts from human hosts did not draw any of their energy. In fact it seemed to give them strength.

The minutes and lives ticked away.

The Skinwalkers, now in human form, shepherded the frightened, confused humans up the hill to the Memory Walkers and Peacemakers, who would help them return to their lives without any recollection of this terrible day.

Samantha kept looking for Alon. When she found Aldara hurrying toward her, she rushed to meet her halfway.

"Is Alon all right?" asked Samantha.

"He is."

Samantha felt a dizzying rush of relief, and some of the tension left her shoulders and neck.

Aldara's eyes sought Blake, now speaking to his mother some thirty yards off.

"I came to see that you are all right," said Aldara and then swept Samantha's body with her gaze as if checking for injuries, lingering at her middle before meeting her eyes once more. The look was not sexual but certainly intrusive. Samantha frowned.

Aldara knew. Samantha was certain. She met the Ghostling's eyes.

"Am I?" whispered Samantha.

Aldara nodded.

"They're still here?" Samantha pressed both hands to her flat abdomen.

Aldara nodded. "I returned their souls myself."

Samantha threw herself into Aldara's arms and felt the Halfling stiffen.

She drew back. "Thank you, Aldara."

"Don't thank me yet. None of our mothers ever survived our births."

"Humans."

Aldara nodded. "But I would stay with you until your time to be certain you survive."

Samantha smiled and squeezed Aldara's hand. "Yes. I'd appreciate that." She stared toward the Ghostlings' camp. "Does he know?"

The quick shake of her head sent her feathery hair flying. "He'd come back if you tell him of the babies."

Samantha looked away. "I won't use them to hold him."

Aldara's gaze drifted back to Blake. "Tell your brother that I've finished my work here and I would like to see him before we go."

Go?

Dread settled over Samantha as she realized what this meant. Alon had seen her safe and had seen her to her parents. His obligation was finished.

A buzz of apprehension grew in Samantha's belly. What if he never came back?

Chapter 19

Alon had received Nicholas Chien in his tent and declined the offer to join the Skinwalkers at council the following evening, but tendered an offer that Sebastian was welcome in his camp and guaranteed him safe passage.

At sunrise, Samantha's father, Sebastian, the War Chief of the Skinwalkers, arrived at their camp. He was escorted to Alon, who had slept little and was now organizing the fifty-some surviving Ghostlings to bury their dead. Just entering their camp showed his courage, for many here hated the Skinwalkers for their hunts of newborns.

Alon met him before the gathering of the Betas, Gammas and the new Delta Pack. Sebastian again requested that Alon and four others of his choosing accompany the Skinwalkers to council that evening.

"Who wishes our company?" asked Alon.

"I do. My people do."

"But not the Spirit Children?" asked Alon.

Sebastian blew out a breath. "My son has convinced the council chiefs that it is safer to have you as an ally."

"Than an enemy?" Alon finished.

"You are invited to meet with both Niyanoka and Ianoka. It is my hope you will accept."

"The last time I spoke to your son he told me that we were not welcome here and that he could not prevent his people from killing mine. Now that we have won the battle for him, he invites me to parlay."

"Your actions have proved us all wrong. We owe the victory to you and your people." Sebastian followed this with an inclination of his head, a salute of sorts.

"Nagi is defeated. The Spirit Children and the Skinwalkers have no more need of us and we have none for them."

The gathering muttered their approval of this.

"I am grieved," said Sebastian. "But I will deliver your message."

Alon waited but the great bear did not depart. At last he spoke again.

"I am in your debt for guarding my daughter and for saving her soul—all of our souls. Should you ever need my help or assistance, you need only ask."

"I have one request," he said, wishing he could ask about Samantha but knowing he could not. He had hurt her enough already. "Please tell our parents, Cesar Garza and Bess Suncatcher, that we love them and respect all they have done for us, but we are not returning to them. From here forward, the Ghost Children will gather our own orphans and raise them. *We* will teach them what they must know."

"If that is your wish. I will deliver your message." Sebastian continued to speak, raising his voice so the others could hear. "So with respect, I ask that you tell the Ghost Children that the Skinwalkers are your allies. Those who formed vigilante groups to attack your young will be brought to justice and their cowardly actions condemned."

Alon turned to the gathering. "Objections?"

None spoke so he turned back to Sebastian, also raising his voice to be heard. "We will respect your word, Sebastian, for we saw you fight bravely while the Niyanoka hid behind their earthen wall. We accept the alliance with your people. Tell them that we will teach our descendants to respect the Balance and not to hunt the Skinwalkers, even when they are in animal form. Tell the Niyanoka, if you care to speak to them, that we will not attack the humans they protect. But we have no accord with them and advise that they keep their distance."

"I will tell them." Sebastian offered his hand.

The men shook. Alon was surprised at Sebastian's grip and the fierceness in his eyes. Alon knew Sebastian would make both an imposing ally and a terrible foe. The War Chief of the Skinwalkers turned and left the camp, alone as he had entered it.

Aldara moved to stand beside Alon. "Are you sure you don't want to see her again?"

He gave her an exasperated look.

"But she said she wants to see you."

"She's a healer and I reap evil ghosts. It's over."

"But she's—"

He held up his hand and she stopped speaking. Silence stretched. His arm dropped heavily to his side. After several ragged breaths he managed to find his voice, but it was a weak and strangled thing.

"She told me." He swallowed back the self-loathing. "She wants to use her powers. If she stays with me, they will banish her, too. I can't do that to her. I want her to find her true soul mate. Can you understand? That's not me." His head hung. "It can't be."

Now it was Aldara's turn to fire off a condemning stare.

"Are you coming with us?" he asked her.

Her jaw was set and her eyes blazed with blue fire. "No, I'm not."

"Aldara, he doesn't want you."

She glared. "I know that. I'm not going to him, but I'm not going with you, either."

"Where then?"

"I'm staying with Samantha."

Which made no sense at all. Was this a hopeless effort to reach Blake through his twin?

"We're leaving tonight, with you or without you."

Blake sat at the council table with the four chiefs of the Niyanoka. As each spoke, his heart sank more and more. None saw that the way they had invited the Ghostlings to parlay was insulting. Rather they were offended that Alon had refused their summons.

He waited in the circle until the talking stick was passed to him, for only the one holding the stick could speak and it was rude to hold it for too long. He gripped the handle, which was covered with seed beads, their pattern forming a cross to represent the four directions. He stared for a moment at the coyote skull, festooned with a feather, glass beads and hanks of horse hair wrapped in bits of bright red cloth, as he gathered his thoughts.

Blake stood, holding the talking stick in two hands. "We have won a great battle. Nagi has retreated to his Circle and will think long and hard before coming again to our Living World."

Several nodded their approval of this.

"We acknowledge the bravery of our people and the Skinwalkers in this fight. But the victory goes to the Ghost Children."

Blake gripped the stick, knowing that what he was about to say would ruin his chances of becoming a leader of the Niyanoka, but he would say it anyway because it was right.

"We have not acknowledged the part the Ghost Children played in the victory against Nagi. None of our people went to their camp. None thanked them for saving us all. And then we are outraged that Alon will not be summoned like a hound. They fought against their sire to save us all. It is a disgrace to pretend otherwise. This council will meet with the Skinwalkers in only a few hours, making this a historic day. But this council cannot ignore the third Halfling race, who has surely earned a place at the peace talks. We must send a delegation to the Ghostlings before it is too late."

He handed over the stick to Chief Rice, who said, "I will not go to these terrors. They have the power to steal our souls. Going to their camp would be suicide."

He passed the stick to the next. Each member refused to send representatives to the Ghost Children. Blake waited for the unanimous vote rejecting his proposal. When the stick returned to him, he rose once more.

"I resign my candidacy for any position for which I might be considered. If the Niyanoka will not go to the Ghost Children, then I will go myself to thank them for their part in this battle and the victory that they have earned. I renounce my citizenship and all rights. I am proud to have led the Spirit Children in battle, but I am not proud now."

He passed on the talking stick and left the circle.

No one spoke.

Outside, the sun was fast setting, though the days were slowly growing longer as spring crept toward summer. Blake found his father, Sebastian, waiting alone in the twilight. Blake saw his deep blue aura capped with rusty brown before he even saw his silhouette.

"Brave words and ones to make a father proud," said Sebastian.

"Too little too late," muttered Blake. These were words he should have said before the battle.

"What is it, son?"

"Before the fight, Aldara stayed with me, protected me from attacks by Nagi's ghosts. When her brother suggested an alliance with the Niyanoka, I told them both that I could not jeopardize the agreement with the Skinwalkers by including the Ghost Children."

"You were right. The Skinwalkers would have withdrawn and the alliance would have crumbled. As it is, we may form a new treaty."

"I was wrong. This is why Alon will not come. He tried to bring us all together before the battle and I said no. Now that they have brought us the win, now that we see what they are capable of, only now we seek them out. It is a double insult."

"You did what you thought was right. Now you feel differently. So you will act differently."

Blake gripped his hair at both temples and tugged. "But I knew it was wrong at the time. I felt it and I still rejected her."

His father peered at him. "Her?"

Blake dragged his hands over his face before meeting his father's inquiring gaze.

"Dad, Aldara was more than my bodyguard."

His father's expression registered momentary shock, but he recovered quickly, rubbing his neck as he looked away. "I see."

"And I kept her hidden, like some dirty little secret. She left me. I don't blame her. I deserved it, but now that she's gone, I realize how much she means to me. I don't want to lose her, but I already have."

His father rested a hand on his son's shoulder, offering silent support as Blake struggled to find a way to win her back.

"If I went to the Ghost camp, if I found her, do you think she would listen to me?" asked Blake.

"I only know that if you don't go, she will never know that you are sorry." His father squeezed the muscles of Blake's shoulder. "Do you love this woman?"

"She is the bravest, most wonderful woman in the world."

His father gave a laugh. "No, son. That would be your mother."

Blake smiled, suddenly grasping what his parents shared and wanting that for himself.

"I love her, Dad. I just want her to forgive me."

Something flashed before them. Sebastian roared and pressed a hand to his chest, calling the change. An instant later his father took animal form. But Blake did not follow him, for he recognized the flash of greenish light and waited. It was a Ghostling, changing form.

A moment later Aldara appeared naked in her human shape and threw herself into Blake's arms. His father reared up and then huffed.

"Dad, this is Aldara."

His father blew out a breath and then lumbered off.

"You heard?" Blake asked, hugging her, willing her to never leave him again.

"Yes, yes, everything. What you said at council and what you said to your father. Why didn't you tell me before?"

"I didn't know. I only…it only sunk into my thick skull when I saw you fighting. I was so scared I'd lose you. It made me realize that I couldn't live without you and that you were right about everything."

She drew back to stare at him, still clinging like a monkey, her legs locked about his waist and her hands laced behind his neck.

"You really love me?"

In answer, he lowered his head and kissed her. When they both came up for air, Aldara allowed him to set her gently on her feet. He removed his blazer, shook it and offered her a lovely lavender cape, made of wool, lined in satin and trimmed in soft wolf fur. She slipped it on, grinning, and slid her arms through the slits so she could grasp hold of his shirt with both fists.

"I don't want you to lose all that you worked for, just for me," said Aldara, her expression now earnest.

"I worked for a victory. It's done. From now on I will do what *I* choose, and I choose to make you my wife, if you will be willing to marry a Seer who somehow could not see that the best thing in his life is you."

Aldara started to cry. But she nodded her acceptance and managed to say, "Yes."

Blake took her away from the Spirit Children and the Skinwalkers and the Ghostlings, traveling over the open plains to a spot on a hilltop with a view of the sunset and later of the whole wide universe. This time their joining held the sweetness of two who understand that such a union is made from the most intimate kind of worship. Afterward, when they lay upon the grass, their bodies still flushed and damp from their exertion, Aldara recalled something.

"How is Samantha?"

"She slept most of the day away. I checked on her at noon and she still slumbered. She is recovering, but very weak. Jessie Healy Chien is visiting her dreams, and my mother is with her. I'm sure she will feel stronger when she wakes."

"Alon sent her away. He thinks he is not suitable for her."

Blake said nothing to this.

Aldara scowled. "You agree with him?"

"Of course I agree. She's my sister!"

"Because he is a Toe Tagger?" She was already on her feet, naked, fist clenched, ready to fight him again.

He sighed. "Because he is a man."

Aldara's face registered confusion and her hands relaxed. "What?"

"He's a man and nobody is good enough for my baby sister."

Aldara made a sound that human females make when presented with a kitten. She sank to her knees. "That's so adorable. I could fall in love with you all over again."

He held her, loving the way her soft breasts pressed against his chest.

Aldara drew back. "Blake, I think Samantha loves Alon. And Alon loves her. I'm sure of it. That's why he sent her away. He's afraid."

"I saw your brother fight, Aldara. Alon is not afraid of anything."

"You're wrong. He fears that being with him will keep

her from finding her true soul mate. He thinks that he, us, all those born of Nagi have no souls."

Blake felt sick, but he came to her defense. "That can't be true." He pinned her with a look of horror. She could not hold his gaze. "Is it?"

She shook her head. "I don't know."

"But we're going to cross the Ghost Road together. We are going to spend eternity in the Spirit World." His voice was adamant, as if the saying would make it so.

Aldara gave him a look fraught with pain. "I hope so, Blake. But truly, I do not know."

He gripped her fiercely then, trying to protect her from this new threat. "It can't be so," he whispered. "They're wrong. All of them."

She nestled against him and rested silently for a time. Then she spoke again.

"I have something more to tell you about your sister."

Somehow he knew he did not want to hear it. He wished he could stop her, but instead he braced for what she might say. The worry and pain in her voice only added to his anxiety.

"Then tell me quickly," he urged.

Her words spilled out in a rush. "When Samantha's soul was torn free, Alon retrieved it."

Blake sat in grim silence at this, wondering who had retrieved his soul and thankful that Alon had rescued his sister.

"He returned her soul, but he didn't see the others."

"What others?"

"Twin souls, just tiny wisps, but still, they were there. I retrieved them, but I didn't tell Alon. I didn't think it was my place. He doesn't know and Samantha may never tell him."

"Aldara, you're not making any sense. Tell him what?"

"Twin souls, Blake. Your sister is pregnant with Alon's children. She's going to have twins."

Chapter 20

Samantha awoke stiff and disorientated in the darkness in a small, unfamiliar room. She hobbled from the strange bed to find her mother and father in the main room of the two-bedroom cabin. They told her that she had not slept a few hours as the night sky indicated, but nearly twenty-four hours.

The news jolted her awake. "Alon?"

Her father informed her that the Skinwalkers and Spirit Children had signed a new treaty, but the Ghost Children had refused their invitation and had left at sunset.

Carried on a cresting wave of dread, she ran to the place where Alon's tent had stood to find only a circle of flattened grass.

Her anxiety turned to grief and she crumpled to the ground in stunned silence. It was Aldara who found her there. One look at the pity on her face and Samantha understood the truth. Alon had done as he had promised. He had seen her safe and he had left her.

After that she didn't recall what was said. She didn't remember what she did. It was like a big black hole had opened and she had dropped in. It took weeks to crawl back out.

She knew her mother and father had taken her home. She knew Blake and Aldara were making a life together. She seemed incapable of feeling happy for them. She felt frozen over inside.

It was Aldara who finally snapped her back to reality when she bluntly told Samantha that she had to eat because the babies were growing weak. Samantha would not have that. She still crept through the days, but now she had purpose. The babies were here and they needed her.

Samantha now set about the job of seeing she stayed fit and healthy. She had a reason to rise and wash and eat and move. Her heart still ached and her mood easily turned blue, but she fought now, determined to see her children born and determined to live to raise them.

Her mother was delighted at her news, but her father was worried. He knew from Bess how the Ghostlings were born. But no Halfling had ever birthed such children. The uncertainty did not weigh on Samantha. She had Aldara to watch over her and keep her from venturing off alone to bear her children.

With a father and a brother who were both healers, she thought her mother's precautions to send for a midwife were unnecessary. But she accepted the arrival of Virginia Thistleback, a wise, old Skinwalker swan who had delivered both Samantha and Blake. She had also fostered Alon's mother, when Bess Suncatcher first grew her feather cloak and changed into her raven form.

Virginia was nearly three hundred, but strong and hearty as a hickory. Her hair was as white as her feathers and had always been so, according to Samantha's mother. She examined Samantha and announced that the twins were growing more quickly than Skinwalker babies and would arrive within the month.

Three months into her pregnancy, Samantha was getting larger by the minute when Bess Suncatcher arrived to speak to Aldara. She was shocked to see Samantha's condition and then overjoyed—until she discovered that Alon was the father.

Samantha had been unable to keep Bess from going to seek her oldest son. It was a terrible time, because Samantha feared he would return only out of duty and was equally afraid he would not return at all. She didn't know which would be worse. She only knew that she loved Alon and he had set her aside as promised.

To him, she was a responsibility successfully discharged. The lovemaking that had changed her world and brought her this gift of children was a mistake for Alon never to be repeated.

Samantha found little joy in the recognition that she could now use her Seer gifts to expel ghosts and help those souls who were too confused to cross to the Spirit World. She could heal the ill and injured. Her family had all survived the war and, for the first time in their lives, they did not have to run.

But Blake and Aldara were planning to move to their own home as soon as Samantha delivered. And that forced Samantha to recognize that she was approaching her third decade and had never had a home of her own.

She wanted one with Alon and their babies. It made her feel ungrateful, since she had been given so much.

The first pains shot through her lower back and abdomen. She stood to discover her water had broken.

The twins were coming.

Samantha was filled with the sudden irresistible urge to move, to go to the forest alone to deliver her babies.

Alon smelled the wolf first, and a moment later he spied a familiar raven circling the camp. His mother had found him. He guessed the wolf was Nicholas Chien, a tracker and his mother's old friend, but he did not make an appearance. Apparently finding Alon was all his mother required.

She landed in a branch above the rough-hewn bench upon which he rested. He had carved this bench with his claws, and it sat on the edge of the little compound they had created in the Canadian Rockies, between two high peaks, where humans rarely ventured.

"So here is my little hermit." Her voice was high and raspy when she was in bird form, but from her tone and the ruffled feathers at her nape, he knew she was in a foul mood.

"Hello, Mother."

"Oh, so you still call me this? I thought you had renounced all ties to the evil Skinwalkers. Since you still acknowledge my relationship to you, I will tell you that this is no way to treat those who love you."

She dropped down to the bench beside him. His second in command, Cody, whom he had known almost since he was born, stepped forward.

"Mother?" he said.

"I'll deal with you in a minute. Now I need some privacy to speak to my eldest son."

None was as fierce as Cody in battle, yet a reprimand from their mother sent him scurrying for cover.

There was a flash of white light, like a lightbulb blowing out, and his mother sat beside him. She changed her feather cape so fast he nearly did not see it at all, for in only an instant she was dressed, from her high-heeled boots to her fashionable woolen jacket, in black. This was not a signal of her ire, which he marked now only by her flashing eyes, but the color she wore in both forms. He'd once asked if she was married in black and she said she had been, but would be buried in white to mark the passing of her soul across the veil that separates the Spirit World from the Way of Souls. Unlike the rest of the Halflings, his mother had actually seen that veil.

"You are breaking your father's heart," she said and then pinned him with her fixed stare.

It was a struggle not to squirm before her. But in the three and a half months since his departure, he had accomplished much. And in his heart, he knew this was the right course. The Ghost Children were Halflings, but they were different from the Skinwalkers and Spirit Children. They were not born in human form. They were capable of hunting from birth, and they had no souls. And so, no soul mates, no eternal love. He thought again of Samantha and felt the familiar stabbing pain strike his heart.

"It is not your obligation to raise Ghost Children. We agreed that it would be best to alleviate both of you of the responsibility of caring for us."

"Did you, now? How noble. Did you also decide it would be best to alleviate us of the greatest joy in our lives, alleviate us of our children, our grandchildren?"

Alon felt the certainty that had sustained him for months begin to erode, like ice beneath warm water.

He tried once more. "We never meant to hurt you."

"Small consolation," she said, giving him her elegant profile.

"Mother, we know you love us. But we're not like Skinwalkers. The young ones are dangerous." He recalled that they had nearly killed Samantha when she had first arrived at their home. "They pose a threat to others."

"That's not so!"

She never could see the worst in them. But mothers were like that.

She faced him, her expression earnest and resolute. "Not one of you ever attacked Cesar or me. If you are so dangerous and deadly. If you are born killers. If the world must be protected from you, as they all say—then why did you not kill a small raven and her helpless Spirit Child mate? I have no fangs, Cesar has no claws. Easy prey. Yet here I am. Why, Alon?"

The muscles in his jaw unlocked and his mouth dropped open. Why hadn't they? Both of his parents were strong, but Bess could not outfly him and Cesar could not outrun him. Yet they let these two scold and teach and direct and nurture. Was she right?

"But..." He could not come up with a rational explanation.

"You never attacked us, even when you did not like the consequences we set for you. You never threatened me and you never hurt Cesar, until now."

"I never meant to hurt either of you."

"We are not the only ones you have hurt."

Did she refer to Samantha?

"I told her I would keep her safe. I made no promises I did not keep."

"How earnest of you."

"She has likely moved on." He feared this was true, though it broke his heart to say it aloud.

"Really? Well, I know otherwise. She told me she never saw a better fighter than you. She said you were the one and only man who ever made her feel completely safe. That does not sound like a woman anxious to be rid of your odious company."

"She said this?" He could not have her, could not let this tiny silver flash of hope lure him like a bait fish thrashing on a hook. Yet, he clung to his mother's words, starved for more.

"Yes. She told me at your sister's *wedding*."

Alon's attention snapped back to his mother.

She nodded the confirmation to his unspoken question. "She is married to Blake Proud. Apparently Aldara does not feel she must spend her life like some outcast. You are part of this world, son. It is past time you claim your place."

Alon covered his face with his hands. His mother still did not understand. She was blinded by her love and could not see them for what they truly were—soulless hunters, incapable of loving or being loved.

Bess rubbed his back as she had done when he was a boy and still unable to hide his true form.

"Tell me why, Alon. At least give me that."

He lifted his weary eyes to meet her piercing ones.

"Mother, when Nagi tore the souls from the other Halflings, we alone were standing."

"Yes?" Her brows tented in question, for she still did not understand.

"He could not tear our souls from our bodies, because, like him, we have none."

She was on her feet an instant later. "What?"

He stood, as well. "Without souls. That is why he could not take them. He said so, told us. Do you understand now why I can't go to her?"

Bess sank back to her seat and stared off into space. He could only imagine the shock of this. To realize that all the children she had adopted were not children, not eternal souls trapped in ugly little packages—but unnatural monsters.

When she finally met his gaze, he was taken back. He had expected to see pity or pain, or perhaps even sorrow. Instead, he saw a familiar gleam that in younger days would have sent him headlong in the opposite direction.

"You *have* a soul, Alon. All living creatures have a soul."

"We don't."

They stared in silence, deadlocked. His mother dropped her voice to a soothing coo. "Is this why you left Samantha?"

He nodded.

"Do you love her?"

"What does that matter? I can never be like you and Dad. I can't cross with her to the Spirit World."

"You do this thing because you love her?" Bess coaxed.

"Yes!" he snapped, folding his arms across his chest. "Because she deserves her true soul mate."

His mother used her thumb and index finger to rub her eyes. Then she glanced skyward, as if calling for help from above. At last she turned to her eldest son and took both his hands. He resisted a moment and then allowed her to unfold his arms. She stared up into his eyes.

"Alon, my dearest boy, you have a soul. The Guardian of the Way of Souls told me so long ago."

He looked away. His mom squeezed his hands. Alon kept his head averted, but now glanced at her from the corner of his eye. He did not like the hope that crept back into his belly, swelling like a sponge in warm water. He couldn't bear it if he gave in to the hope only to have it crushed out of him once more.

"I spoke to Hihankara. She said that *all* the children of Nagi bear the markings necessary to gain entrance to the Spirit World. She said she thought only Soul Whisperers were born with such marks. But that all Ghost Children bear them, too. Do you hear me, son? You have a soul and you will one day enter the Spirit World. Hihankara told me so."

"She could be wrong," he whispered, longing to give in to the possibility even has he dug his heels in further.

"Alon." Tears filled her eyes. "I saw Gregory and Gail on the Road."

He stilled, thinking of the brothers and sisters he had lost. Gregory and Gail had fallen early in the battle.

"I called to them, but they begged to go. I had not the heart to force them back to us. Do you understand? I saw their souls, brilliant silver and shining bright as the face of the full moon. You have a soul, Alon. And you are born with your feet already upon the Red Road. Your love will not hinder Samantha. It glorifies her, it strengthens her and it protects her."

Alon sank back against the bench. His heart now raced and his ears were ringing as if he flew very fast.

"Is it true?" he whispered. "Can it be?"

"Yes."

"Then why could Nagi not tear our souls away with the others?"

"I know only that it is *not* because you do not have one."

He did not remember standing, but suddenly he found he was on his feet.

"I have to go to her," he whispered, more to himself than to his mother. "Where is she?"

"Back with her parents in Yellowknife."

Alon was already airborne.

"Wait! I haven't finished." His mother's words receded as he flew fast. He needed to get to Samantha.

Alon rocketed through the skies, night to day to night once more, not stopping, racing higher and faster than he had ever gone. He rose so high he saw the glittering path that led to the Spirit World, and he saw the shining silver souls walking along the path.

Then he came down, low to the ground, sighting the topography, searching for the Great Slave Lake, which would mark his arrival. He found Yellowknife and recalled Samantha telling him that Nagi found them because she had expelled a ghost from a boy in a place called Dogrib. He started there, finding a Skinwalker, a wolf, whom he recognized by his scent. His name was Nodi, a tribal leader, and he said he had fought with Sebastian in Wyoming. He did not recognize Alon in this form, but seeing him turn to his fighting form convinced him. Nodi provided him with clothing, jeans, boots and a navy blue jacket with a king salmon embroidered on the breast. After he learned Alon was Aldara's brother, he agreed to lead him to the Prouds' home.

His arrival was not as private as he would have liked. Nodi, his elder escort, brought him to Sebastian, who looked less than pleased to see Alon. His wife, Michaela, welcomed him to their large, three-story home, though Alon perceived from her breathing and heart rate that his unexpected appearance made her anxious.

Blake turned up next and clearly wanted to kick his ass, but his new wife, Aldara, held on to his arm. He appreciated her support until she told Blake that if anyone was going to pummel him, it would be her.

It was unanimous. None of them wanted him here. They stood in the living room, like a stone wall.

"Samantha?" he asked again.

"She doesn't want to see you," said Aldara.

He lowered his chin and glared at his sister. "That wasn't what I asked."

"You have been absent for months. You did not even attend your own sister's wedding. Why now?" asked Michaela Proud.

"My mother tracked me down. She told me…" How did he say this? "She told me where to find her."

Her dad took a menacing step in Alon's direction, but his wife's hand stayed him.

"Let him finish," said Samantha's mother.

Alon knew he had been a fool and that his misguided effort to protect Samantha had actually hurt her deeply. He did not blame her loved ones for trying to protect her from further harm.

"I thought…" He stopped, checked himself and then realized he would not be able to keep his dignity. He would not be able to appear as anything other than what he was, a fool who had used their daughter and then tossed her aside. If he was going to get to Samantha, he'd have to begin with that. "I have feelings for Samantha."

Her dad's hands curled into fists.

He hurried on. "But I didn't believe I was right for her."

"You left without a word because you cared? Is that what you expect us to believe?" asked Blake.

"I did."

The lines about Aldara's mouth softened and her brow lifted, giving him the first sign of a willingness to listen. "What changed your mind?"

"I was wrong, Aldara. What I said to you, what I believed about us. All wrong. Mom told me she saw Greg and Gail on the Spirit Road. She saw their immortal souls. We have them, Aldara. We all do."

Aldara's shoulders slumped and she swayed against her husband, who wrapped his arms about her instantly. She nestled against Blake, buried her face in his coat and wept out her relief. Blake's eyes pinched closed and his head bowed. Alon understood then. She had told him and he had accepted her anyway.

"Blake? What?" asked Sebastian.

Michaela spoke now, moving past her husband to stare at Alon with a look of absolute astonishment. "You doubted this?"

He nodded, grimly. "I was certain…so certain that I made a grave mistake."

"Letting her go?" asked Sebastian.

"I need to speak to her." He put it all out there, telling them the truth, not trying to keep his pride, for he had none left. "I need to tell her that I was wrong, that I'm sorry and that I love her. I just wanted her to be happy, and I couldn't see that I could ever make that happen. But if she'll give me another chance, I'll spend the centuries trying to make up for what I've done."

The room fell so silent that he could hear his own stomach growling. No one moved as his gaze flicked from one frowning face to the next.

At last, Blake stepped aside and extended his hand toward the twin staircases that rose from the foyer to the second floor.

"I'll take him," offered Aldara.

Michaela glanced to her husband, who nodded his consent, then her attention swept back to Blake.

Alon followed his sister up the stairs, across the landing that overlooked an enormous grand room. The

Prouds all stared up at him as he crossed to the hallway and out of their sight.

Aldara paused partway down the hall. "So we have immortal souls?"

"Yes."

She drew a great, long breath. "I've been afraid to have children. Afraid they would be soulless like us. But now…"

The bright smile radiated hope for a moment and then gradually faded as she returned her focus to him.

"You've got an uphill climb, brother. She's been grieving for months. Inconsolable. The entire family has been worried. If not for…" She stopped herself.

"For what?" he coaxed.

"For your sorry ass and your assumptions none of this would have happened. You would have been with her all along instead of having to crawl back here with your mea culpas. And, brother, she needed you. I don't know how you'll make this right, but you best give it your all." She lifted a finger and pressed it deep into his chest. "Don't screw up again."

With those final words of encouragement, his sister paused, drew a breath and then lifted her hand to knock on the closed door.

Samantha's lovely musical voice responded, calling out a question.

"It's Aldara. May I come in?"

Samantha invited his sister to enter. When he tried to follow, she pushed him back in the hall.

"You got by them. But you don't get by me unless she wants to see you. Wait here."

The door slammed in his face.

Chapter 21

Samantha closed the door to the nursery where her two newborns slept at the same moment the knock sounded on the door to her suite. Aldara called a greeting and Samantha bade her enter. Aldara did so, firmly closing the door behind her.

Samantha noted her sister-in-law's rigid posture and tight expression. Something was wrong.

"He's here," said Aldara without preamble. Her penchant for bluntness struck Samantha like a slap to the face.

She did not need to ask who "he" was. She knew and suddenly it hurt to breathe.

"Here?" She glanced to the door of the room where the twins slept. If her babies followed their usual pattern, they would sleep for at least another hour.

"He asked to speak to you. If you don't want to see him, I'll send him away, but…"

She let that sentence hang. But—the children were her brother's, as well. But—he had a right to know. But—she should at least listen to what Alon had to say.

"Is he here for the twins?" These were *her* children and she'd fight anyone for them, even him.

"I don't think he knows of them. May he come in?"

"Where is he?"

Aldara motioned to the closed door. "Just outside."

Samantha drew herself up to her full height and resisted the strong impulse to shift to her more imposing bear form. But then she could not speak to him. She stared at the closed door, then cast a quick glance to Aldara, nodding once, then immediately returned her attention back to the door.

"Would you like me to stay or go?"

Samantha knew this meeting must be private. She did not want Aldara to witness Alon telling her again that he did not want her or his babies. Well, *she* wanted them and, contrary to his expectations, she had bore them and lived.

"Leave us, please."

Aldara opened the door and stepped out into the hall. Samantha heard Aldara speak to her brother. "She'll see you. Try not to screw this up…again."

A moment later Alon's wide shoulders filled the doorway. Her eyes gobbled up the sight of him. Her fingers itched to stroke his strong jaw and dance through the fine, soft hair on his head. His clothing looked as if he'd found them in a Dumpster, baggy jeans, worn hiking boots and a pull-over jacket that stretched tight over his broad chest. He looked tired, she realized, and his expression pinched his handsome face.

The hope that fluttered within her was crushed by his forlorn expression. He seemed like a man about to tackle a very unpleasant task. So her fears were realized. She had become a burden to him.

"Samantha." He paused to stare at her, his gaze sweeping down her body and then back up once more. Did he mark the increase in her bust? "You're too thin."

Her eyes narrowed. "Why are you here?"

He glanced about her bedroom as if looking for the children that she feared he might suspect were here. Could he smell them? She moved to block the nursery door. He sagged then rebounded off the door frame as if he needed the solid structure to propel him forward.

"My mother told me about Blake and Aldara."

"A little late to join in the festivities."

"I'm a fool," he said.

Samantha's ears perked up. Alon was many things, but never a fool. She had seen him in battle, fearless, powerful, a consummate fighter. She'd never seen him make a mistake. Except about motherhood. He'd been wrong about that.

"I don't understand." She took a tentative step in his direction.

"I never meant to hurt you. I only did what I thought was best. I believed you'd be better off without me. I wanted you to be a great healer and a member of the Niyanoka. I didn't want to be the cause of your banishment."

"So you made the decision for both of us."

He bowed his head. "Yes."

"Alon, you left me without a word. You hurt me, deeply."

He bowed his head. "At the time, I thought it was best."

"Did you? It must be wonderful to know what is best for another person without even asking her. Did you really believe that I'd forget you, forget what you mean to me and just find some replacement?"

He met her gaze. "I'm sorry, Samantha. I believed that if I stayed, I would keep you from your true path."

He still had not said that he wanted her. Only that he was sorry for hurting her. She covered her mouth with one hand to keep herself from speaking, from crying and against the pain that now clawed at the lining of her throat.

"After the battle, Nagi told me I'd never cross the Way of Souls."

She recoiled at this horrible lie.

He kept going, as if in a rush now to get it all out. "How could I be your soul mate if I had no soul? How could I stay with you, knowing that?"

She stared a moment, taking in this news. Finally she shook her head in flat denial. "Don't you believe him!"

That brought the flicker of a smile. "My mother came to me a few days ago, to tell me of Aldara's marriage. She also told me that she saw Ghost Children cross into the Spirit World. I was wrong. Terribly wrong, and I am here to beg your forgiveness. I never meant to hurt you. I only wanted you safe and happy."

She reached for him and then held herself back. "Alon?"

"Yes?"

"You said you were protecting me. Was that only because of your promise?"

"No." He extended his open hand, but his expression was bleak. "At first it was obligation, but then I fell in love with you. I have loved you since the day you offered to bury the Delta Pack. I never expected to find a woman who would try to protect me or one who could see in me something other than a monster."

"You're no monster!"

Alon smiled. "Still my fierce little defender. But I wonder if you can forgive me. I wonder if you could ever love me or if I have lost your heart through my mistakes. Please tell me it isn't too late for us."

His hand lay open and outstretched. She wanted to take it, wanted to believe him. A touch would tell her what he felt.

"Let me stay with you."

She took his hand. He enfolded her in his arms and kissed her with a sweet tenderness blended with longing. The guilt and sorrow struck her first, but when their mouths met she experienced the sweet longing he still held for her. She gave over to the sensation of their reunion. At last he pulled back, resting his forehead upon hers.

"I have been as the dead these last few months. It nearly killed me to stay away."

"I wish you hadn't," she admitted. "I needed you so much."

"Can you ever forgive me?"

She rubbed a hand over his broad, muscular back. "In time."

He captured her hands and dropped to his knees. "Samantha, I love you with all my heart and soul. Will you honor me by becoming my wife?"

She drew a breath, overwhelmed by the sincerity of his emotions and the fluttering hope he held in his heart. She drew back, breaking the contact, for her thoughts were still too private to share.

"No, Alon, not yet." The look of pain flashed across his face and pierced her heart, but she continued on. "There is something you don't know."

He interrupted her. "We could find a way to be together that wouldn't threaten you. Blake and Aldara have done so. We could, as well."

She wanted to tell him he had been wrong about that, that she had delivered the twins. That they were perfect and beautiful and mysterious. But she had to tread cautiously. She did not know how Alon would feel about discovering he was suddenly a father.

"I have to show you something first, and then, if you still wish me for your wife, I would be honored."

She drew him up and he rose, cautious, uncertain as she led him to the closed door to the nursery. She paused with her hand on the knob and stared into his worried blue eyes.

Alon did not like the conditional acceptance. What was behind this door that she believed might change his mind about her? There was nothing, nothing in this world that could make him love her less. So why then was his heart pumping like a piston and his forehead slick with sweat? Had she found another? Was he there beyond that door?

Samantha pushed open the door with caution, as if something might spring at her as she peeked inside. Alon braced for attack, mentally choreographing his moves, including pulling Samantha behind him. His senses rose to alert, but he heard nothing and smelled only powder and clean linen. Then it reached him, the scent of his own kind. The hairs on his neck rose.

He pushed past her to meet this challenger.

"Alon," Samantha whispered, capturing his arm in a surprisingly strong grip. "Quietly."

If she expected to sneak up on a Ghostling, she did not know his kind. None ever found them sleeping.

Alon stood in the strange small room, sweeping the

corners for some threat. His head turned, his eyes darted and he saw nothing, no one.

Samantha pushed in, standing beside him. He remained on alert.

"Where is he?" Alon asked.

"Where is who?"

"The male Ghostling. I have his scent."

The furniture was odd. The dresser held a small plastic pad upon it, and there was a low rocker, two covered baskets and what seemed to be a topless cage made of wood that sat on wheeled legs. Blankets and bedding filled the little container. Above it hung a series of small fluffy creatures tied on strings.

He did not know what this was or why he could not see his rival. He searched the ceiling for the familiar gray smoke but found nothing.

"What is this place?" he said, now keeping his voice hushed as uncertainty filled him.

"Haven't you ever seen one like it?" she asked.

Was that *amusement* in her voice? He glanced toward her and saw her smiling.

"Never."

She snuggled against him, resting her head upon his shoulder. Clearly *she* perceived no threat. He allowed her to bring him forward toward the square box with wooden slats along one side and a funny little blanket draped over the other.

"Here they are," she whispered.

They? Alon followed Samantha's lead, leaning to peer into the raised box. Inside were two tiny pink babies, sleeping side by side with their hands clasped.

He rocketed upright and backed away. He did not stop until he hit the windowsill. Alon tried and failed to speak and succeeded only in lifting one hand to point at the infants.

Samantha crossed to him. "Alon, breathe. You're turning purple."

His mouth gaped like a hooked bass, and finally the air returned to his lungs.

"Babies!" he gasped.

She giggled. "Babies," she agreed, capturing his raised hand and lacing her fingers into his.

His gaze jumped from the sleeping box to her. She smiled indulgently at him as she stroked his cheek with her free hand.

His head spun. He could swear the floor beneath him heaved, for he had to stagger a step to keep from being tossed to the carpet. Samantha held on, an anchor in his stormy sea.

Fingers of anxiety squeezed his larynx. "Mine?"

But they couldn't be. They were pink and perfect. She shook her head and he covered his eyes as the truth tore into him. She had found another, had had another the entire time she was with him. Who was he? Where was he? And why had he left her here alone to raise these children?

"Alon, look at me." She lifted his chin and waited until he opened his eyes. He stared down into the perfection of her face and the lovely dark calm of her eyes. "They're not yours. They're *ours*."

And he knew it was so, could feel the truth of her words echoing in his heart, but more than that. He perceived her anxiety over his reaction to this news, her hope that he would accept them and her dread that he would not. What was happening here? He released her hands and clasped her shoulders so he could stare at her smiling face.

"Ours?"

She nodded, her sweet, lush mouth curling into a smile as pride beamed in her eyes.

"Yes. Ours. You're a papa. This was what I had to show you. If you still want to marry me, you will not gain just a wife, but also a family."

"But how?"

She laughed and patted his hand. "The usual way."

Her love for him vibrated through him from the point of contact and traveled to his heart.

"But you're alive. The birth, I don't understand."

She snuggled against his side, wrapping her arms about his torso as she rested her head against his chest.

"Helped to have two healers and two Seers and a Ghost Child in the family. Oh, and a midwife, too."

He looked horrified and she realized what he thought. "Did it hurt?"

"Just the usual amount. A normal C-section and my dad healed me the same day."

Alon gathered her up in his arms as relief swept through him. It was one of his fears, that she would want babies, babies that he did not dare to give her.

They stood that way a long time and then more questions sprang up in his mind, one after the other, like new green shoots amid a forest blackened by fire.

"What are they?" he asked. "I was born in my fighting form. And I was never pink and..." He stopped himself before he said "weak and helpless."

She read his thoughts. "They're not helpless. They can already roll over."

She clasped his hand and drew him back with her to look at the twins.

"I'm not sure what gifts they have yet. But I know, whatever they are, that they will be wonderful."

Such complete confidence she had, while he was still drowning in panic.

"What if they attack your family?"

"Don't be silly. They're infants."

He knew better. The yearlings of his kind were as dangerous as hungry tigers. But then he recalled what his mother had said. They had never attacked her or their father. They never killed humans, either. How did they know?

"I could fly at birth," he said absently, gazing entranced at the two little souls.

"I'll keep the windows closed." She giggled and looped an arm about his waist.

"They don't look like me," he said. But they smelled like him, he realized.

"Oh, no?" She lifted the closest baby, who woke with an irritated cry and blinked open its eyes. "This is Andrew."

Samantha rested the infant on her shoulder and cradled the small, fuzzy head as she turned so Alon could see his son's tiny face. The baby boy blinked open his eyes and stared at Alon.

"This is your papa, Andy."

Alon gaped in astonishment at the haunting yellow eyes that were so familiar in his kind. But his eyes were that color only when he was in fighting form and never while in human form. The contrast of familiar and unfamiliar increased his anxiety.

"Take him."

She didn't give him time to refuse. Suddenly he had a little malleable lump of baby boy molded to his shoulder. He was warm and fragrant, with hair as soft as the belly of a rabbit. Alon's heart squeezed with joy. He closed

his eyes to savor the lightning bolt of emotion that left
him full of hope and joy.

"It's a miracle," he whispered.

Samantha laughed. "I'm glad you think so. They need
feeding every three hours."

He wondered what they ate. Alon turned to grin at
Samantha, still clasping the little bundle. "I love him
already."

Samantha blew out a breath as she nodded. Was that
relief? Did she really think he could look at these babies
and not want to keep them right here next to his heart?

"I still want to marry you," he said.

She rested a hand on Andrew's small back. "Then
that is what we shall do."

Alon swallowed past the lump in his throat. "I'm so
sorry I wasn't here for you. That I left you alone—"

He was about to say "alone to give birth," but she cut
him off. "No more of that now. My family was with me."

*You and I will build from here, from this moment
and this love.*

She never spoke the last part, but he knew her
thoughts. How did she know what he was going to say?
How had he known what she was going to answer?

And then he recalled what she had once told him
about her parents and how they knew they were meant
for each other. His parents, too, had this connection,
this way of reading thoughts and emotions by a touch.

The soul mate bond, he thought and she nodded.

"Yes."

Behind her came a tiny huffing sound. She turned
and bent over the bedding.

"Let me introduce you to your second son, Ian." She
held up the boy, who kicked his tiny legs and frowned
at Alon.

"Ian? But Ghostling twins are always a boy and a girl."

"Are they? I didn't get the memo. And these are not only Ghostlings, they are also one-quarter Skinwalker and one-quarter Spirit Child."

It was so. His children were of all the Halfling races.

"What will they grow to be?" he asked, full of wonder and a hope that was as bright and unfamiliar as sunlight after months of darkness.

"Whatever they grow to be, they will be loved."

Samantha clasped his waist with one hand and inclined her head for a kiss.

Alon pressed his mouth to hers, tasting again the familiar sweetness. She was his bride, the mother of his children and, as soon as possible, his wife. He drew back to stare down at her.

"I'm the luckiest man in the Living World."

"And in the next," she said, snuggling closer.

He could see it now, their future. Raising babies and walking together through the centuries, for he knew that his descendants truly held a place in the Living World. Because of her, Alon now anticipated the years and also the end of years when he and Samantha would walk the Ghost Road and into eternity together.

* * * * *

Terminology

DREAM WALKER*
A NIYANOKA with the ability to visit another person's dreams and work mental and/or physical healing during the visitation. The human visited has no memory of the visit.

CIRCLE OF GHOSTS
The final home of all GHOSTS who once led evil lives and are punished when HIRHANKARA pushes them from the SPIRIT ROAD into the CIRCLE, where they drift for eternity in endless circles. This ghostly prison is presided over by NAGI. Some GHOSTS have been released from this prison by the prayers of those who live a pure life.

CLAIRVOYANTS*
A NIYANOKA who has the gift of sight. He can see all a person's possible fates through touch. The number of possible outcomes can be vast and vary wildly depending on outside forces and personal decisions. In rare instances at least two or more outcomes conflict, making their advice sometimes contradictory and confusing.

GHOST
The remains of humans after they have left their earthly vessels.

GHOST CHILDREN*
(See NAGINOKA)

GHOSTLING*
(See NAGINOKA)

GHOST ROAD
(See SPIRIT ROAD)

HALFLING*
Any creature with one SPIRIT and one human parent.

HANWI
THE MOON *is a reflective female SPIRIT who warms* MAKA *when the* WI (Sun) *is absent.*

HEYOKA
SPIRIT *of chaos who is a double-faced SPIRIT with a split personality and emotions. He represents joy and sorrow, war and peace and all other opposites. Humans who see* WAKINYAN (THUNDERBEINGS) *become living* HEYOKAS *and do the opposite of what is expected.*

HIHANKARA
The crone who guards the SPIRIT ROAD. If the soul has walked the RED ROAD and led a righteous life, he bears the proper tattoos and is allowed to pass. If he has led a wicked life, she pushes him from the road and allows him to fall into the CIRCLE OF GHOSTS.

HUMANS
Mortal creatures without firsthand knowledge of the SPIRIT WORLD or SPIRITS.

INANOKA*

Mortal beings born of a human female and the SPIRIT TOB TOB. *They are* SKINWALKERS *who shape-shift into the animal of their mother's tribe at will and maintain all attributes of that animal while in human form. They are called* HALFLINGS *and live an average of four hundred years. They are despised by* NIYANOKA *for being beasts and possibly because they live longer. They protect animals from capricious* SUPERNATURALS. *Each animal is gifted with a different power:*

BEAR: *Has the ability to heal all injuries and wounds.*

BUFFALO: *Is a creature of sacrifice that can absorb injuries, illness or grief into its body and then heal at a rapid rate. They are not healers and must feel all the pain they take from the ones they relieve. It is said they can raise the dead, but only at the expense of their own life.*

HAWK: *Receives messages from the* SPIRITS *and sees into the future. But they are helplessly blind to their own future or the future of those they love.*

MOUNTAIN LION: *Has the power of sight and can perceive things far beyond the realm of normal sight. This gift gives cats the appearance of telling the future, but they really see things as they occur in other locations. They are especially good at seeing what is happening to those they know well.*

OWL: *Has the ability to exorcise disembodied souls* (GHOSTS) *from their unwilling hosts but cannot send them for judgment on the* WAY OF SOULS. *They also can predict a human's death. It is for this reason that seeing an owl is considered an omen of death.*

RAVEN: *The only creature that can travel the SPIRIT ROAD and speak to the souls in the SPIRIT WORLD.*
WOLF: *Can track anyone on earth by their scent trail.*

KANKA
OLD WOMAN SORCERESS. *She travels in dreams and helps people purify themselves. She can see the past, present and future and is a SUPERNATURAL.*

LIVING WORLD*
The world of all things alive, also known as the earth, distinguished from the SPIRIT WORLD and the Realm of Ghosts, where only Superior Spirits and the souls who have crossed can reside.

MAKA
MOTHER EARTH, *who holds the female power of birth and is a sacred SPIRIT.*

MEMORY WALKER*
A NIYANOKA with the power to make another forget a person or event. He cannot erase another's memory, but only make slight alterations. This gift is helpful to reduce grief after a loss and to allow a person to go unnoticed by erasing the memory of an encounter.

MITAKUYE OYASIN
A closing for a blessing. It literally means "All my relations included" or "We are all related" and reminds us that humans are connected to everything of the earth.

NAGI
This shadow creature is the ghostly guardian of the CIRCLE OF GHOSTS and is a SPIRIT.

NAGINOKA*

Mortal beings born of the union between the SPIRIT NAGI, *Ruler of Ghosts, and a human or children descended from these beings. They are the third* HALFLING *race and take three forms, an ethereal smoke capable of flight, a hideous but highly effective fighting form and their most human form noted for its otherworldly beauty. Also called* GHOST CHILDREN *and the derogatory* TOE TAGGERS *and Deathlings. Their purpose is to find evil* GHOSTS *who remain in the* LIVING WORLD *and send them to the* SPIRIT ROAD *for judgment. They have a life span of three hundred to four hundred years.*

NIYAN

A SPIRIT BEING *that teaches man to understand the cycle of life and death and the return of the body to* MAKA *(the earth) as the spirit returns to the* SPIRIT WORLD. NIYAN *is a* SPIRIT.

NIYANOKA*

Mortal beings born of a union between NIYAN *and a human. They are called* SPIRIT CHILDREN *and are charged with protecting humans from the interference of* SUPERNATURALS *and* SKINWALKERS. *In addition they consider themselves shepherds of Mankind, working for their benefit, helping them walk the* RED ROAD *and preparing them for the* SPIRIT WORLD. *They have a life span of three hundred to four hundred years.*

PEACEMAKER*

A NIYANOKA *with the power to influence the moods*

and emotions of those nearby. They are highly persuasive and sought after for their ability to assist in all forms of negotiation. Since their suggestions are difficult to defy and their proposals hold such influence, their ethics must be above reproach.

RED ROAD

The RED ROAD *is a metaphor for the correct way to live. One who walks the* RED ROAD *exists in balance with all things of the earth, behaving in a manner that is both proper and blessed. Walking the* RED ROAD *allows for entrance into the* SPIRIT WORLD, *while ignoring the proper way might lead to being cast from the* WAY OF SOULS *and into the* CIRCLE OF GHOSTS.

SEER OF SOULS*

A NIYANKOKA *member of the Ghost Clan, thought to be extinct. Such a* HALFLING *has the ability to see not only* SPIRITS, *but earthbound souls in the form of disembodied* GHOSTS. *They have the power to speak to* GHOSTS *and to send them to the* SPIRIT ROAD *for judgment. (See:* HIHANKARA)

SKY ROAD

(See SPIRIT ROAD)

SOUL WHISPERER*

A NIYANOKA *of the Spirit Clan with the power to bear witness to a death by touching the corpse. The* WHISPERER *sees exactly what the departed saw in the moments prior to his death and also experiences his* thoughts. *This makes WHISPERERS essential for solving crimes such as murder, but also makes them unclean in the minds of their kind, making them outcasts. None will touch them for they are believed to be unclean.*

SKINWALKERS
Another word for INANOKA, the HALFLING children of TOB TOB the SPIRIT BEAR. Legend says these are animals who remove their skin to masquerade as humans, but their ineptitude often reveals them.

SPIRITS
All of these creatures are immortal.

SPIRIT CHILD
Another name for NIYANOKA, a HALFLING child of NIYAN and a human parent.

SPIRIT ROAD
(SKY ROAD, SPIRIT ROAD, WAY OF SOULS, GHOST ROAD) The milky way that is the path leading to the SPIRIT WORLD. Those without the proper tattoos are pushed off the trail and wander endlessly in the CIRCLE OF GHOSTS. Souls without the proper markings have led an evil life on earth and do not merit entrance to the SPIRIT WORLD.

SPIRIT WORLD
The home of all souls that have successfully crossed the SPIRIT ROAD because they walked the RED ROAD while in the LIVING WORLD. Also the home of Superior Spirits, such as TOB TOB and NIYAN.

SUPERNATURALS

There are eight SUPERNATURALS, including KANKA. They are immortal but less powerful than SPIRITS. They live on earth.

THE BALANCE*

This refers to the balance of nature, the fragile connection that the IANOKA protect from careless or malevolent damage by supernatural creatures, NIYANOKA and humans, who all tend to feel a certain entitlement to the earth.

TIME TURNER*

NIYANOKA with the power to move forward and backward in time. But while traveling they use time twice as quickly and so cannot be seen by others.

TOE TAGGERS*

Derogatory term for GHOST CHILDREN, who are the HALFLING children of the SPIRIT NAGI and a human female. They are also called NAGINOKA.

TOB TOB

Translates as "Four by Four," meaning a creature that goes on four legs. This great SPIRIT BEAR has wisdom and healing powers. TOB TOB is a SPIRIT.

TRUTH SEEKER*

A NIYANOKA who can divine the truth to any spoken question, merely by touching the one he questions. TRUTH SEEKERS are hard to deceive and make excellent judges in the NIYANOKA community.

WANAGI
The soul of a dead person, a GHOST.

WAKAN TANKA
THE GREAT SPIRIT, THE GREAT MYSTERY, *Creator of all. A holy immortal entity who is more than SPIRIT.*

WAKINYAN
THUNDERBEINGS (THUNDERBIRD, THUNDER-HORSE). *The power of electric energy on earth. Thunder comes from the opening of the THUNDERBIRD's eye and from the drumming of the THUNDERHORSE's hooves. WAKINYA are SPIRITS. They also cause clouds, hurricanes, tornadoes and storms. They are known to strike dead any human foolish enough to lie while holding a sacred pipe.*

WAY OF SOULS
(See SPIRIT ROAD)

WI
The Sun. WI represents power and sustains life. He is a great teacher and a SPIRIT.

WONIYA
The soul of a living person.

*These terms/beings are fictional and do not exist in Lakota legend.

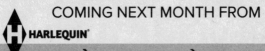
#159 KEEPER OF THE SHADOWS
The Keepers: L.A. • by Alexandra Sokoloff

Rosalind Barrymore Gryffald is a news reporter and a Keeper, one of an ancestral line of extraordinary mortals charged with keeping the peace between humans and shapeshifters. When she discovers an eerie parallel between two murders and a fifteen-year-old Hollywood tragedy, Barrie reluctantly teams with the gorgeous and enigmatic Mick Townsend, a rival journalist on her newspaper. As they dig into the cold case, more victims surface, and Barrie can trust no one, least of all Mick, who may well prove to be as inconstant as the shifters Barrie is sworn to protect.

#160 TAMING THE DEMON
by Doranna Durgin

Devin James wields a demon blade...and the demon blade wields him, creating an irrevocable bond that leeches into his soul, setting him on a path of loss and destruction. Natalie James is a woman who knows how to see through the darkness to Devin's heart. But neither of them realize that her mentor will stop at nothing—not betrayal, murder or selling his own soul—to acquire Devin's blade.

REQUEST YOUR
FREE BOOKS!

2 FREE NOVELS FROM THE
PARANORMAL ROMANCE COLLECTION
PLUS 2 FREE GIFTS!

YES! Please send me 2 FREE novels from the Paranormal Romance Collection and my 2 FREE gifts (gifts are worth about $10). After receiving them, if I don't wish to receive any more books, I can return the shipping statement marked "cancel." If I don't cancel, I will receive 4 brand-new novels every month and be billed just $21.42 in the U.S. or $23.46 in Canada. That's a savings of at least 21% off the cover price of all 4 books. It's quite a bargain! Shipping and handling is just 50¢ per book in the U.S. and 75¢ per book in Canada.* I understand that accepting the 2 free books and gifts places me under no obligation to buy anything. I can always return a shipment and cancel at any time. Even if I never buy another book, the two free books and gifts are mine to keep forever.

237/337 HDN FVVV

Name _____ (PLEASE PRINT) _____

Address _____ Apt. # _____

City _____ State/Prov. _____ Zip/Postal Code _____

Signature (if under 18, a parent or guardian must sign)

Mail to the **Harlequin® Reader Service:**
IN U.S.A.: P.O. Box 1867, Buffalo, NY 14240-1867
IN CANADA: P.O. Box 609, Fort Erie, Ontario L2A 5X3

Want to try two free books from another line?
Call 1-800-873-8635 or visit www.ReaderService.com.

* Terms and prices subject to change without notice. Prices do not include applicable taxes. Sales tax applicable in N.Y. Canadian residents will be charged applicable taxes. Offer not valid in Quebec. This offer is limited to one order per household. Not valid for current subscribers to Paranormal Romance Collection or Harlequin® Nocturne™ books. All orders subject to credit approval. Credit or debit balances in a customer's account(s) may be offset by any other outstanding balance owed by or to the customer. Please allow 4 to 6 weeks for delivery. Offer available while quantities last.

Barrie Gryffald was heading for the local crime editor's desk
when she saw the one person she didn't want to see coming
toward her.

Mick Townsend.

A newbie on the paper, and a thorn in her side from the
instant he'd show up. For one thing, jobs were scarce enough
without extra competition. But that wasn't even the start of it.

Townsend was *w-a-a-a-y* too good-looking to be a journalist.
In a city of surreally gorgeous people, he was truly heartstopping.

Only movie stars were supposed to look like that; there was
something almost preternaturally beautiful about him. Dark
gold hair and green eyes under perfectly arched eyebrows,
cheekbones you could cut glass with. The way he held himself,
that casually aristocratic elegance that was the territory of actors
and, well, aristocrats. He moved like a cat, strong as a panther
and just as lithe. He was tall, too, which made Barrie glad she

was wearing some serious heels tonight, Chanel pumps to go with the little Balenciaga number she'd found in her favorite thrift store.

Mick Townsend stopped right in her path, towering over her in an alarmingly commanding way. "Gryffald."

Barrie put up all her defenses as she coolly replied, "Townsend," and was proud that she didn't blush.

"You're looking very Audrey Hepburn tonight," he said lazily, and looked her over, a direct look that managed to be slow and sexy and aloof all at the same time, which didn't help her state of mind at all.

She sidestepped him and kept walking toward the crime editor's desk. Unfortunately, he turned and walked with her.

"A lady on the scent of a story, if I ever saw one."

"Looks like there's only one story tonight."

"Ah, yes. The Prince of Darkness. *Requiescat in pace.*" *Rest in peace.*

But there was a bitter quality to his voice that belied his words; it seemed more than mere journalistic cynicism, but some deeper feeling.

Interesting, she thought. *I wonder what that's about?*

**Find out in KEEPER OF THE SHADOWS
by Alexandra Sokoloff, available May 7, 2013,
wherever books are sold.**

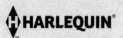

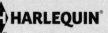

NOCTURNE™

Devin James wields a demon blade…

And the demon blade wields him, creating an irrevocable bond that sets him on a path of destruction. Natalie James can see through the darkness to Devin's heart, but neither of them realizes that her mentor will stop at nothing to acquire Devin's blade.

TAMING THE DEMON

by

DORANNA DURGIN

**Available May 7, 2013,
from Harlequin® Nocturne™.**

HARLEQUIN®

A *Romance* FOR EVERY MOOD™

**Stay up-to-date on all your
romance-reading news with the
Harlequin Shopping Guide,
featuring bestselling authors, exciting new
miniseries, books to watch and more!**

The newest issue will be delivered right to you
with our compliments! There are 4 each year.

Signing up is easy.

EMAIL

ShoppingGuide@Harlequin.ca

WRITE TO US

HARLEQUIN BOOKS
Attention: Customer Service Department
P.O. Box 9057, Buffalo, NY 14269-9057

OR PHONE

1-800-873-8635 in the United States
1-888-343-9777 in Canada

Please allow 4-6 weeks for delivery of the first issue by mail.